Masterpiece
Marriage

Other books in the Quilts of Love Series

Beyond the Storm
Carolyn Zane

Tempest's Course
Lynette Sowell

A Wild Goose Chase Christmas
Jennifer AlLee

Scraps of Evidence
Barbara Cameron

Path of Freedom
Jennifer Hudson Taylor

A Sky Without Stars
Linda S. Clare

For Love of Eli
Loree Lough

Maybelle in Stitches
Joyce Magnin

Threads of Hope
Christa Allan

A Stitch and a Prayer
Eva Gibson

A Healing Heart
Angela Breidenbach

A Promise in Pieces
Emily Wierenga

A Heartbeat Away
S. Dionne Moore

Rival Hearts
Tara Randel

Pieces of the Heart
Bonnie S. Calhoun

A Grand Design
Amber Stockton

Pattern for Romance
Carla Olson Gade

Hidden in the Stars
Robin Caroll

Raw Edges
Sandra D. Bricker

Swept Away
Laura V. Hilton & Cindy Loven

The Christmas Quilt
Vannetta Chapman

Quilted by Christmas
Jodie Bailey

Aloha Rose
Lisa Carter

A Stitch in Crime
Cathy Elliott

MASTERPIECE MARRIAGE

Quilts of Love Series

Gina Welborn

Abingdon fiction™
a novel approach to faith
Nashville

Masterpiece Marriage

Copyright © 2014 by Gina Welborn

ISBN-13: 978-1-4267-7363-1

Published by Abingdon Press, P.O. Box 801, Nashville, TN 37202

www.abingdonpress.com

Published in association with the Steve Laube Literary Agency

Macro Editor: Teri Wilhelms

The persons and events portrayed in this work of fiction
are the creations of the author, and any resemblance
to persons living or dead is purely coincidental.

Scripture quotations from The Authorized (King James) Version. Rights in the
Authorized Version in the United Kingdom are vested in the Crown. Reproduced by
permission of the Crown's patentee, Cambridge University Press.

Library of Congress Cataloging-in-Publication Data has been
requested.

Printed in the United States of America

1 2 3 4 5 6 7 8 9 10 / 19 18 17 16 15 14

To Becca

Thank you for being a needed friend, counselor, inspiration, cheerleader, and brainstorming partner on this book and beyond. Starbucks Monday?

Acknowledgments

This book would not be what it is without the blessings Jesus gave (and continues to give) in the form of:

My husband and kids for helping cook and clean and for all the dinnertime prayers asking God to "help Mommy finish her book" and that "the food isn't poisoned." I love you!!!

My agent, Tamela Hancock Murray, for telling me "you can do it!" again and again and again.

My Inky sisters—Anita, Barb, C. J., DeAnna, Deb, Dina, Lisa, Jen, Niki, Suzie Jo, and Susie—for listening, counseling, distracting, and laughing.

To Deb, Lisa, Niki, Becca, and Laurie for the quick and helpful critiques.

To Bonnie "Ordinary World" Calhoun for the wise words she shared at the ACFW gala dinner, helping me realize I needed to rewrite my first three chapters.

To Deb and her team at the Cache Road Starbucks for keeping me well supplied with iced coffee and providing me a once-a-week escape.

To Ramona Richards and the Abingdon editing, sales, and marketing teams for support they've given my book and the entire Quilts of Love series. I am honored writing for you!

Within is a country that may have the prerogative over the most pleasant places knowne, for large and pleasant Rivers, heaven & earth never agreed better to frame a place for man's habitation; were it fully matured and inhabited by industrious people.

Captain John Smith
The Generall Historie of Virginia

The LORD will perfect that which concerneth me: thy mercy, O LORD, endureth for ever: forsake not the works of thine own hands.
PSALM 138:8 KJV

1

May 9, 1891

In all his thirty-one years, Zenus Dane had never expected to see seven inches of rainfall during a six-hour period.

He trudged through the flooded floor of the textile mill he was able to inspect since the fire marshal had declared it safe. Still, the water reached the third metal clasp of his vulcanized rubber boots, a product he wished he had invented, but was thankful Charles Goodyear did. Although, at the moment, he felt more nauseated than thankful. Through the hole in the roof, the morning sun revealed the full extent of the destruction caused by Friday afternoon's deluge setting a record for one-day rainfall in Philadelphia.

April was the month for deluges. Not May.

His mouth sour over the damage, Zenus looked to his foreman at the other end of the mill. The man didn't have to speak for Zenus to know he shared his grim thoughts.

Zenus stopped at the loom farthest from the collapsed roof. A floral cotton print lay half-woven in the machine. Unlike the bolts of textiles in the storage room, the print was as dry as his gabardine suit. It was also water-stained on the bottom portion of the roll. As he had with the other machines, he examined the loom's frame, the crankshaft, tight-and-loose pulleys, picker stick, shuttle, and race plate. All damp. Oxidation here, too, on the bolts where the floodwater reached its highest level. The looms hadn't even had a month of usage, and now rust?

As if his flooded warehouse of raw cotton bales wasn't a torturous enough loss.

A fitting *why God?* moment if there ever was one.

Zenus whipped his newsboy's cap off his head, ran his hands through his hair, then put the cap back on. Living by faith could be hazardous.

With a shake of his head, he released a breath.

No sense bemoaning fate. Count it all joy—it was the only contingency he had. And he *would* count it all joy that he'd fallen into this trial, because the testing of his faith was producing patience in him. He didn't consider himself an impatient man. His well-planned schedules allotted time for the unexpected and diversions; they resulted in maximum efficiency. Everything would work out, in time. Optimism: the first necessary ingredient for success. Don't lament the obstacles was the second. A few days were all he needed to solve this setback.

He could—no, he would—do it.

After a slap to the loom beam, Zenus stood.

"Cousin Zenus!"

He looked across the mill's vast floor to the entrance. His ten-year-old goddaughter Aimee stood with her father, waving frantically, while wearing her perpetual smile. The parts of her blue dress not stuck in her rubber boots grazed the surface of the floodwater.

He waved back with a silly expression, knowing it'd make her giggle.

And she did.

"Morning," his cousin Sean Gallagher called out, his voice echoing in the practically empty mill.

Sean said something to the fire marshal then touched Aimee's head. The fire marshal, nodding, motioned Sean to enter. As they did, he resumed pointing to the second-story rafters and speaking to three other firemen, likely, about the hole in the flat roof.

Sean gripped Aimee's hand. He slogged forward with the pants of his gray suit tucked inside his own pair of shin-high galoshes, his arm and Aimee's a pendulum between them, their legs creating ripples in the water.

"I should've insisted you buy flood insurance," Sean said.

Zenus's lips twitched with amusement. Typical of Sean to cut to the *should've*. "Buying flood insurance wasn't logical. When was the last time this part of Philly flooded?"

Sean gave a yeah-you're-right shrug as he waded through the water.

"I'm sorry about your mill," Aimee said in almost a whisper.

"It'll be all right, sweetheart." He gave her a gentle smile. "Did Noah have flood insurance?"

She shook her head, her dark corkscrew curls swaying.

"Did he survive?"

She nodded.

"Then things will work out for me as well."

"Sometimes your optimism annoys me." Sean stopped with Aimee one loom from where Zenus was. He rubbed the back of his neck as he glanced about the mill, his blue eyes even lighter in the morning sun. "You'll need a new roof before production can resume. Insurance will cover it. Unfortunately, it won't cover damage caused by rising water."

Zenus motioned to the looms around the mill floor. "Is any of this fabric covered by insurance because the damage was caused by the collapsed roof brought on by an act of God, not by flooding?"

"Yes, but" —Sean removed folded papers from his suit coat's inner pocket—"let me see what your policy says."

Zenus blinked, stunned his cousin actually remembered to bring the policy. Details, Sean never forgot. Items—always. If the man ever married again, his wife would have to accept Sean would remember their anniversary, but wouldn't remember to get a gift. Or if he did remember to buy a gift, he would leave it at his law office or in the cab or at the café where he always had a coffee after leaving work.

Good man. Honorable. Just forgetful.

"What isn't excluded," Sean said, "is included, so it's covered. But from what I can tell, none of the fabric on the looms looks damaged."

Aimee ran her hands across the orange-and-brown plaid, one of his new textile designs. "It's not wet."

"Because it dried overnight." Zenus trudged to the loom where Sean and Aimee were. He looked to his cousin. "Even if the textiles don't have stains, I have to declare they were exposed to water and sell them at a drastic discount, which means no profit. I lost all the raw cotton bales in the warehouse, too."

Sean repocketed the policy. "You'll get insurance money to help you equal out. Why are you shaking your head?"

Zenus leaned back against the loom. "I have forty-seven bolts in the storage room"—Aimee touched his hand, and his fingers immediately curled around hers—"all damaged or partially damaged by the flooding."

"How much fabric is it?"

"A hundred yards per bolt. Each bolt, fifty-four inches wide."

Sean opened his mouth then paused, clearly thinking, running numbers through his head. "Were those bolts already paid for?"

"Almost all. They were scheduled for cutting and delivery this Monday. Forty-five days of weaving will go to fulfilling those orders." Zenus loosened his tie. "Insurance money will go to repairing the roof and making my loan payment. I have enough left in savings to make payroll for a month."

"Maybe this is God's way of telling you to sell the business and do something different."

Zenus nodded thoughtfully. Maybe this was God at work. He'd go to his grave believing God worked in mysterious ways. He also knew God generally did not cause a field of wheat to grow unless a farmer sowed said grain. Made no sense for God to tell him to expand his business if God wanted him to sell the business. The loan he took out to buy the looms—to "grow his flock"—could now cause him to lose everything.

He needed guidance. Heavenly guidance. Jesus-inspired guidance.

"Maybe," he answered.

Sean stared at him in shock. "Maybe?"

"I should consider all my options."

"How adventurous of you, Queen Victoria."

Sean's face shared how much he believed Zenus was capable of doing something different. It pricked. Court a mail-order bride. Take out a loan. What else did he need to do to prove to Sean he was open to change? And he *had* changed.

Zenus withdrew his pocket watch, holding it in his palm. "The problem is the MacKenzie brothers' offer was made before rain created a hole in my roof," he said calmly, restraining the twinges of irritation from growing into a roar. "Would be foolish to presume their offer stands as-is."

"Then take a lesser offer and be done with—"

"Boss," his foreman called from the exit doors, "I'll get some mill hands to start clean-up here and at the warehouse."

Zenus nodded and hollered back, "I'll lock up." He looked to Sean.

"No. I can't risk my employees losing their jobs. A quarter are unmarried women—" His gaze shifted to Aimee long enough for Sean to understand his silent *with children.*

Sean leaned against the loom, his shoulder slightly touching Zenus's. "All right, Coz, selling isn't an option then. Insurance will help you through a month, maybe two. Then what?"

"You could ask Great-Aunt Priscilla," Aimee cheerfully offered. "She likes helping people."

If his eyes rolled, Zenus would not admit to it. His aunt was the last person he'd go to for aid.

"Thank you for the suggestion, sweetheart." Zenus gave her hand a little squeeze. "But I can't ask her."

"Why not?" she asked.

"I'm not allowed back into her home."

"Until he apologizes," Sean tacked on.

Aimee's confused gaze shifted between them. "For?"

"Being me," Zenus answered.

Sean, to his credit, did not snicker.

Aimee looked at Zenus with some surprise. "I don't understand. What's wrong with you?"

Sean chuckled. "His sentiments exactly."

Zenus quirked a brow. "Flaws, I have, as everyone does, and I can admit—"

"Confession is good for the soul." An unusual edge tinged Sean's words. His gaze never wavered from Zenus, never flickered, never stopped hammering nails right there in the center of Zenus's chest. He couldn't know. Couldn't.

Zenus looked away. Not everything needed to be confessed.

"The problem is," he said to Aimee, "Aunt Priscilla sees flaws which do not exist. She is quite secure in her opinions, thus she and I are at an impasse."

"Impasse?"

"It means when neither person can win," Sean answered. "What about the girl from Boston you've proposed to? Maybe her family could loan—"

"No." Zenus's response sounded a little tight, which betrayed a lot of emotion to anyone who knew him well, and Sean did. Fact was being emotional about another failed courtship would not do, considering Zenus had not yet formed an attachment to the lady in question. "No," he repeated this time in a lackadaisical tone. "My courtship of Miss Boesch has reached a mutual conclusion."

"You proposed in your last letter." While Sean didn't add a *didn't you?* the implication was clear.

Zenus checked his pocket watch. He needed to get to the next item on today's agenda. "Yes," he answered, pocketing his watch again. He began the slow walk back through the mid-calf-deep flood water to the mill's entrance, Aimee clinging to his hand.

Aimee looked over her shoulder. "Papa, can we have ice cream for lunch?"

"Certainly. Your mother would have insisted," Sean said, the water sloshing against his boots as he caught up to them. "I'm confused. The time line doesn't make sense. You mailed the letter on Wednesday, three days ago. Mail doesn't travel overnight even to Boston."

Moments like this were when Zenus wished his cousin was less tenacious. He gave Sean a bored look. "She mailed her proposal acceptance before I mailed my proposal offer."

Sean's frown deepened with his continued confusion. He grabbed Zenus's arm, halting him. "Explain."

"The proposal she accepted was from a Wyoming rancher to be *his* mail-order bride."

"Ouch."

Ouch, indeed.

"Do you mean you aren't getting married?" Aimee asked, brow furrowing.

Zenus shook his head.

"Are you sad?"

He ignored the interest on Sean's face from Aimee's innocent question. Irritation, not sadness, was his more prevailing emotion.

"Things always work for our good." Believing that didn't ease his sour mood. He resumed their trek, the water splashing and rippling, Aimee singing "Row, row, row your boat."

Five months of courting Miss Boesch through letters. Five months of weekly correspondence. Five months of examining his schedule for the next year and finding the best date for a wedding and honeymoon to Niagara Falls so he wouldn't miss . . .

(1) Thursday Canoe Club meeting, or
(2) Friday symphony attendance (both had free nights on the fifth Thursday and Friday of a month), or
(3) Saturday hunting trip (off-season), and
(4) he would have been home in time for Sunday morning worship.

Five months wasted. Why? Because even when he'd had hours—days even—to plan what to say in his letters, she chose another man over him. He was cursed to remain a bachelor. And someone with his qualities and assets shouldn't remain a bachelor. Women should be fighting with each other to marry him. It was a logical and self-possessed—not vain—assessment.

His current financial quandary aside, he was well-to-do: owned his own business, house, two canoes, and a box at the opera house. Zenus also faithfully attended church, where he taught a Sunday school class for boys, and dutifully gave to charities. Yet, upon at least two occasions, he'd overheard women describe him as "a Gothic rogue, so aloof and cold." Even though he and Sean had the same dark-hair-with-blue-eyes coloring—not surprising considering their mothers had been identical twins—Sean always earned a sigh and a "he's *so* charming."

A man's appearance should not define him as a rogue.

Nor should his past forever delineate him as one.

He should count it joy God spared him from the wrong match with Miss Boesch because there was a better-suited woman for him. If only he could find a way to convince the lovely and vivacious Arel Dewey to see him for the charming, devoted man he truly was.

"Too bad you couldn't figure out a way to repurpose the damaged fabric," Sean said, breaking into Zenus's thoughts.

"What?"

His voice raised an octave. "I said it's too bad—"

"No, I heard you." Zenus stopped at the opened double-door entrance and met his cousin's gaze. Repurposing the fabric? He should have thought of it on his own. "I could cut up the fabric to sell as packaged scraps and then I could charge at least the minimum market price. Or . . ." Think. He closed his eyes and pinched the skin between his brows.

Aimee kissed the back of his other hand, then let go. Sloshing. Humming.

There had to be some way he could repurpose the fabric and get a better return.

"I should introduce you to Miss Corcoran," said Sean.

"Uh-huh," Zenus muttered.

What if he added something to the fabric? Like a bonus. The prime buyers of his textiles were women who purchased them at the mercantile who bought them from the distributor. He needed to become the distributor himself to increase his profits. He needed something to entice his prime buyers to buy small pieces of fabric instead of yard sections.

"You aren't such a bad catch," Sean continued.

"Uh-huh."

With his eyes closed, Zenus could hear the fire marshal yelling to his men to leave. Could smell the dirt in the floodwater. Both distracted him from focusing. Think. Ignore Aimee's humming too. Find something to lure buyers. Who wants fabric even if it's water-stained? With a little washing, the fabric would look like new anyway. He needed a woman who would settle—no, who actually desired something less than perfect. A cast-off. Leftover.

" . . . my new transcriptionist."

Zenus opened his eyes, absently noted the pirouette Aimee performed with all the grace her mother used to have. "What?"

Sean was grinning. "I said I am going to introduce you to my new transcriptionist."

Aimee didn't stop pirouetting to say, "She's nice."

Zenus kept his grimace internal. The dozen of secretaries and transcriptionists Sean had hired in the five years since his wife's death all looked the same: lackluster black hair with unmemorable faces that had forgotten how to smile. "Does she look like your last one?"

"She's not married, knows how to read and write, and is still within childbearing age," Sean said in a most pitying tone, "and it makes her the prime matrimonial catch for you."

Aimee nodded. "And she's nice."

Zenus let out a low growl. "Having Aunt Priscilla fail to matchmake me last Christmas with the niece of her quilting friend was humiliating enough. You were there. You saw how—Whoa! That's it." He held his hand up, stilling his cousin from speaking. "Wait. Quilters use every textile known to man. They love scraps." He snapped his fingers and pointed at Sean. "They're what I need."

Sean's brow furrowed. "A quilter?"

"Quilters. Plural."

"Trust me, you don't want more than one wife."

"I'm not talking for marriage, Sean. I'm talking about buying my textiles."

"Miss Corcoran doesn't look like the sewing type."

Aimee stopped pirouetting. "What's a sewing type?"

Sean scratched his dark bristled jawline, having clearly not taken time to shave this morning as Zenus had. He didn't appear to have any more of an idea of what the sewing type looked like any more than Zenus did, beyond being the female sort and domesticated.

Zenus stepped to the threshold. He patted the top of Aimee's head, murmured "Keep dancing, sweetheart," and then reached in his suit pocket for his set of keys. "Sean, I need you to hire a couple of guards today to watch over the mill during the night while I go arrange for the roof repair." He withdrew the keys, finding the one for the lock. "Offer a week's pay, although I doubt I'll need them so long. Hopefully when I return, the mill can resume operations."

"Return from where?"

"Belle Haven. I'm leaving early Monday morning. Return Wednesday."

"Why not leave today?" True to lawyer form, Sean focused on the least significant detail in what Zenus had said.

"Why doesn't matter," Zenus bit off.

"I think it does." A knowing smirk on his face—

With a growl under his breath, Zenus grabbed the left door's iron handle and drew it closed.

Sean let out a bark of laughter. "Church is tomorrow, and you don't want to lose out on another perfect attendance pin. Isn't eight enough?"

Zenus grit his teeth. "It's not about the pin." He drew the right door closed then threaded the chain through the handles. "As a Sunday School teacher, my responsibility is to model faithfulness to those boys."

"You have a point there."

For as many years as they'd known each other, Zenus couldn't consistently tell when his cousin was being sarcastic. It was disturbing.

Zenus knelt down and kissed Aimee's cheek. "See you tomorrow, sunshine."

Her curly hair and bubbly effervescence were all her mother's. Aimee should have been his daughter, not Sean's. Clara Reade should have been his wife, not Sean's.

She kissed him back. "I love you, Cousin Zenus."

"I love you too."

Sean held out his hand, and Aimee took it. "So you are actually going to your Aunt Priscilla for help?" was what he asked. Unstated was *Have you forgotten what she said to you last Christmas?* and *I'm glad I have no blood relation to her.*

Zenus stood and gripped the iron lock, cold against his palm. He hadn't forgotten. In fact, what Aunt Priscilla had said spurred him into deciding to stop playing life safe. The next day he'd filled out a loan application and begun the courtship of Miss Boesch, the niece of a deacon in his church. He'd been determined to disprove Aunt Priscilla's assessment of him and his apathetic (pathetic, according to her) approach to finding a wife. His first two risk-taking attempts both ended in setbacks, which he wouldn't bemoan. Every failure brought him one attempt closer to success.

Despite his optimism, Zenus did nothing more than nod his response to Sean. The thought of having to grovel before his aunt soured his mouth, churned his stomach, and warmed his cheeks with embarrassment. Her last lecture included "mule," "pig-headed," and "scaredy-cat." Nothing like being viewed by a woman as a barnyard animal.

But she was his best hope. No one knew quilts like Priscilla Dane Osbourne.

No quilter had national name recognition like her either.

To save his business, home, livelihood, and future, all he had to do was the impossible: Convince a fiercely protective quilter to give him one of her precious patterns. This was one wooing at which he could not—would not—fail.

2

Eastern Shore, Virginia

The following morning

Headmistress Whitacre warned that a lack of dedication to drawing class would one day lead to ruin.

Mary Varrs refolded the letter from her father, the fold of each crease earning a shake of her head. Left. Then over. Once more. Then, with precise care, she returned it to the envelope. Wax-sealed. Not gummed like practically everyone else in the world used. Only fools tossed away tradition for ease, or so her father believed. Her eyes burned. What was wrong with photographs? They captured accurate images. Botanical illustrations were nothing more than Gibson Girl versions of the truth. All she had worked for during the last two years—her future—now hinged on a set of botanical illustrations. Illustrations she had absolutely *no* ability to draw.

Two years. Wasted.

She twisted the edges of the envelope. It could have been mailed four months earlier after Director Preston—her father's supervisor—had been hired. His waiting until this stage . . .

He couldn't want her to fail. Could he?

Mary sniffed, rubbing the tip of her nose, blinking rapidly to rid the tears before anyone noticed. Before someone asked what was wrong. Before she broke.

She laid the envelope on the table then stared absently at the Bumblebee Café's Sunday Breakfast Special: chicken spinach quiche with a side of fresh fruit. The plate had been delivered while she read her father's latest correspondence and as a burnt smell from the kitchen spread into the eating area. All the relaxation brought from her hour-long walk disappeared. Two years of dedicated work and persistent hope.

Wasted. Wasted. Wasted.

The motorized ceiling fans turned the air about in the stuffy, open-windowed room. Yet perspiration beaded on her forehead like the condensation on her goblet of lemonade.

Her stomach growled. Mary blinked repeatedly to ensure every last tear was destroyed. Then she forked a piece of quiche and ate with precise monotony. One bite. Another. The usually well-prepared lunch here in this tiny hamlet in the Commonwealth of Virginia fed her stomach but did little to ease the ache in her soul. She swallowed the dry-as-her-straw-hat quiche before sipping the lemonade and almost spitting the watered-down beverage back in the goblet. Her list of the day's frustrations kept increasing.

(1) Napoleon's gastronomic distress
(2) A broken bulb in her germination light heater
(3) A flat tire on her bicycle
(4) This tasteless food
(5) The letter from her father should have been received yesterday, but Postmaster Hamilton "miraculously" found it on the floor of the post office this morning when he returned for the spectacles he'd "accidentally" left there the night before. Of course, knowing she always took her meals at the café, he insisted on "personally" delivering the letter.
(6) Herself for whining about all she had (justifiably) to whine about. This was not the person she wanted to be.

Mary rested her goblet on the table with a soft thud, earning her several curious glances. None of the dozen Belle Haven residents in the café needed cause to look her way. From the moment she arrived in town, she'd become their object of curiosity and obsession—and much disdain like a stunning heiress in her London debut. Few would

21

declare her a classical beauty. Too sun-lightened brown hair. Too sun-bronzed skin. Too deep-set eyes. Nor was she an heiress. Although, she was the granddaughter of a marquess, which counted for little in the academic field—the one world in which she desired success.

She sighed. Her heart hurt too much for her to care who heard the dejection in the sound.

Eleven days—all the time she had left to produce those illustrations. Her father would not give her another chance to prove her merit. Mother would not give her more time to be free. And Prince Ercole . . .

My darling Mary, I expect to see a great return on my investment.

For all he had done for her, she owed him.

She stabbed a melon wedge, then, upon second thought, laid her fork across her plate. Harvested too soon, the melon tasted like cucumber. She didn't dislike cucumber. It merely tasted better combined with, say, tomatoes in vinaigrette.

"Excuse m-m-me, M-M-Miss Varrs?" came the voice, deep for a woman.

Mary glanced up to see the café owner's gaze intent on her letter. More likely intent on the Blacksburg postmark.

Those in the café went silent.

Mary left the envelope where it was, because snatching it from view would look suspicious. "Yes, Mrs. Taylor?"

"Would you c-c-care for a slice of blackberry p-p-pie? Fresh baked."

"Your pies are commendable, but today I shall pass." Mary placed her napkin on the table, avoiding the gaze of all in the café. "Thank you for the offer." She reached inside a pocket in her Turkish trousers to retrieve the coins to pay for her meal.

Mrs. Taylor wiped her hands on the apron she wore around the skirt of her simple yet practical calico gown, typical of what she wore while working at the café. "M-m-my sister's grandson attends Virginia Agricultural and M-M-Mechanical College. First in the family."

Mary didn't even try to look shocked upon the news Mrs. Taylor knew someone who lived in Blacksburg. Three hours from now, during church, at least a dozen Belle Havenians would feel the need to inform her of a friend or family member who lived in Blacksburg.

And then they would wish to discuss who she knew who lived there. The more the Belle Havenians determined to see who could discover the most information, the more she determined to keep as much as possible private.

What did shock her was this shy woman who rarely spoke to anyone—and who was rarely spoken to—because of her stutter had begun a conversation. With her. And Mrs. Taylor seemed to want to continue it because she was genuinely proud of her great-nephew's achievement.

"Virginia A&M is an excellent school for those interested in the sciences," Mary responded, placing the coins next to her half-eaten meal.

"He's m-m-majoring in it. Science, that is. Chemistry."

"It's a fitting career path for men," Mr. Hamilton, the postmaster, called out from the table he shared with the mayor. "God created women to be a man's helpmate, not scientists."

Listen to me, Mary Varrs, women are not meant to be scientists.

Headmistress Whitacre's words a decade earlier during one of Mary's "improving" sessions lived in perpetuity in her mind. Someday, though, the evergreen belief espoused at Wellons & Whitacre School for Young Ladies in Brighton—and in Mr. Hamilton's words—would come to an end. Had to.

"Mrs. Taylor, I see a prosperous future for your sister's grand-son." The moment the words left her mouth, Mary wanted to take them back. She sounded as pompous as the fortune-teller Edward had coaxed her into seeing in Paris. Life's decisions should not be left to the roll of the dice or turn of a tarot card.

Mrs. Taylor glanced from Mary to Mr. Hamilton then back to Mary. "I suppose," she said quietly, "a p-p-person would need to be dedicated to earn a science degree. Let alone two."

At this tidbit of gossip—a minor detail Mary had shared with Arel Dewey when they first met—Mary looked to the café owner. Really looked. No more eyes demurely fixed on the ground. Mrs. Taylor gazed at her with awe. It was as if she was saying, albeit silently, *I am impressed with your accomplishment, even if no one else is.*

Mary's eyes burned again. How she envied the Americans' ability to treat everyone, even those common, like a familiar friend. She wanted to. One simply did not forget all she'd been taught as easily as shedding a cloak. Not as if she hadn't tried. Those few attempts at allowing people into her life, into her heart, always resulted in a disaster.

She offered a timid smile in return. "Mrs. Taylor, I appreciate being able to take meals here. You are"—her voice tightened, weakened—"a blessing. Please save me a slice of pie for lunch."

Mrs. Taylor nodded.

Mary nodded too, because . . . well, nodding was an easier form of response than crying. Ugh. What had come over her? She had never been such an emotional person before today.

"Mrs. Taylor, by chance, do you draw? Sketch?"

She shook her head.

Mary looked about the room. Twelve sets of eyes watching her. Regardless if they heard, she would not pose the question to them. She claimed her letter from the tabletop and slid it between the wide triangular front collars of her brown tailored jacket. The blue poplin bloomers and double-breasted jacket, crafted for a cyclist, were ideal attire for tending to her garden. Not the ideal attire, though, for blending in.

Her chair scraped against the pine floor as she stood and turned to leave.

"Who do you receive weekly letters from?" Mayor Erstwhile asked, blocking Mary's path to the exit. His head tilted as he looked up at her. "I've heard of a group of socialists who meet in Blacksburg. Are you a spy for England? Darwinist like the Linwoods? Union worker?"

Mary winced at the hardness Americans gave to words ending in "r."

"Why are you *really* here?" he said with his dark eyes narrowed.

"Harold," Mrs. Taylor warned. She took a step closer to Mary. "M-M-Miss Varrs, you don't have to answer him."

Mr. Hamilton, sitting at the table next to Mary's, leaned back in his chair, crossed his legs, and slid his hand between the first and second button of his black suit coat. "I *wager* Miss Varrs has a *suitor* in Blacksburg." Like many Americans she'd come across in her travels, the postmaster spoke slowly and tonally. "It *would* explain the twice-weekly correspondence *to* and *from* there."

How gracious of him to share.

"I hope the news was good," the woman who lived across the street from Mary practically yelled, as if Mary being English also meant she was deaf.

"Miss Varrs picked at her food, sister," said the gray-haired woman at the table with her. "A lady does not do so if the news is good."

Their eyes focused on Mary, expecting her to explain. As if they, save Mrs. Taylor, all believed with their collective mind power, they could pressure her into a confession. The only pressure Mary felt was tension between her temples.

The rotating *whuuump whuuump whuuump* of the overhead fans filled the awkward silence. Only two escape routes. Either past the stout and almost-a-foot-shorter Mr. Erstwhile. Or past a still-silent trio of ladies whose names she couldn't remember, but whose disapproving and judgmental glares she knew too well. Despite the desire to slump and lower herself to a more womanly height, Mary held her shoulders level.

"I am neither socialist, unionist, Darwinist, nor spy," she answered with a tug at her jacket's buttoned-front. "Now, if you would excuse me, I must hurry home and ready for church." She tipped her head in their direction. "Good day to you all."

Mary eased past Mr. Erstwhile and quickly exited the café.

She stepped into the immediate stickiness from the May humidity. Thankfully, when she began her sunrise constitutional—a brisk walk instead of her usual bicycle ride—the temperature had been moderate. Her straw hat shielded her face from earning additional bronzing as she strolled down the sidewalk toward her spring home. Occasionally the heels of her black boots would hit an errant brick, jutting slightly where flooding from last summer's hurricane damaged the sidewalk. Carriages, wagons, horse riders, pedestrians, and bicyclists added to the traffic and morning noise.

Any one of them could be an artist. But how could she go about asking without dozens claiming skill for the purpose of learning why she needed help?

Tomorrow she would post personal ads in the *Richmond Times* and the *Maryland Gazette*. God would bless her with an immediate answer. She chose to believe it. To be hopeful. To ignore the doubts.

Mary breathed in the clean, salty air, satisfied with her strategy. Sea breeze. Loblolly pines. Dogwoods in bloom. For all she didn't like about the snoops of Belle Haven, she loved how Virginia smelled.

As she passed a lamppost, the pair of seagulls resting on it jolted into flight. They raced across the street and landed on the lamppost besides a two-story brick building. Little Archie Blanchard paused in washing the window of his father's mercantile. He waved, and she returned the motion. For a child of ten, he was clever and restrained. Perhaps she would accept the Reverend Jaeger's invitation for her to attend Children's Hour at the library and to speak about botany. Every child and youth she had met, thus far, in Belle Haven behaved like Archie. The simple truth—and one quite contrary to the prevalent view that being a mother was a woman's highest calling—was that disliking children did not go hand-in-hand with not wishing to have any of one's own.

"Mary Varrs! Miss Mary Varrs!"

Mary stopped at the intersection. She glanced over her shoulder to see who called. "Splendid," she muttered under her breath.

Arel Dewey, the leading local suffragist, came running up the sidewalk. Six of her friends followed. Each wearing similar cotton blouses and pleated linen skirts. Each holding a wooden sign. For women who championed individual thought and equality, they came across as nothing more than pretty sheep to Miss Dewey's even-prettier shepherdess. Unless Miss Dewey elected to attend college, she doubted any would consider venturing into academia.

Mary turned to face them as they stopped in front of her, their gazes all direct and unshrinking. A bit unnerving. "Yes?"

Miss Dewey reached forward and shook Mary's hand. "Arel, Arel Dewey. It's so good to see you again, Mary Varrs." From their first meeting and subsequent ones, the gregarious younger woman began the conversation by introducing herself and shaking hands, which had not taken Mary long to learn she did with everyone who she didn't know well.

"Is there something I can help you with?" Mary asked, more so because it was polite than because she had the inclination.

Miss Dewey smiled. "In fact, there is."

Panic slid along with beads of perspiration down the sides of Mary's face. The day was too humid to have a conversation outside.

Yet the petite beauty named Miss Dewey didn't look to have a drop of sweat on her. "Tomorrow we are participating in a rally. We depart for Richmond on the four o'clock train today, and we wish for you to come along as our mentor and chaperone." Her fun-loving grin was as tightly fixed in place as her wheat-colored chignon. "It's vital we take a stand, as our forefathers did more than a hundred years ago against a deaf tyrant, and ensure our voice is heard. The women's revolution is at hand."

"We've made signs," a curly-haired lamb explained, holding hers up. Painted in red were the words *Marriage = Slavery*.

Oh, good gracious. Mary managed to keep her eyes from rolling.

"Since 1869," a lamb Mary thought was Postmaster Hamilton's daughter, said, "women in Wyoming have been allowed to vote, which has set a precedent." The brown-eyed girl looked to Miss Dewey, who nodded approvingly at words Mary remembered hearing in the first conversation she and Miss Dewey had had two months ago, an hour after Mary had arrived in Belle Haven.

Whatever could be said of Arel Dewey, she was the most welcoming person in town. And the most talkative. The fact she couldn't bake an edible pie made the list, too.

Mary looked from girl to girl whom she guessed to be between the ages of sixteen and twenty-two. All idealistic, adoring, hopeful, and a bit angry. *Papa, why is he so angry?* she'd once asked after her grandsire returned home after the year's first Parliament session. *Politics steals one's joy,* her father had interjected, and it must have been true because Lord Iddesdowne never denied it.

She focused on Miss Dewey, who still didn't look to have a drop of perspiration on her. "As someone who is not a citizen of this land, I am unqualified to be your political mentor. Nor do your parents know me well enough to approve me as your chaperone. Do know, however, I am honored you thought of me."

"But—" Miss Dewey's eyes, as dark and large as an owl's, shifted to Mary's Turkish trousers. "You are one of us."

Mary released a frustrated breath. The pertness of American girls—and their candor—never ceased to surprise her. "My clothing choice, Miss Dewey, is a matter of practicality, not political posturing. Now if you would excuse me, I need to ready for church."

She turned and hurried across the street.

"I'll see you there!" Miss Dewey called out.

Mary raised a hand high enough to acknowledge young lady's words.

While she understood, even applauded, the reasons for votes for women, she had too many of her own woes to manage.

The mile walk from the café never seemed so long.

Mary reached the front yard of the three-story, white-framed house, the lone residence on the street surrounded by an iron fence. The gingerbread trim, dark blue shutters, and abundant flora in the front and back of Linwood House reminded her of the Honeymoon Cottage on Grandsire's country estate. She hurried over the bricked path and up the steps to the covered porch. The Linwoods' piebald English bulldog, Napoleon, peeked between the curtains and the window and whined.

She moved to open the door, something ivory catching in her peripheral vision. She opened the door to let Napoleon out, then stepped to the wicker table. In the center sat an envelope atop a napkin-covered plate. The script on the envelope unrecognizable, yet elegant.

Miss Mary Varrs

"I see we had a visitor," she said as Napoleon attended to his business. She opened the flap and withdrew a card.

Dear Miss Varrs,

You are cordially invited to attend my annual Quilting Bee beginning this Monday and continuing each weekday over the next two weeks. We will be working on a Bride's Quilt for Miss Lydia Puryear. Breakfast will be served promptly at eight, with quilting immediately following the meal. Lunch is potluck. Following the evening meal, the menfolk will join us for outdoor festivities. Music by the esteemed Lovell Brothers. I do hope you will come.

Sincerely,

Mrs. Priscilla Dane Osbourne

P.S. I do pray the elixir helped Napoleon.

A quilting bee? Needles, thread, fabric, and room full of talkative women?

Mary shuddered.

Yet, as the moments passed, Mrs. Osbourne's missive in her hand weighed as heavy as the letter from her father inside her jacket. Neither invited her to something enjoyable.

Heart chilled, she sat in one of the wicker chairs and looked to the Georgian-style house next door where Mrs. Osbourne lived. Napoleon curled at her feet. She had far greater issues to occupy her day than to stitch a quilt with those whose prime mission was to find out everything they could about "the strange and aloof Englishwoman." Namely, her.

Unless those ladies were more like Mrs. Taylor than like Mr. Hamilton and Mayor Erstwhile. Could she be sociable? Was it worth the risk?

Her gaze fell to the covered plate. Curiosity getting the best of her, she lifted the napkin. Shortbread biscuits with some type of yellowy glaze. Perhaps lemon.

"Look here, Napoleon," said Mary, "Mrs. Osbourne made us biscuits. What do you Americans call them?"

Napoleon whined.

"Oh yes, cookies. Alas, your persnickety bowels need none." From the looks of the finger-length biscuits—and the smell—they were freshly baked. The last time she had tried to bake biscuits, the

29

dough wouldn't adhere into a workable consistency until she added additional water. They'd tasted like sugary sawdust.

Her stomach growled. Considering how unappetizing her meal at the café had been, a midday snack couldn't harm anything. Besides, after the day she'd had so far, she needed a moment of bliss. She exchanged the card for a biscuit. As she took a bite, the almond-flavored crust crumbled onto her tongue and dissolved. She closed her eyes in delight.

"Mmmm." Perfect lemon buttery blissfulness.

Napoleon sat up and whined.

She looked at him. "No."

He whined again.

"Shall I give you more elixir?"

He flopped down, head resting on her boots.

"Smart boy." Mary grabbed another biscuit. She took a bite of the crisp shortbread and groaned again, licking the crumbs off her lips.

If she knew her way around a kitchen like the woman who made these biscuits, she would never visit a café for another meal. She popped the remaining bit in her mouth, brushed the crumbs off her hands and lap, and then took another biscuit from the plate. As she ate, her gaze settled on the card. She turned it over and stopped chewing. Brow furrowed. Head tilted.

Goosebumps raced from one arm to the next.

There, on the front, was an expertly sketched illustration of a dogwood branch in bloom. In the corner—the initials PDO.

"Priscilla Dane Osbourne drew this?"

She looked across the yard, mouth gaping, heartbeat pounding in her chest. The answer to her dilemma lived next door. But between now and the deadline to have her study submitted to Director Preston at the Virginia Agricultural Experiment Station, the esteemed Widow Osbourne was hosting a quilting bee. The same bee to which she'd invited Mary. The woman had won numerous county, state, and world's fair ribbons with her quilts, *and* she didn't share her patterns with anyone—information Miss Arel Dewey provided during their first meeting. She wouldn't relinquish quilting and hostess duties to draw pictures.

Unless—

"Napoleon, do you think she would work a trade with me?" She looked down, but his eyes were closed.

Leaning back in her chair, Mary nibbled on another biscuit she didn't need to eat but, heaven help her, they were so delicious. She had to think of something to offer to be enticing enough to sway Mrs. Osbourne away from quilting and into sketching. Even if she had exorbitant wealth to offer beyond the dwindling allowance set up by the prince, the railroad investor's widow didn't need more.

And Mary's abysmal cooking skills were Arel Dewey level.

The singular worthwhile skills she had were gardening and canning, both part of her duties to the Linwoods this spring in exchange for living in their home—and for caring for their pampered *he never likes to leave home* dog. None of which Mrs. Osbourne needed. She could also fish and hunt (thanks to Prince Ercole) and maneuver a canoe through a swamp, the latter skill learned by necessity, not desire. Upon occasion, she made a tasty porridge, the only food she could cook well.

But . . . quilting?

She picked up the card and reread the invitation. The palpitations in her chest increased. In rhythm. In noise. Go. Go. Go. GO.

She tossed the card back onto the table. "I shan't."

There had to be another person in Virginia or Maryland who could draw botanical illustrations. Had. To. Be. To find someone else meant spending time searching. Spending time searching meant wasting time. Why waste any time when she knew a skilled artist lived next door? Who was also hosting a quilting bee. To which she'd invited Mary. Oh dear.

Go go go go gogogogogo.

She leaned forward. Elbows on knees, forehead against open palms. She breathed deep. Slow. Steady. To ease the anxiety in her pulse. In her spirit. In her mind. If she wanted to be a research assistant at the Virginia Agricultural Experiment Station in Blacksburg, she needed to ask Mrs. Osbourne for help. Had to. Today. After church.

It was the best solution.

And the worst.

3

Later that morning

I made you your own rally sign." Miss Dewey's words were punctuated with a squeal reminiscent of a piglet's first gleeful discovery of slop.

Arel Dewey slid into the padded mahogany pew as Mary opened the hymnal to the first song listed on the board. Most people were still finding seats or already seated and in deep conversations. Unlike anyone else in Belle Haven, Miss Dewey dared to share a pew with Mary. Her sheep always assembled with their parents. Today, their ninth Sunday service together, Miss Dewey sat so close their thighs touched. She had also uncharacteristically changed clothes. Next to Mary's simple black-and-white-checkered dress, her yellow one with its pink and orange trim looked like a bouquet.

Speaking of flowers . . .

Miss Dewey's new and cloying perfume cloaked Mary in a garden cloud she suspected would leave them both scented for hours. She sniffed. Lilac. With a touch of magnolia, heliotrope, and nectarine. Sweet and fruity. Like lemonade with berries. Not altogether unpleasant if doled out in moderation.

Moderation seemed not to be a virtue Arel Dewey espoused.

"It's very—" Mary hesitated. Kind? Thoughtful? Imposing? Unsure of the least offensive yet most appropriate adjective, she settled on, "You didn't have to."

"Oh, but I did." Miss Dewey leaned in. Her heavily lashed brown eyes sparkled and widened, making them appear even more owlish. "It's what friends do, one for the other." The heavens would open and the ocean beds would split to flood the earth again before it was possible for Miss Dewey's voice to hold any more delight.

Mary dropped the open hymnal into her lap. Her every muscle, tendon, joint, bone, and strand of hair tensed. Perhaps she exaggerated a bit on the latter, but—friends?

Acquaintances, yes.

Perhaps friendly acquaintances.

Being friends meant spending time together, having deep intimate conversations where one shared mistakes, dreams, fears, and desires, and it was *not* going to happen if Mary had any say in the matter. If she were to have a friend, and she would like a confidante when her life had settled down, she certainly wouldn't choose a happy-as-a-piglet one who was preternaturally disposed toward conversation.

Mary leaned back and looked past Miss Dewey to spy Mrs. Priscilla Dane Osbourne. Now there was someone with whom she needed to become friends, or at least friendly acquaintances. The dark-haired widow, elegant as ever in her blue walking suit, sat beside her housekeeper, Mrs. Binkley, who was clad in a dove gray gown with a white lace fichu, as elegant a scarf as Mary had seen. A cough broke free from Mrs. Binkley's chest. She opened her pocketbook and withdrew a handkerchief. She then slid what looked to be a butterscotch candy into her mouth.

"Mary, don't forget we're leaving on the four o'clock train."

She looked back to Miss Dewey and chose her words carefully, as to be as clear and direct—as American—as possible. "Spare no time waiting for me, for I shan't be your chaperone."

Miss Dewey's eyes rolled and head bobbed in a faux offended manner, her straw hat not shifting an inch on her braided wheat-gold chignon. "Oh, pishposh, of course you will," she said calmly. "You can sit with me and we can catch up on old times."

Mary blinked. They've been in each other's acquaintance for two months. Spoken upon no more than twenty-three occasions, during which Miss Dewey did most of the talking. No old times to be found. Nor would they sit in a railway car together on way to a rally. On the way to anywhere.

She shifted on the pew to put several needed inches between them. "Miss Dewey," she started, "I must elucidate—"

"Call me Arel." Her sparkling grin filled her face. "For you are simply Mary to me."

No. Not Mary. Not Arel. Not either of them using each other's Christian names, and they certainly were not friends who had old times to reminisce over—despite Miss Dewey's delusion.

Miss Dewey's head tilted to the side. She was still grinning. "I must admit I view you more as an older sister than"—her face quirked as if she licked a lemon and her voice sounded like a chipmunk—"a mere friend."

There was morning effervescence. Then there was Arel Dewey. Five minutes in her presence was enough to compel Mary to require a nap from sheer social exhaustion.

Mary gripped the hymnal as she resisted the urge to punch a fist through her own straw hat. She didn't dislike Miss Dewey, but how was one to be friends with a wild girl with no sense of proper decorum? Miss Dewey was the antithesis of the ideal English lady.

Mary eased another few inches away from Miss Dewey then shifted to face her pew mate. "Miss Dewey, I—"

"Arel," she corrected, placing her hand on her bodice, just under her red lily corsage bearing her *Deeds Not Words* pin and yellow *Votes for Women* ribbon. "As in Arl. One syllable. Think of it as Karl without the K. Everyone pronounced my name correctly until Zenus called me Owl last summer during the croquet tournament, and when Zenus Dane speaks, people listen and follow and adore. He's Mrs. Osbourne's nephew, in case you don't remember. He hasn't been to visit since Christmas because she attempted to match-make him with Lydia Puryear, who I made sure to warn away because Lydia deserved someone less . . ."

Her upper lip curling, she uttered an I-am-so-revolted-by-him *errrg*.

Mary looked away long enough to notice the dozens of Belle Havenians watching them from the pews behind, next to, and in front of them. Her neck and face felt unusually warm. She closed the hymnal and slid it into the pew back next to the congregational prayer book and Bible. If she left now—

She couldn't leave. She needed to stay and talk to Mrs. Osbourne.

Miss Dewey gripped Mary's clenched palms and didn't respond to Mary's immediate flinch.

"Zenus Dane believes *he* is a Titan and *we* are insignificant mortals," she groused. Her voice became happy again. "Be thankful you will never meet him. He had a fight with Mrs. Osbourne last Christmas, and now they aren't speaking." Arel's lips curved in a contented smile, and Mary presumed it meant she had finished talking.

Thank you, Jesus.

Mary withdrew her hands from Miss Dewey's grasp. She fiddled with the pearl earring in her right ear, not because her skin itched but to disguise her reason for pulling away. Whoever this Zenus Dane was, Miss Dewey had an abnormal fixation on him. Mentions of him crept, ever so often, into Miss Dewey's conversation. If she didn't like the man, why talk about him? What Miss Dewey needed was something more noble to occupy her thoughts. Something like—

Despite the volume of the congregational noise, Mary lowered her voice to keep those watching them from hearing. "Can you draw? Sketch plants or leaves?"

Miss Dewey looked mildly offended. "Why?"

"No reason," she answered with a dismissive wave and a disappointed sigh. At least she tried. She reclaimed the hymnal and flipped through the pages.

"Four o'clock train."

Mary flinched, startled by the sound of Miss Dewey's voice so close to her ear.

"Don't. Be. Late," Miss Dewey added, reaching to claim a Bible from the pew back.

"Regarding the railway, I—"

"Oh, and bring the necessities for four days in Richmond." She looked to the wallboard that listed the day's scripture location. "I'll bring your sign."

Mary released a frustrated breath. "I am sorry to say you have mistaken the degree of our acquaintance and made presumptions upon my acquiescence regarding your trip to the Commonwealth's capital. You will have to—must, actually—rally without me."

Miss Dewey stopped flipping through the Bible and gaped at Mary. Then she blinked. "No matter what British people say, they sound smarter. It's the accent. My dearest and bestest sister Mary, this is why you must come with us. We need an educated woman such as you to communicate our passions and convictions in such a manner."

"A collegiate education is available for anyone who seeks it." In fact, college would be good for Miss Dewey, whose mouth gaped again.

Her mouth gaped again.

Oddly encouraged by the silence, Mary continued, "There are over ninety mixed-sex colleges alone in your country." Which she knew because she'd researched them all looking for a professorship. As the other conversations in the chapel began tapering off, thankfully with gazes focused more on the podium than on them, Mary whispered, "You should enroll. Secure for yourself the education you admire in me."

Arel Dewey continued to stare as if the thought of earning a higher education never occurred to her. At twenty-two and the youngest of five children, heir to a substantial inheritance from her fishing empire father, and under no pressure to marry and produce grandchildren thanks to her prolific older siblings (information Mary never asked to know), Miss Dewey had a world of opportunities and adventures before her. There was nothing wrong with her suffrage cause. It was merely a case of how she was going about it, which was rather off-putting at times.

Mrs. Binkley fell into a fit of coughs.

Mary mimicked the gaze of everyone on her side of the meetinghouse and looked to where the gray-haired woman now stood.

Mrs. Binkley motioned to Mrs. Osbourne to remain seated. Then with her kerchief covering her mouth, she eased out of the pew and down the back of the room to the door.

"Let's bow our heads in prayer."

The exit door opened then closed.

Mary turned to the podium to where the Reverend Jaeger now stood. He bowed his head, giving all in attendance a prime view of his balding scalp. She followed suit, desperate for a moment away from her chattery pew mate to focus her thoughts. She'd been raked across the conversational yard by Arel Dewey. The poor girl was going to be devastated—but hopefully disillusioned—when Mary did not show up for the four o'clock train. But she couldn't. She had no time to be distracted by other causes. Or people. Once the service was over, she had to find a way to convince Mrs. Osbourne to agree to turn her plant photos into illustrations.

As far as what to do about Karl without the K . . .

She peeked to see Arel holding the open Bible to her chest and mouthing her own prayer while Reverend Jaeger was praying aloud. One more thing to say about Arel Dewey: She had the courage to be herself. English society trained a woman from the cradle to be pleasing, thereby obliterating her individuality in the process. Mary certainly felt obliterated.

She looked away. What would life be like if she were free to be herself? Free to express her feelings and opinions, even disagreeable ones?

Free like Miss Dewey.

A strange warmth rushed through her, bubbles of—dare she say—hope. Never before had anyone insisted on being her friend or viewed her as a true sister. Not even her brothers claimed her as one. To them, she was the unspoken black sheep of the family, a female Varrs with two baccalaureate degrees. Worse, even, than her mother. Horrors upon abnormal horrors.

My dearest and bestest sister Mary . . .

Not just friend but—

Sister.

For one second—just one—Mary yielded to a slight smile.

A quilting bee would, simply, not be the death of her.

Mary nibbled on the last lemon-glazed biscuit and held the curtains back to spy on the house next door. Another quilting lady entered Mrs. Osbourne's home. Ten ladies so far this morning. Not including Mrs. Osbourne or her housekeeper Mrs. Binkley. A coughing fit like the one that had caused Mrs. Osbourne to leave the service early to care for Mrs. Binkley would not derail her plans.

Her own fears may.

Mary glanced at the crumbs on her fingers, the sweetness of the biscuit no longer a tasty trifle on her tongue. Monday morning arrived all too soon.

Napoleon whined.

She knelt, holding her fingers out. "How can I go to a quilting bee?" she asked as his sandpaper tongue found every last crumb. She'd never felt comfortable talking to strangers.

If only she had the extraordinary vivacity of Arel Dewey.

"Should I go"—she sighed—"or put an ad in the paper and hope someone answers immediately?"

Napoleon stopped licking. He didn't have to speak for her to know what he would answer. Mary scratched behind his ears until he stopped arching his head for her to scratch more. She then stood and walked to the kitchen to wash her hands. The water cooled her skin but not her nerves. Her hands shook. Her heart pounded in her chest. She turned off the water and gripped the edge of the porcelain sink. No reason to panic. Stop panicking! Be calm. Somehow, she and Mrs. Osbourne would work a trade, and it wouldn't include Mary spending one minute quilting. Simple and easy.

The idea brought a morsel of comfort.

Mary toweled her hands, retoweled, wiping until not a drop of moisture remained. Then she folded the towel in proper alignment and laid it over the edge of the sink. Nothing else to do. Nothing else to stop her. Go. Go. Go. GO.

"All right, I will," she muttered.

Mary dusted the front of her bodice, brushing away any biscuit crumbs. She smoothed the belt around her waist. Her gaze shifted to the straw hat on the kitchen table, still where she'd left it, following her morning constitutional. Wear it? Not wear it? Stop stalling.

Go. Go. Gogogogogogogo.

Fine!

"Wish me luck," she said to Napoleon as he trailed her to the front door.

Before she talked herself out of it, she was at Mrs. Osbourne's house. Standing at the bottom riser. Not moving. Don't think. Just go.

Mary raised the front of her white skirt and hurried up the stairs, crossed the porch, reached for the door, and gripped the handle tight. A wave of dizziness hit, blurring her vision. She desperately held onto the door. Not now.

Closing her eyes, she breathed deep.

Speak of nothing save the weather and other idle chatter. All would be well and easy and comfortable and fine.

She relaxed her hold on the door. Opened her eyes. Steadied her shoulders.

After another deep breath, she walked into Mrs. Osbourne's house in the same manner as she'd observed the other quilting bee attendees do—without knocking. Not a soul stood in the open foyer to welcome her except an orange feline on the carpeted stair runner. Its tail flicked with a *you may pet me if you must*.

Mary laid her calling card in the empty gold-plated receiver, her fingers hovering over the white card. Leave it. Don't leave it. What was the proper Virginia protocol?

"We're in here, Rheba," someone called out. "Leave your pies on the table. I'll take care of them in a moment." Sounded like Mrs. Osbourne, but since they'd only spoken upon a handful of times, Mary couldn't be sure.

Mary looked around. Covered baskets rested atop and underneath two folding tables that looked to be handcrafted from rosewood and inlaid with ebony, similar to a design she once saw in

Paris. Wait. Pies? She cringed. *Lunch is potluck* the invitation had specified. She should return home for some canned jalapeño pickles.

Splendid idea! If she wished to lose what courage she'd built up coming here.

Mary rested her hands on the increasingly tight, black v-shaped belt she wore with her pique skirt and pink-with-gray-dots blouse, an outfit usually worn when golfing, which she enjoyed often during her studies in Florida. Despite bringing her clubs, she had yet to find a golf course. But she hadn't tried looking. She ought to. In fact—

She released an unladylike grunt. Golf and fashion? She had far more pressing worries at the moment than golf and fashion.

Still, the white bow tie around her shirt's high collar now felt like a grip around a putter. The internal tension from interrupting a quilting bee was enough to strangle her. And she missed calculating the trajectory of the ball, the influence of the wind, the—

Dawdling is what she was doing.

Stop avoiding the inevitable!

She breathed deep. Her lungs had to have the capacity of an ocean steamer. She released the breath and walked to the parlor.

Underneath the ornate chandelier and surrounded by gold-painted, velvet-cushioned furniture were the quilters. Ten to be precise. All gathered around a rectangular wooden frame covered with muslin. Each wearing dark skirts with white or gray blouses, hair drawn back in simple buns, instead of the elaborate braided and twisted chignon Mary wore. Without taking turns, they spoke. Five, six maybe, conversations going.

So many people talking at once. So much laughter.

Instead of covering her ears and running from the house, Mary opened her mouth. "I am not Rheba."

Silence blanketed the room.

All gazes turned her way, emotions clear on their faces. Shock: *You?!* Then suspicion: *Why are you here?* Finally, rejection: *This is a private event; we don't have a place for you.* Responses similar to those she'd endured since she was ten. Their gazes shifted to Mrs.

40

Osbourne, the singular soul in the room looking delighted to see Mary.

"Miss Varrs," she said, standing and stepping back from the quilt frame. "I am thrilled you decided to attend." Her words held a sincere graciousness.

About this. She wasn't actually attending if she could get out of it.

"I have no pies." *That* was the best she could say in response. Pathetic.

"No need to fret," Mrs. Osbourne said sweetly. "You're my guest."

Mary nodded to the ladies in the parlor. "But they are your guests, too, and they brought . . . on the tables . . . the invitation said potluck. I wasn't thinking and . . ."

Oh, good gracious, she was babbling like a brook. Her pulse even raced like a kayak down said brook. All panicky. Just like the day Headmistress Whitacre drew her to the front of the great hall. *Ladies, this poor soul needs improving to become a lady.*

Mary gave her head a shake to dispose of the memory. She smiled as best she could to appear at ease. "Mrs. Osbourne, might I have a word with you?" She motioned to the foyer. "In private."

"Certainly." Mrs. Osbourne touched the shoulder of the quilter on her right. "Peggy, take over for me please, and remember to continue layering the scraps out from the center." She then walked to Mary and stepped with her into the parlor, leaving whispers in her wake. "Did the elixir not help Napoleon?"

"It did. He and his bowels have returned to docility."

"Then, if this is about not bringing a dish, you need not feel embarrassed. We always have enough food."

"It's not —. I—" Her throat choked as the words *I need your help* petrified inside her larynx.

Mrs. Osbourne took Mary's hands, surrounding them together with hers. A tender action. A typical American action. "You look ghastly," she whispered. "What's wrong?"

She didn't look at Mrs. Osbourne's hands clasped around hers, nor did she draw away despite her desire to escape being at the complete mercies of her neighbor who had invaded the private—and

GINA WELBORN

comfortable—bubble surrounding her. Yet, she relaxed her grip, in hopes Mrs. Osbourne would receive the action as a subtle clue to let go, like other people had when holding her hands. Instead, Mrs. Osbourne held tighter.

Speak and ignore her touch.

"For the last two years, I have lived around the world doing a study on tomatoes," she rushed out. "My intention has been to submit it to the Virginia Agricultural Experiment Station with the express purpose of obtaining a research assistant position. The VAES is open to hiring females."

Mrs. Osbourne nodded for her to continue.

Mary glanced down at their joined hands and pinched her eyes closed, drawing in a steadying breath doing nothing to ease the nervous tumble of her pulse. Do not insult her by pulling away. She looked up, meeting her neighbor's compassionate gaze, a gaze clearly aware of her unease. Why? A caring person would not force closeness. Even animals knew to respect another's territory. Granted, their establishment of territory required the use of urine, which was not an option for her.

Abruptly Mrs. Osbourne dropped Mary's hands and, with a gentle smile, took a step back. "About your tomato study . . .?"

"Yes, I, uh . . ." Mary clasped her hands together with a concerted effort to look relaxed. "I have recently learned the photographs I've taken for my study will nullify my application. I need classical illustrations of my photographs"—she nipped the corner of her mouth—"and I have no artistic ability."

For the longest moment, Mrs. Osbourne just stood there, giving Mary time to notice how her ski-slope nose tipped up at the bottom. The little bump made her classic features more amiable. Even with heavy wrinkles and gray-sprinkled dark hair, the woman was aging well. Of course, what she was thinking, Mary could not fathom. While she knew little about her temporary neighbor, she sensed the woman was old enough to be her mother and did not suffer fools.

"And?" Mrs. Osbourne finally prompted.

"When I saw the drawing you did on the invitation . . ." She gave a little shrug. "I need a botanical illustrator. I need . . . you."

Understanding dawned in Mrs. Osbourne's blue eyes, and she released a pent-up breath. "Is this all? I would be happy to help."

Mary blinked, stunned. "You would?"

"It brings me joy to help others." Said with enough maternal concern to cause Mary's eyes to feel unusually moist for the third time today. "When do you need them?"

Mary cleared her throat. "Ten days."

"Ten days? Dearest, my quilting bee—"

"Yes, I know," cut in Mary, "and it is the quandary I am in. They need to be in the mail by next Wednesday in order to arrive by the submission deadline. I would seek aid elsewhere, but I am desperate, and your sketching is beautiful. I'm willing to negotiate a trade of my time for yours."

Mrs. Osbourne fingered the falls of lace at the neckline of her gray-on-gray-striped blouse. "How many illustrations do you need?"

"For a study of this size," Mary explained, relieved by the comfortable topic, "five types per species is common, along with a rate of growth related to nutrients and sunshine, and I have seven major varieties per type, although I have fifty-three different seed plants, including cultivated and wild and—"

Mrs. Osbourne's brow rose in a headmistress manner. *Minimum requirement, please.*

Mary cringed awkwardly. "Um, well, for the top tomato in each of the five types: germination, mature plant, leaf, fruit size and shape, and a cross section of a mature tomato. Each illustration approximately palm-size."

Mrs. Osbourne smiled warmly in return. "So five individual drawings on five separate canvases?"

"Yes, mum," Mary said with an embarrassing exuberance in her tone spewing forth before she could contain it. This time the racing of her pulse made her feel giddy, hopeful. "Each set of sketches needs to fill a traditional sheet of art paper, not canvas. The mercantile had drawing and charcoal paper. I bought both this morning not knowing which you would prefer."

"If it must be paper, then Bristol board would be better."

"I purchased it in two-ply and three-ply, white, but if you prefer ivory, I could—"

Mrs. Osbourne just arched her brow. Again.

Mary avoided wincing this time.

"Your diligence to be prepared for all scenarios reminds me of my nephew."

"Thank you."

"It was not a compliment." Mrs. Osbourne's gaze shifted to the parlor, where not a peep could be heard. Wherever her quilting friends were standing and listening, they were far enough back not to be seen.

Afraid to say more and risk losing her neighbor's willingness to help, Mary eyed the cat. The cat—with its *you poor worrisome human* flick of the tail and an arrogance befitting Marie Antoinette—lifted its paw, rubbed its head from back to front, then proceeded to lick its paw as if it literally did not have a care in the world.

Oh, to be a cat.

"I will help you, Miss Varrs." Mrs. Osbourne turned her full attention on Mary. She took a step forward, closing the comfortable distance between them. "I will sketch in the day during my quilting bee, and in exchange, you will take my place embroidering the quilt."

Mary could do nothing to stop her eyes from widening and jaw dropping in a most unladylike manner. "Embroidering the quilt?" she echoed. "But—"

Mrs. Osbourne's brow rose again, and Mary held back any further argument.

Mrs. Osbourne patted the side of Mary's arm with a *you'll do fine,* then added a verbal "You do know how." Not a question, but a statement made in confidence. Likely from the assumption all Englishwomen knew how to embroider; thus, Mary knew, simply by location of her birth. Which was an unfair presumption. One would not have to do a case study to prove not all Englishwomen were intrinsically skilled with the needle. This said, her needlework skill was passable. When she concentrated on giving her best effort, some—all right, one: the prince—even declared her skill to be exceptional.

Mary nodded.

"Excellent," was said with all the delight Arel Dewey had when discussing votes for women. Mrs. Osbourne smiled. "Now, Miss Varrs, while I collect my pencils and easel, you will bring over the Bristol board and your first set of photographs."

Lifting the front of her black skirt, she moved up the stairs, around the cat continuing to flick its tail even with its eyes closed.

"Holly Jane Ferris," she intoned, "in recompense for listening to a private conversation, please find Miss Varrs a chair between you and Peggy. The rest of you, get back to work. Posthaste."

Mary didn't move. She had hoped for a trade. For an exchange of goods, perhaps. She clenched her hands together, nipping her bottom lip, staring nervously at the parlor's entrance. But—

Embroider a quilt? Heaven help her, what had she gotten herself into?

"Miss Varrs?"

Mary looked to the top of the stairs where Mrs. Osbourne stood. "Yes?"

"A quilting bee will not be the death of you." She paused, smiled. "I promise."

4

Her fingertips literally throbbed from a longtime lack of sewing. Tonight she would soak them in Epsom salts.

Mary wiped the beads of perspiration on her forehead. Her lemonade sat on the nearby coffee table. Her wanting a sip, sadly, wasn't as strong as her not wanting to get up.

She punched her needle through the underside of the tightly pulled muslin with a crisp pop, pulling the yellow floss through. She should have found the courage to keep the nondescript white she'd chosen instead of the bright contrasting yellow Mrs. Osbourne handed her along with a needle and petite embroidery scissors. Being skilled in the Art of Pleasing Others truly did obliterate her individuality. No wonder the average English girl was viewed as decidedly dull by the Americans. Years of being "improved" made her this way.

At least it made *her* this way.

After a few initial and not too personal questions, the eleven quilters and Mrs. Osbourne had abandoned her to a small corner of the quilt, a section most likely to be hidden under pillows. No offense had been taken at their presumption her stitching would be poor quality. She would have put herself in a corner, too. Unlucky thirteenth quilter.

Mary niftily knotted the underside of the star she'd finished then began a new one, taking care to ensure it was in proper alignment with the others. Better to take one's time than rush and lose precision. One angled + atop a second angled +. Each angle, hopefully, mimicked those of the other stars.

She smiled to herself.

Pleasure in symmetry. Pleasure in monotonous repetition. And it was about the only thing providing any semblance of order on the chaotic quilt top.

Although she had to admit the quilting process was rather simple, albeit whimsical, for this Bride's Quilt the women were making for Miss Lydia Puryear in honor of her upcoming October nuptials. The groom's unmentioned name was one everyone knew except her. (Asking what it was required speaking, and speaking would lead to them to remember she was present, and remembering she was present would lead to personal questions.) What impressed her was how each quilter brought a basket of scraps, including padded and embroidered appliquéd pieces. Not unwanted scraps. Favorite ones. Treasured ones. Mrs. Marvin had even embroidered *Welcome my friends all!* onto a rectangular scrap of white cotton to be included in the quilt. The same Egyptian cotton she'd used to sew her granddaughter's christening gown.

Her back to the foyer, Mary finished her yellow star stitch and began another where the plaid calico laid atop a scrap of rough wool intersecting with two pieces of silk and embossed velvet. The differing shapes and the contrast of textures and weights of the fabrics felt erroneous. A *faux pas*. Like wearing plaids with stripes. Or navy with black. Or sprinkling bacon atop ice cream or watermelon.

Yes, it could be done, but *could* didn't mean the same as *should*.

The gentle hum of the stand fans in front of the open windows circulated air about the warm room. And the grandfather clock in the foyer chimed the hour: ten o'clock. They would be breaking for lunch in an hour.

At least now, the conversation had fallen into a comfortable lull.

Mary sighed. Contentedly? It made her pause. Perhaps she was content, to a degree, despite the warmth in the room. Attending a quilting bee wasn't as insufferable as she'd expected. Better than, say, a Votes for Women rally.

Mrs. Osbourne left her easel to examine the quilt top. "Ladies, this is the progress I like to see." She paused next to Mary, touching her shoulder. "Nice work."

Nice work? Did Mrs. Osbourne not care she'd yet to finish embroidering her first set of basted scraps?

Her cheeks warmed. "I, uh . . ." *am sorry I'm slow.*

"Sometimes a simple thank-you is enough," Mrs. Osbourne said gently.

"Thank you," Mary muttered, falling into an absent stare at the quilt.

Mrs. Osbourne patted her shoulder, all tender. All sincere. She then moved on to the next quilter, inquiring about the lovely fabric choices, listening as Mrs. Lee responded.

Mary spared a glance at the raven-haired quilter to her right. Mrs. Holly Jane Ferris, a ravishing widow, who recently celebrated her thirty-second birthday, was the only other young woman in the quilt group. All the other quilters in the sunshine-brightened parlor were at least double in age. Yet, her lesser years did not lessen her skill. Each of her blue turkey trot stitches matched perfectly.

"My favorite scraps are from my trousseau material," interjected Mrs. Ferris the Younger as she tied off her thread then positioned her next set of scraps. A velvet ribbon remnant. Three mismatched cotton prints. A padded hen and rooster appliquéd onto a scrap of green satin. An odd collection. Yet, once she basted them in place then selected different colored threads, presumably for varying stitch patterns, her choices blended well. As well as any of the hodge-podge scraps could on this harlequin "crazy" design.

Mary stabbed her needle into the muslin again.

"Shall we tell *her* about last summer's quilt?" asked Mrs. Turner, indicating Mary.

"Do tell." Mrs. Osbourne returned to her place by the easel.

"A white-on-white whole cloth Trapunto," Mrs. Rutland explained. "The most beautiful one we've made thus far." Her blue eyes glinted with excitement while she worked with a nimble and swift skill similar to the other quilters. Stitching while talking was apparently necessary to produce a quilt during a two-week bee.

"We each contributed to the design," Mrs. Lee boasted.

Mrs. Ferris the Older patted the muslin, near where Mary was working at a less nimble pace. "A whole cloth Trapunto should not to be confused with whole cloth Provençal."

Obviously.

Mary smiled and hoped it was enough of a response.

"Remember the Provençal bride's quilt we made for Holly Jane?" Mrs. Mackey said wistfully.

The quilters all looked to Mrs. Ferris the Younger. "I cried when I first saw it. It's still my most treasured quilt." She turned to Mrs. Clemmer. "Wasn't your Bride's Quilt a Windmill Blade?"

And with the question began a slew of incomplete sentences and interruptions, rushing from one Bride's Quilt to the next, opening a floodgate of words leaving Mary looking from one quilter to another in order to catch what was being said. So many quilt designs! So many quilter names to remember! Like a room full of Arel Deweys. Her head was splitting.

"Priscilla," Mrs. Ferris the Elder ordered, "bring out your entry for the Keller Agricultural Fair." And the topic changed once again.

Mrs. Ferris the Younger leaned against Mary's shoulder. "The fair is in August," she whispered. "She always snares blue."

Blue? Oh, a blue ribbon.

Mrs. Osbourne didn't look up from her easel. "You can see it at the fair."

"You say that every year," Mrs. Van Mater called out.

"We want to see it early," Mrs. Jaeger added.

Pleas rose from each of the quilters, until they evolved into clapping and one unified "show us," in which Mary joined.

What was so mysterious about this quilt Mrs. Osbourne would keep it a secret from her dearest friends? Even she wanted to know.

Mrs. Osbourne looked up from her easel, her eyes shifting from one quilter to the next. For a moment, it looked like her gaze settled on Mary. She moistened her lips. Eyes dropped. Head shook. "I can't."

"You can," Mrs. Turner said crisply. "You don't want to."

"You're right, Nicola. I don't want to." Mrs. Osbourne picked up her pencil. "To be candid, I don't think I will be entering it in the fair after all."

A united gasp. Minus Mary.

Instead, she frowned at the lack of sureness in her neighbor. Unusual. Shocking.

Mrs. Marvin shook her head, disappointedly. "Your problem, Priscilla, is you don't trust us to keep it a secret."

"We're not going to steal your design," Mrs. Jaeger added with tenderness in her tone.

The front door opened. "Aunt Priscilla!"

Mrs. Ferris the Younger gasped. "It's him." Squeak. Then, breathlessly: "Zenus."

"In here," answered Mrs. Osbourne without moving off the stool she sat partially on.

Mrs. Ferris the Younger frantically brushed the loose threads off her clothes then stopped. She breathed deep, rolled her shoulders back, clasped her hands together in her lap, and pursed her lips in a coy manner befitting any London debutante.

The door slammed.

Mary looked over her shoulder to see the entrant.

A man strode into the parlor. A tweed Irish eight-piece cap was cocked jauntily atop his dark hair. Raincoat draped over an arm. He stopped near Mrs. Ferris the Older, who partially blocked Mary's view of him. The flushness to his face did not lessen the striking contrast of his walnut hair and pale blue eyes. While he didn't appeal to her, she understood why some women would behave as Holly Jane Ferris.

"Aunt Priscilla, I took the first train out of Philly this morning because I need—"

"Slow down, Zenus." Mrs. Osbourne rested her pencil on the easel. Her ever-communicative eyebrow rose.

Mary straightened in her chair. *This* was Zenus Dane? The one Arel Dewey oft mentioned in not-so-flattering terms.

He yanked off his cap. "Ladies, nice to see you all again," he said, barely giving them a cursory glance. His discourteous gaze focused on the back of the room. To his aunt. To the only person in the room who clearly mattered to him. No wonder Miss Dewey abhorred the man.

"I need your help," he begged.

"And you want it in a hurry."

"Of course, time is—"

"Of the essence. As it always is with you." She snapped her fingers and pointed to the Queen Anne chair between her easel and the unlit hearth. "Zenus, sit. Ladies, keep working."

Mary rested her needle on the quilt top.

She didn't have to take her gaze—narrowed and observant—from him to know the man in the well-tailored, brown pin-striped suit with the impressive watch chain had attracted the attention of every quilter. And . . . he knew he attracted their attention. Reveled in it. Holly Jane Ferris was close to drooling. Widow Marvin at the end of the quilt frame opposite Mary looked a bit starry-eyed. Over a man half her age.

Mary released a *pffft*. He could take his Titanesque attitude elsewhere. *She* had claimed Mrs. Osbourne's help first.

He walked past the quilt frame, a direct cut to Mrs. Ferris the Younger and her I'm-so-delighted-to-see-you wave, and stopped at his aunt's easel. "In this case, Aunt, time is truly of the essence. Philly experienced a deluge on Friday causing massive flooding. I need one of your quilt designs to help me salvage my damaged textiles. The design needs to be simple for a beginner, but still enjoyable for the expert, one using fifteen to twenty textiles and requiring no more than a yard of each print. Amounts needed must vary."

She angled her cheek toward him. "First things first."

He leaned down and planted a kiss.

"And?"

He let out a loud exhale. "I am sorry it took a flood to motivate me to visit. You were correct in everything you said last we spoke." He laid his raincoat and tweed cap on the chair next to her. "I am willing to make adjustments."

Mrs. Osbourne flashed him a smile. Part *pleased to hear it*. Part *I don't believe a word you said.*

"Now this wasn't too painful. I forgive you for leaving abruptly and for arriving just as abruptly." She smoothed the front of his matching brown pin-striped waistcoat. "I see you had the tarnished buttons replaced like I suggested. Like your wife, if you had one, would have suggested."

She stopped him cold.

She waved at the air. "Pay me no mind, dear nephew. I'm delightfully delighted to see you again. As far as my quilt patterns go, I give them to no one."

"We're family," he blurted, as if it obligated her.

With another *pffft*, Mary took offense on Mrs. Osbourne's behalf.

"No one." Mrs. Osbourne's smile froze on her face. "Ever."

A muscle in his strong, slanted jaw flinched. "Then design me a new pattern, an original."

"No."

"I'll pay. Give you four percent of all sales."

"Noooo," she said, elongating the word.

"You will be fully credited for the quilt design," he countered.

She rose off the stool to stand toe-to-toe with him, even though she had to look up. "Do you not hear me?"

"But—"

"*No.*"

Even from her corner at the quilt frame, Mary could feel the tension emanating from the pair. It gave her a headache. She wiped her forehead. The breeze coming in through the window must have stopped because the room was sweltering. And she wasn't the only one who noticed because the other quilters had stopped sewing and were fanning their faces with their hands.

Mary joined in the face fanning.

"Please, Aunt Priscilla," Mr. Dane begged. He gripped her hands. "I'm desperate. I'm willing to do whatever I must for your help."

"Now *that* I believe." Mrs. Osbourne slowly exhaled. "If—and I am only saying *if*—I decide to create a design for you, how soon do you need it?"

"Tomorrow."

"An impossible deadline."

Mary silently cheered. Stand your ground, Mrs. Osbourne.

He walked to the nearest window. "I am willing to negotiate," he offered as he scooted the ornamental brass fan closer to the opened panes, "because your quilts are nationally recognized, and deservedly so." He drew the curtains back more and then tilted the fan, sending the air to the ceiling. Crossing the room to the next window, he said, "People will buy these quilt kits solely because your name would be on the packaging." He stopped at the other fan and repeated the process. "Two days doable?"

Two days? Mary's temple began to throb.

One of Mrs. Osbourne's dark eyebrows rose, in a *you are taxing me* manner to which Mary had become accustomed. This time she savored it.

The man groaned. "I hate it when you look at me so." He paced in front of the unlit hearth, a hand rubbing the back of his neck. "Five days tops," he countered. "Production must begin immediately. I know you can do this. You've created blue-ribbon-winning patterns in half as much time. Don't answer. Just consider it first."

Mary growled under her breath, shaking her head, which wasn't smart because of how much it was pounding. Mrs. Osbourne had agreed to help her. *Her*. Nothing Zenus Dane could say would make his need for help any more important or pressing than hers was. She had spent every day of the last twenty-five months working on this tomato study. She'd forgone relationships. Friendships. Endured humiliation, for the sake of earning—for *proving* she deserved—the position of research assistant amid academia who gave little support to women scientists and doctors. Even put her future in the hands of an Italian prince.

This man, Zenus Dane, would not ruin her chances.

She refused to allow him to waste the last two years of her life.

She sought Mrs. Osbourne's gaze. Gave her a silent *we had an arrangement first*. But the woman kept her attention on her wily, silver-tongued nephew.

"Why do you need this so desperately?" Mrs. Osbourne asked.

"In less than a month," he explained, "if I have nothing to make payment or to show the potential for payment, the bank will call in my loan. I—"

"Wait," Mrs. Osbourne interrupted. "*You* took out a loan?"

He stopped pacing and gripped the fireplace mantel with one hand, his knuckles turning white. "Yes."

"But—" Mrs. Osbourne sat back on her stool. "Taking out a loan is risky."

"I know." His eyes pleaded as much as his tone. "Aunt Priscilla, if you don't help me, I will lose my business. Over forty families rely on me. Me. Many are mothers who are their family's sole support. I can't let them down."

Holly Jane Ferris gasped, placing her hands over her heart. "Oh, the poor man."

Poor man? Mary wanted to gag.

First of all, there was insurance. Second, there were eleven other expert quilters in Priscilla Dane Osbourne's parlor. Not to mention how many others lived in Belle Haven alone. Any one of them could design a quilt pattern this let's-presume-the-worst-will-happen cassowary—this lofty ostrichlike man—needed. She refused to allow him to sweet-talk his aunt into caving to his will.

Poor man. Ha! Men like him—

Mary gritted her teeth. Oh, she knew about men like him.

She'd been engaged to one.

This nephew of Mrs. Osbourne would not bamboozle her of her future, like she'd allowed Edward Argent to do. She wasn't a naive, love-struck girl anymore.

Mary stood, with more verve than she'd felt since Edward terminated their engagement. This Mr. Dane was not getting what he wanted from Mrs. Osbourne. Not if she had a say in the matter. She took no care in brushing a single loose thread off her clothing—what he thought of her mattered not—and made a beeline to the man who now stood facing the hearth, both his hands gripping the fireplace mantel.

She held her hands together in front of her. She tipped her head toward Mrs. Osbourne, giving a *would you introduce us?* look.

Mrs. Osbourne stood there. Silent. As if Mary's respect for protocol was lost on her.

Oh, good gracious. If she didn't take the initiative, who knew how long she would be standing here. As St. Ambrose said, "*Si fueris Romae, Romano vivito more; Si fueris alibi, vivito sicut ibi.*" When in Rome . . . well, when in America—

Although it went against all she knew as apropos, she lightly touched the center of his back. Then jerked back, lest anyone notice. "Excuse me. I am Miss Mary Varrs, your aunt's neighbor for the spring."

He turned around, giving her a blank stare, elevating the hair on the back of her neck. He smelled aristocratic. Unexpectedly pleasing and familiar. Lemon, sandalwood, and petitgrain oils combined in the same Astor cologne her father had been wearing for the last decade. From where she'd sat, he hadn't looked as tall as he was. At five foot, eight inches, she rarely met men who made her feel dainty. Neither had she ever met one whose hands she could feel on her waist, drawing her to him, even though he wasn't touching her. Yet the possessive look in his summer-sunshine blue eyes—

His lips parted.

Warmth spread from her neck to her ears, and Mary took a precautious step back. The Book of Proverbs and *Good Housekeeping* both warned of men like him.

Instead of backing further away, she stuck out her hand. "Arel— as in *Arl*—Dewey has mentioned you to me." Feel free to take it as warning. "It's nice to finally meet you."

"Venus Dane," he said with a firm grip as he shook her hand, "it's nice to marry you."

5

The look on her exquisite face matched what Zenus felt—mortification. He also felt lightheaded with a rapid heartbeat, but he had no idea if she experienced the same. *Venus Dane, it's nice to marry you.* Venus wasn't his name. Or hers. Mentioning marriage two seconds after greeting a comely woman was a faux pas if there ever was one. Should he clarify, or would it make matters worse to say, *I meant it's nice to* meet *you? Not* marry *you.*

He should stop staring at her.

Or release her hand that suddenly went limp.

Or mutter an apology for his misspeak.

Or remember why he was standing in his aunt's gaudy red-and-gold parlor in the first place. Or at least remember what the woman said her name was. Her skin glowed golden and adventurous. Her voice, a cardinal's song. Her scent—of fresh earthen works—pine, dirt, and herbs. Her eyes hazel, like the camouflage to shield the hunter from his prey. Her lips red as the blood of a mighty elk.

No. Not that last. But . . . say *something* charming before she flees. Like—

"I am Zenus Dane of Philadelphia." Excellent. He gave her hand another shake. "I did not intend to imply I'm a Venus or you are one either."

Her lovely face lost all color.

Not excellent. Not excellent at all. Not charming either. "Ahhh, I meant to say it is nice to meet you," he clarified, still shaking her hand. "I do not wish to marry you." Zenus closed his eyes in misery. Stop. No more talking. Not to her. Not ever again.

Being insulting would not do either. Fix it!

He looked at her. "No, I'm not refusing your proposal." What? No. Fix that! "No, I'm not suggesting you proposed," he hastily added, "but had you, I would not have refused." No. It's not what he meant either. Zenus bit his lip to halt further words from passing forth. He sounded like a petulant idiot. Because he was an idiot. *She* made him an idiot by her very—and vastly tempting—female existence.

She tugged at his firm grip. Shot a desperate glance to his left.

With a soft groan, Aunt Priscilla stepped forward, separating their hands and drawing the woman another step away from him— which meant something. His aunt's action was so protective he instantly knew she liked her new neighbor (not surprising) and wanted him to know her neighbor was not for him (completely surprising). After all, his aunt was a matchmaker to her core and, except in his case, successful at it.

"Ladies," she said, "Miss Puryear's quilt won't sew itself."

While their gazes shifted back to the quilt top and hands returned to stitching, not a word came from The Eleven's mouths. Eavesdropping was easier when not talking.

Aunt Priscilla lowered her voice. "Zenus," she said with a consoling pat to the woman's hand, "Miss Mary Varrs is a botanist from England, a guest in our country. This is where you should be polite and express a greeting. Such as *welcome*."

From England? It explained the melodious tenor to Miss Varrs's voice. Zenus didn't say anything. Wasn't going to. Ever again. Nor would he look her directly in the eye, for doing so made egg of his thoughts: scrambled, over easy, boiled—any way, he couldn't think straight. As long as he couldn't bridle his tongue, he wasn't saying anything.

He folded his arms across his chest. And said nothing.

"A greeting," she repeated. "To Miss Varrs." The arch of her brow never ceased to be annoying.

"Welcome to the Commonwealth." Finally, something not sounding idiotic.

Miss Varrs's lips curved. Head nodded for a quick—and clearly reluctant—*thank-you*. Yet her chin rose as she looked down her nose at him. Judging. Measuring him short.

Uppity Englishwoman.

"Zenus, she's leaving Belle Haven in ten days."

"No, in June," Miss Varrs supplied, smiling at Aunt Priscilla, who had finally released her hold on Miss Varrs's hand. "Once the Linwoods return from Europe. My *study* must be in the mail in ten days. Or sooner."

"Thank you for the clarification," Aunt Priscilla went on. "I am not sure how I misunderstood."

"I could make a timeline for you," Miss Varrs offered. All daughterly.

"Thank you, dearie." She patted the side of Miss Varrs's arm. All motherly. "It would be so helpful. Zenus has been telling me for years I wouldn't forget things if I kept a schedule."

They spoke as if he weren't in the room.

Zenus interjected, "The Linwoods have relatives in England?"

Miss Varrs looked at him strangely. Because he'd spoken in a nonblundering manner? Or because she'd forgotten his presence? He'd wager the latter.

Then she gasped, "Oh," and touched the center of her chest and said, "Because I am from England, you thought the Linwoods and I . . ."

Zenus waited, giving her an I'm-waiting-for-you-to-finish-your-sentence look.

Nothing. Just a raised chin and another appraisal down the length of her smug aristocratic nose. *You are a sad one of your sort* her look implied. Pity she was so handsome. Harridans generally were old, warty, and bore the name Evil Queen.

"Miss Varrs," his aunt explained, "is caring for the Linwoods' home and dog while they are on holiday and while she completes her tomato study, with which I've agreed to assist her. Thus, I cannot help you—"

"I'll be your helpmate," came from the center of the room.

"Holly Jane, be quiet and focus on the quilt." Aunt Priscilla looked to The Eleven. "Ladies, this is a private conversation, which will not leave this room. Understood?" Said in a tone to have stopped ten-year-old Zenus from much foolhardiness and spared him a broken limb if he hadn't been bored . . . and male . . . and ten.

All the quilters nodded.

Aunt Priscilla turned back to Zenus. "I cannot help you *unless* you are willing to agree, as Miss Varrs has, to my terms. Help me and I will help you"—he'd swear her lips curved upward—"help both of you get what will make you happy."

Then she gave him the look. The one that said *you know what I'm referring to.*

If he didn't know better—and he always had his doubts when it came to Priscilla Dane Osbourne—he'd think she had an ulterior, even altruistic, motive for wanting to help. But it would mean trusting her. It would mean believing she wanted to help him get what *he* wanted, not what she wanted him to want. His aunt, his summer mother, desired one surety yet from life: to see him married and producing the closest thing she'd ever have to grandchildren. She'd failed matching him with Lydia Puryear. It left the one lady in Belle Haven she knew he wanted, and the only lady she refused to aid him in courting.

Arel Dewey.

The swan of Belle Haven. The epitome of womanly perfection. And the only woman he dreamed of marrying since Clara.

Zenus uncrossed his arms.

Marrying Arel Dewey will make me happy. Help me court her!

The least manly begging he could have ever done. But he'd been desperate. And frustrated. Despite reaching his wit's end, she'd still refused his request for help during their argument last Christmas. The intensity in her gaze now gave him hope she'd changed her stance. To court Arel—finally. Now. Even after he'd called her Owl last summer. Christmas morning giddiness tickled his spine. The best—only—person to help him solve his quandary, once again, was Aunt Priscilla.

Zenus shifted his stance to give his electrified feet something to do. "Are we of the same mindset about what I want?" He managed to say it in a tone without conveying an ounce of the eagerness rippling through him.

A sparkle of delight grew in Aunt Priscilla's eyes. She was getting exactly what she wanted. "We are."

"I'm listening."

Aunt Priscilla's gaze shifted to her easel with a partial drawing attached.

Zenus leaned forward to get a better look. A tomato? Why was she sketching *that*?

The minutes passed. Slowly. Tediously.

He didn't have to look at Miss Varrs to sense her disapproval or know her lips had tightened and tiny white lines had formed at the corners of her mouth. She didn't like him. Arel, in her innocent gregariousness, had likely shared about his folly. But once Arel listened to his apology, realized his feelings were true, they could put his unfortunate misspeak behind them.

Aunt Priscilla continued to think at leisure.

Zenus tapped a hand against a thigh. They were wasting time.

Patient. Be patient. Needing a distraction, he gave his attention to the eleven women sitting around the rectangular quilt frame. All had known him since he was in knickers. Each had witnessed his verbal stupidities in the last eight years. Most, pitying his repetitive moments of humiliation, had attempted, by the by, to matchmake him. Holly Jane, obviously, for herself. Before her marriage, during, and a year to the day following her husband's funeral. The last quilter he'd turn to for assistance would be Holly Jane Ferris, née Randolph. Asking her the time of day was akin to a marriage proposal.

Zenus checked his pocket watch. Almost eleven. No quandary needed as much thought as what his aunt put into one. Especially this one.

A *humph* slipped from his throat, drawing her attention and Miss Varrs's glare.

Aunt Priscilla slapped her bejeweled hands together.

All in the parlor looked her way.

"Ladies," she said, "I know this has been an eventful morning. With Mrs. Binkley's illness, with the delightful arrival of my neighbor and guest, Miss Varrs, and the unexpected arrival of my nephew, both of whom seem to have equal reasons for needing my assistance."

"Are you cancelling the bee?" Mrs. Scarborough asked.

"Of course not," Aunt Priscilla reassured her. "Miss Puryear needs this quilt for her bride's chest. Everything will continue as usual. The minor adjustment will be instead of me quilting, Miss Varrs will take my place. As long as it is acceptable to each of you."

The Eleven exchanged glances.

Mrs. Peggy Ferris answered, "She works slow, but her skill is acceptable."

Miss Varrs nodded as if it was a fair assessment.

"Excellent." Aunt Priscilla gave Miss Varrs's hand a quick squeeze. "Then the hours prior to lunch, I will work on her sketches. Post lunch, I will work on creating a quilt pattern for my nephew, who will serve as host and my errand boy until Mrs. Binkley recovers from her illness or until I have his pattern completed."

Holly Jane nudged Mrs. Clemmer's arm, whispering, "Ask her."

"So we won't be rotating hostess duties?" Mrs. Clemmer said.

Aunt Priscilla shook her head. "Zenus will attend to it all, as long as necessary, so we can focus on the quilt at hand."

Holly Jane softly clapped.

Zenus groaned. A pounding behind his eyes. As long as necessary? With the shark named Holly Jane circling?

He looked from the quilters to his aunt. To be her host and errand boy meant staying in Belle Haven all week. Or longer. He had church on Sunday, which he couldn't miss. Not to mention Tuesday night book club, Wednesday church choir and board meeting, Thursday Schuylkill Fishing Company meeting, Friday symphony attendance with Aimee, and on Saturday, he and Sean were doing their once-a-month fishing cruise down the Wissahickon Creek. All of which Aunt Priscilla knew. Once again confirming her lack of respect for his schedule.

"I had planned on returning to Philly tomorrow with the design."

Aunt Priscilla's nod and pinched expression conveyed every bit of her disappointment. "I can see how this will be a problem for you." The *and your schedule* was clear despite being unsaid. "Oh, and you must be my escort to the Johns Hopkins Faculty and Alumni Brunch next weekend."

"It's a Sunday."

"I know."

Zenus kept his face even. His aunt would not get the best of him. Or worst.

"Nevertheless," she continued with a dismissive wave, "if you wish me to help you obtain what will make you happy—and I will do so for free since we are family—then you must agree to my terms."

Miss Varrs and her snooty *please leave* look would not get the best—or worst—of him either.

"Aunt Priscilla, be reasonable," he put in. "I have a flooded mill to manage."

"And we both know Sean will oversee it during your absence. If what you want is in Belle Haven," she said pointedly, "then in Belle Haven you should be, until what will make you happy is yours." Her shoulders rose in the closest thing his aunt had ever done to resemble a take-it-or-leave-it-I'm-fine-either-way shrug. "You have the liberty to go to one of my quilter friends for assistance. Holly Jane has already expressed her willingness."

And with her statement, he knew she was no longer referring to the quilt pattern he needed.

Zenus looked back to The Eleven. To the hunger on Holly Jane's face. To the matchmaking gleam in the other women's eyes. Women who all had unmarried daughters or nieces, and none of whom would assist in his courtship of Arel Dewey, despite her being, justifiably so, the town's favorite daughter. The quilt top they were sewing resembled colorful mud pies thrown against a bed sheet with

Frankenstein stitches to hold them in place. Whatever the crazy design was, he didn't want it for his quilt kits. Although . . . for his bags of scraps, it was perfect.

His shoulders straightened. His heart skipped a beat, and the pounding between his temples eased.

This was workable.

This had promise.

But not with any of The Eleven as his quilt designer or matchmaker.

He needed the woman whose name alone had national recognition in the quilting community. Considering how quickly Aunt Priscilla created new patterns in the past, by week's end, he would have what he needed. More so, he would have time to court Arel with Aunt Priscilla as his helpful sage.

He spared a glance at Miss Varrs.

She stood stoically, like an English queen before her executioner. Or, more fittingly, like she held the blade and he was the condemned monarch. What was she doing in America anyway? He didn't think English ladies *did* anything. This one, though, did one thing well—look down on him as if he were sludge.

She was a rather unfriendly female. Strange. Abnormal.

Gaining Aunt Priscilla's aid in courting Arel Dewey meant him staying in Belle Haven. It meant being in Miss Varrs's presence. He had no choice but to do his best and avoid her.

"I agree to your terms," he answered, ignoring the haughty glare Miss Varrs sent his way.

<hr />

She wasn't ignorable.

From his spot in the dining room corner, Zenus tapped his fork against his dinner plate. Fourteen people scrunched around a table that properly sat ten. No one thought to save a place for him. But for Miss Varrs—they lionized her. All afternoon and into the dinner hour, the peculiar creature was the object of their curiosity and obsession; they acted as if she were Princess Alexandra and he a foul smell. True, he could have found a seat at the table in the music room with Aunt Priscilla and the remaining quilters and their spouses, and spared himself. But something about Mary Varrs intrigued him. Like when Aimee lost her first molar and she couldn't stop gazing in the mirror at the bloody hole in her gums.

Zenus leaned forward. Rested his elbows on his knees. Gripped his plate with his left hand. He jabbed his fork into the pile of green beans with his right, focusing on the conversation.

"So then what brought you to Virginia?" Gerald Turner asked looking around his wife who sat between him and Miss Varrs.

"My botany study," Miss Varrs softly answered.

"On?" Mrs. Turner prodded.

"Tomatoes."

Everyone paused, waiting for her to say more.

She pushed her food around on her plate. "I . . ."

No one spoke.

Zenus chomped down on a mouthful of beans. No woman—least of all an English one—came to Virginia to study tomatoes. She had to have an ulterior motive. For years, European aristocrats had been using their titles to ensnare social-climbing American heiresses, recently one from Philadelphia. Why not do the same by sending their spinster daughters to find bachelor millionaires? His gaze shifted around the room. None of the quilters had sons who met the qualification. In fact, the only unmarried millionaire he knew in Belle Haven was Mr. Xavier B. Dewey, Arel's widowed father.

Mackey nudged Ferris.

"What brought you to America?" asked Ferris, who stayed for the evening meal even though his wife had left with Holly Jane to attend to his ailing grandson.

Miss Varrs sipped her drink. "Soil."

Zenus gave his head a little shake. She must think Belle Havenians were simpletons.

"Soil?" Mrs. Clemmer shifted to face Miss Varrs, who sat on her left. "How so?"

"The, uhh . . ." Miss Varrs put her goblet down, nicking the edge of her dinner place, causing a *ching*. "The Eastern Shore enjoys the agricultural advantages of a mild climate, abundant rainfall, and a long growing season. In particular, the soils of Accomac and Northampton, mostly light, sandy loams, are well drained, easily cultivated, and receptive to the application of fertilizer making them the most productive of the Atlantic Coastal Plain."

Rutland slapped the table so hard the silverware bounced. "I've been saying the same for years!"

Mrs. Rutland followed up, saying, "Daniel owns farmland in both counties."

"Oh," Miss Varrs said, her expression blank. She took a bite of ham.

Mrs. Mackey put in, "Why did you choose Belle Haven?"

Miss Varrs patted her mouth with her napkin. "It was not my first choice."

Silence.

"Then what was?" asked Jude Scarborough.

She moved to spear another bite of ham then stopped. "Onancock or Chincoteague." Her voice sounded apologetic, but Zenus didn't believe it for a second. This woman excelled in playing the innocent.

Everyone looked to her to elaborate.

"Belle Haven," she said, "provided the only suitable real estate with an established garden and empty portion for me to cultivate my tomato plants."

Zenus managed not to roll his eyes in cynical disbelief. She had to be here for Arel's father.

"Where did you live before?" inquired Fitzwilliam Lee.

"In the last twenty-five months"—she spoke in such a detached, unapproachable manner—"I've lived in Italy, Spain, Cyprus, India, Africa, South America, Mexico, and Florida, before coming to Belle Haven."

"And we are so glad the good Lord brought you to us." Hand on Miss Varrs's arm, Mrs. Turner smiled sweetly. As if the practical stranger was her long-lost daughter.

Zenus rolled his eyes.

Miss Varrs cast hers demurely to the table.

Pretense. Pretense. Pretense.

He scooped up another mouthful of salty beans. The woman knew how to use her looks and charm to get what she wanted. Namely, his aunt sketching tomato plants instead of helping him. Family was supposed to put family first. Miss Varrs had manipulated Aunt Priscilla. What kind of woman studied tomatoes for two years? He couldn't think of one fascinating thing about tomatoes. Or seeds. Or fertilizers. If he ever lived in England or Cyprus or India or any of the other places she'd mentioned living in, he certainly wouldn't spend his leisure studying plants, either floral or edible.

Zenus swallowed and choked on a bean. He coughed. Cleared his throat. Eyes watering, he frantically grabbed the lemonade goblet resting at his feet. He took a swig. Coughed and cleared his throat again.

Not a single person looked his way.

Instead, as quickly as Miss Varrs answered, other questions came in succession like the rat-tat-tat of the door knocker. Oohs. Ahhs. How interestings!

Why? Her responses contained the least amount of information a person could share, unless she was discussing flora, fauna, and fungi, about which she rambled incessantly.

A woman couldn't be more uninteresting.

He knew all about women like her. Women who chose to marry "so charming" men instead of the reformed rogues who loved them.

Zenus continued to eat.

And plot.

And plan.

Miss Mary Varrs of Belle Haven, by way of Italy, Spain, Cyprus, India, Africa, South America, Mexico, and Florida had to go.

⤙⧟⤚

"I need to attend to Napoleon," Mary said to Mrs. Osbourne. Nearby, the musicians were fiddling the opening dance. "He hasn't been let out for hours and with his bowels being what they are and all. . . . And he, simply, will not do anything outside once the sun has set." Granted, sunset wasn't for another hour, and she had checked on Napoleon prior to the dinner meal. But still—

She nervously eyed the dancers, swinging and laughing to the festive music. Mr. Dane leaned against the wooden fence surrounding Mrs. Osbourne's garden, his arms folded across his broad chest, his eyes intent on them. Wary. Disapproving. Angry. Why? Did he fault her for making him say something causing him to look foolish? She wasn't to blame. What he thought of her mattered not, but he could at least be a gentleman and hide his dislike.

She looked to Mrs. Osbourne, who was swaying in tune with the music, and all but yelled, "I should really go."

Mrs. Osbourne's attention turned from the dancers to Mary. "I'm sorry," she said as loudly, "what did you say?"

"I said I should go." She tilted her head in the direction of the Linwood's home. "Napoleon."

"Oh yes!" Mrs. Osbourne motioned toward the dirt path leading from her backyard to the Linwood estate.

Mary fell into step with her.

"Did you enjoy yourself today?" Mrs. Osbourne asked once they were beyond the clearing and into cluster of trees and shrubs pruned to create an arched canopy.

Mary nodded. "It was . . ."

Exhausting, but, surprisingly, not too unpleasant. Save for the arrival of Mrs. Osbourne's nephew. During dinner, she simply could not *not* answer the many questions sent her way, but once she began talking, it didn't feel so awkward or imposing. The quilters and their husbands seemed genuinely interested, not in competition. Realizing she had lumped all Belle Havenians into the same gossip mongering pot did not set well in her spirit. Then again, she may be naive and they'd pulled the wool over her eyes as to their true motives.

How odd to think she preferred feeling like a hypocrite than her judgmentalism being proven right.

She said, "It was more than I anticipated. Thank you for inviting me and for agreeing to help with my illustrations. Without you I would be lost."

"Oh, dearie, you are more than welcome." She wrapped Mary's arm around hers. "If Napoleon needs more elixir, let me know. No matter the hour."

"I, uhh . . ."

The telling brow of Mrs. Osbourne's rose. *Sometimes a simple thank-you is enough*, it warned.

"Thank you."

This morning she couldn't have imagined walking along the shrub-framed path in close confidence with her neighbor. Even after waking the woman up at four to beg help with a gastric and bewailing dog. But now . . . this moment . . . it felt . . . nice. Comforting. Right. The last time she'd walked arm and arm with her mother, she'd been ten, and Mother informed her she was taking a holiday to the continent. Alone. *Without you.*

They stopped where the Osbourne land ended and Linwood property began.

"I'll see you tomorrow," Mary said, withdrawing her arm from Mrs. Osbourne's hold. "Good night."

"Miss Varrs?"

Mary paused. "Yes?"

"It's all right to admit the day has been overwhelming and you need time alone." Mrs. Osbourne's mouth curved in an understanding smile. "No one will think ill of you. I won't think ill of you."

Mary looked to the grass under her feet, unnerved by her neighbor's insight. Ladies did not admit they were tired, or overwhelmed, or unable to bear being the focus of attention. Mrs. Osbourne was as true a lady as any. If she were tired, she would be honest and not claim an easy excuse to escape. Mrs. Osbourne would not lie for the sake of appearance.

She met Mrs. Osbourne's rapt gaze. "I rather do need to attend to Napoleon, but you are correct the day has been more than I am accustomed to. Do you mind if I call it a night?"

"Not at all." Mrs. Osbourne enveloped her in a hug.

Mary stiffened. Don't pull away, don't pull away. Do. Not. Pull. Away. She drew in a breath and listened to their heartbeats, relaxing as her tension fluttered away on the soft early evening breeze.

What were the odds of finding the personal ad in the *Richmond Times* seeking a reputable spinster with gardening and canning knowledge to care for a private residence in Belle Haven during the spring? For three months. The almost exact amount of time she needed to stay. Coincidence? Miracle?

Either way, she was blessed. An omniscient God would have known months ago the need she had for an illustrator today. A loving God would have orchestrated events to ensure she found a house in Belle Haven instead of one in Onancock or Chincoteague. The larger the town, the greater chance of not being noticed, which had been her desire. A loving God would have also put a welcoming woman like Mrs. Osbourne next door.

But to believe God planned this for her benefit would mean what happened with Edward had been in God's plan, too, and it was too much for her to believe. Why would God design pain for her? A loving God would not.

"He is not always a bear," Mrs. Osbourne whispered.

Mary took a step back. "Who?"

"My nephew."

"Oh." Mary clasped her hands together, lacing fingers, nudging the tip of her boot into the grass. Who or what Mr. Dane was did not interest her, nor did she wish to discuss him. The man carried a block of resentment on his shoulder. Wisdom said stay away. "I should go."

Mrs. Osbourne nodded. "You are welcome to return for the dancing. Later. If you feel up to it."

"I do have a book I've been meaning to finish." *Anna Karenina.* The Nathan Haskell Dole translation had been delivered to her villa in Cyprus by her mother. Only one of the two stayed past the next

GINA WELBORN

morning. Happy families were all alike. Unhappy families . . . well, the Varrs were unhappy in their own comfortable way.

Mrs. Osbourne's eyes seemed sad. "Good night then."

She turned on her heel and headed back down the path toward the laughter, claps, foot stomps, and fiddling, leaving Mary alone.

Someone called out, "Priscilla, join us!"

Mary looked from the path they'd traveled . . . to the Linwoods' home . . . then back to the path. Levin, Kitty, Anna, and Vronsky could wait another night. She hadn't danced in years. But returning meant enduring more of Mr. Dane's scowls, and years of enduring scowls had taught her the easiest solution was to walk away.

Mary turned from the music and headed to where Napoleon waited.

6

Aunt Priscilla would be his downfall someday. Three moves from checkmate and she *had* to insist he leave his chess match with Mr. Clemmer. To go fishing. And he had to "be quick about it" because the sun would be setting soon. This had more to do with her disrupting his routine than with her needing fish.

Zenus clenched the wicker fishing creel in one hand and rod in the other. He jogged across the street to the path leading to his favorite Chesapeake Bay inlet, which also happened to be the closest one to Aunt Priscilla's house and still on Osbourne land. Dipping his head, he passed under a vine-covered hickory. Used the creel to push back the shrubs. Could have been worse. She could have insisted he dance with Mrs. Marvin or assist the Turners with washing dishes or read *Good Housekeeping* to her ailing housekeeper, Mrs. Binkley. Or, even worse, go next door to the Linwoods to see why Miss Varrs hadn't returned from feeding Napoleon.

Why did everyone feel the need to ask him why she hadn't returned? She wasn't his guest. The fact she hadn't returned made him happy.

Zenus slapped the basket against another shrub blocking the trail. A limb bounced back, smacking his cheek. He swatted the foliage with both basket and rod as he pushed through the verdant woods to the rocky clearing halfway between the street and the inlet. His favorite aspect of the Eastern Shore was how the level terrain comprised a patchwork of fields and woods penetrated by winding tidal creeks.

Breathing in deep, he grinned. It smelled pungently of oaks and sycamores, loblolly pines, and moss.

Heaven on earth.

In all actuality, the earthy scent one typically recognizes as the forest is caused by fungi in the dirt.

Zenus growled. He couldn't even escape her irritably melodic voice in his mind. A man's beautiful wilderness should not be condensed into a description of fungi.

He stepped over a family of rocks, tripping on one, which he aptly named Mary Varrs. He paused to catch his breath. Eye twitched. Teeth grit. She was like fungus on his skin. Bacteria refusing to leave. Contagion.

Zenus kicked the rock for good measure.

No more. He was going to think about her no more. Done. Out of his mind. Poof.

He was only going to think of things that interested him.

He stepped on a wooden flat bridge and entered the long glades, fringed with yellow sedge, affording cover to the birds and protection from the hawks. The absence of trees assured the hunter almost any number of shots. Snipe. Woodcock. Of course, if the inlet were on the sea side, he'd have his choice of waterfowl: wild geese, brant, black mallards, shufflers, or . . .

If he was going to waste thoughts on a woman, and he didn't mind doing so, he ought to at least be thinking about a woman he liked. Such as Arel Dewey, who (according to Mrs. Van Mater), knew Miss Varrs. Who (according to both Jaegers), sat with Miss Varrs every Sunday during church. Who (according to Mrs. Scarborough), had told everyone in Belle Haven Miss Varrs was her mentor.

Mary Varrs a mentor?

He laughed.

As if the woman could improve upon the glorious perfection called Arel.

The best way to curry favor with Mr. Dewey would be to befriend his favorite daughter. But according to Misters Rutland, Lee, and Clemmer, in the two months Miss Varrs had been in town, they couldn't remember hearing she'd even met Mr. Dewey. Never visited Dewey House. Nor stepped foot on Mr. Dewey's steam yacht, *Reverie*. Her plan must be more long-term. Or something different.

Endear herself to a wealthy, childless widow and become her heir.

Aunt Priscilla, whose wealth alone was enough for a money-grubber to try to ingratiate her way into an inheritance, had to be her target.

With Arel not expected to return to Belle Haven until Wednesday night, he had two days of being nothing but an errand boy and Miss Varrs's competitor for his aunt's attentions. She looked miserable during dinner, providing him a bit of solace. If he wasn't enjoying himself, neither should she. But he didn't consider himself a vindictive person.

Something about Mary Varrs brought out the worst in him.

Zenus growled. He stopped before the glades ended and made himself take a calming breath. No sense allowing his circumstances, including one aggravating Englishwoman, to drive his emotions.

No sense begrudging fate.

He closed his eyes. Breathe in. Out. In. Out. Count it all joy. In. Out. It was what he'd do. Through this trial, he was becoming more patient. In. Out. By week's end, he would be the most patient man in the mid-Atlantic, have the quilt pattern he needed, and would be well on his way to wooing Arel Dewey successfully.

Zenus smiled.

Optimism: the first necessary ingredient for success. Don't lament the obstacles was the second. Everything would work out in time. While Monday night was his traditional chess night and fishing was limited to Saturdays, he could adjust.

He was adjustable.

Fishing pole in one hand and basket in the other, he inhaled the woodsy air. More than a sport, fishing was meditative. Quiet solitude found in waiting. In being unhurried. To be lulled away from one's frustrations—it's what he needed. While waiting for a fish to bite, he would watch a steamer or yacht sailing in the bay. In the spring, summer, and, indeed, until November, fine fishing could be had in the waters of both sea and bay. Drum. Sea bass. Trout, mullet, spot, and taylor.

He could count a fishing excursion as joy.

Yes, yes, he could.

He stepped off the wooden bridge keeping his shoes from sinking into the marsh and stepped onto the sandy beach. Took two steps toward the wooden dock. Stopped. Any hope of being lulled fled from him as did the relaxing air in his lungs. There.

There—

In his line of sight where the sun dipped toward the Chesapeake's blue and gold horizon sat a woman. Sitting contentedly. On the edge of the dock he'd helped his uncle build a decade earlier. Holding a fishing pole of all things.

With how his luck had been today, how could the woman be anyone but Miss Mary Varrs?

Straw hat perched atop a braided chignon. Pink shirt with a white skirt. No angler in his—or her—right mind would dress thusly for fishing. Nor was he any more practically attired in his brown suit. He had an hour at most before the sun set. An hour! To catch a basket of fish before his aunt commanded him, as if he were still a child, to be home before dark.

And the next nearest dock was a ten-minute hike away and not the prime fishing available at this secluded inlet.

His inlet. His.

Miss Varrs baited her hook, her long fingers moving effortlessly. She lifted her black hardwood rod and, with an elegant swing, cast the line, reeling in slowly, each turn a fluid movement. The quiet elegance surrounding her came as natural to her as breathing. She wasn't smiling, but he could not see her face to know for sure. But her lips, he knew, had a soft curve as she delighted in the moment. The golden light of the resting sun shaded the lissome contour of her neck, where wisps of hair invited a man's touch, hypnotized his thoughts, and made him want—

Zenus moved to take a step forward. Then stopped.

What was he doing?

She stopped. Abruptly. As if something didn't feel right, as if she felt an inner warning.

She looked over her shoulder to where he stood.

"You," she said, because he guessed it was the most words she would deign to waste on him.

His face warmed from embarrassment—and disgust—over his thoughts. The lissome contour of her neck? Heaven knew he didn't want her. He didn't even *like* her. Whatever glow he thought he saw was the trickery of the dying sun and the romantic bayside.

Zenus adjusted his cap, searched for the right words—any words—to respond.

"Aunt Priscilla sent me to catch fish for breakfast." He started to step forward, but forward meant being closer to Miss Varrs, and closer to her wasn't where he wanted to be. He held his ground. "I should—" *go.* He didn't offer, though.

He shouldn't be the one leaving.

This was his dock first. *His* dock. He built it. The land would someday be his by inheritance. Thus, the fish practically belonged to him, too. By all American standards, if anyone had a right to fish off of it, he did. So he waited, tipping his cap back on his head, giving her time to speak. He wasn't leaving.

Since there wasn't a gentlemanly way of asking her to vamoose, he'd wait her out.

Fortitude held together the bones of perseverance in his spine.

"I'm supposed to bring back a basketful," he called out. He held up the creel, empty save for his tin of worms. "Of fish. I'm supposed to catch. Before sunset." Off his dock. Where she was sitting. Where he didn't want her to be.

Mosey along, Miss Varrs.

The sound of crickets and a few bullfrogs pervaded the silence.

Her gaze fell, but not before he saw—or at least thought he saw—weariness, maybe even a bit of sadness, in her eyes. She focused on the horizon. One click of her reel. Two. Three.

He didn't think she would respond, but much to his surprise, she said, "This dock is large enough for the two of us. You may stay, Mr. Dane . . . if you don't talk."

His dock. His. He should be the one granting permission to stay. Not her.

At the rate he was going, his teeth would be ground down to stubs.

Zenus trudged forward. He didn't like her, or her cold hauteur, so not talking to her suited him just fine. Nor would he lament any obstacles, such as having to share a dock with Queen Mary, because he was an optimist. He would make the best of the situation, too, because he was a patient man.

Since she sat on the west edge between two piers, he took the north edge between his own set of piers. The two boards of dock between them felt like two inches. From this view, he could see she wore a leather apron covering the front of her skirt. She also had a net, which he'd forgotten to bring.

"Might I share your net?" he asked. Begrudgingly.

She didn't so much as nod as incline her head, in a queenly sort of way, as if to say *if you must*.

After a moment of debating if he should thank her, and deciding not, Zenus sat cross-legged and made no further comment. His luck would turn, and their agreed-upon silence would then spread into an awkwardness resulting in the surly girl giving up and leaving. First the dock, then Belle Haven. It was a plan. He liked plans. And he could adjust his plans, if needed, because he was adjustable.

Zenus held back his grin. He opened his bait tin, but before he had a worm on his hook, Miss Varrs jerked her fishing rod back. With the ease of an experienced angler, she lifted the rod and simultaneously reeled in a fish. Then—in what seemed to be the blink of an eye—she leaned down, scooped the good-sized fish into her cotton net, removed the hook with pliers from her apron pocket, and set the fish free without even removing it from the water.

His jaw gaped as much from shock over her actions as from awe of her skill.

"You threw back a perfectly good fish," Zenus said as she baited her hook again.

Her face assumed an exasperated mien at his words.

"Why did you do throw it back?" he ground out.

She seemed to think about it for a moment. She cast her line again.

He waited.

She said nothing.

He waited more.

Then—finally!—she turned to him with a smile making his heart fall like a sinker in his chest. "Because, Mr. Dane, I can. Now, will you please hush?" And she turned back to her line.

Because, Mr. Dane, I khaaan, he mimicked and felt smugly satisfied even though he knew he was being childish. She was quite an unsociable female. She, with her regal carriage and excessive height, might sit as pretty on a horse as she did casting lures, but he couldn't imagine any man wanting to take her to dinner. He'd die of boredom.

"I could have used the fish," he grumbled, because he found it quite enjoyable to be immature and annoying.

She ignored him.

"Would you say it'd been a three-pounder? Five?"

She ignored him still.

So he studied her profile. He made no attempt to be subtle about it either. She had a small scar, barely noticeable in the setting sunlight, near the right side of her upper lip.

"How did you come by the scar?" he blurted.

She turned to him, frowning, confused.

"The one right"—he motioned to his mouth—"about here."

Her eyes, beyond being hazel, glinted with intelligence and more than a bit of sadness. Whoever broke her heart, he hoped to never meet him. Zenus blinked at the thought. Whatever her past, he had no interest in knowing, including any heartbreak. An enigma she was to him, and an enigma she would stay as she took the train straight out of town.

He wasn't surprised she didn't answer.

He'd never met a woman less inclined to talk.

With the best grin he could manage to interject levity in the moment, he inclined his head to his empty basket. "Be ye kind, miss, one to another, or I may be here past my sunset curfew."

To say she looked at him sharply was an understatement. "Don't use Scripture to manipulate me."

Zenus stiffened. Manipulate? "No, no," he rushed out, feeling a trifle queasy, "it's not what I intended by my remark. I meant to be amusing. Ease the tension between us, which I have inadvertently only increased. My apologies, Miss Varrs. Perhaps we could start over? My aunt asked me to catch fish for breakfast. You appear to be an expert angler. I would be honored if you'd help me fulfill her request."

A wrinkle formed between her perfectly arched brows. "Those were the most words I've heard you string together and none be offensive. Why?"

"I . . ." He thought about it. Why her? Why now?

The brief second her fingers had rested upon his back before she had introduced herself, he'd felt warm. Hot. No, more like the cold sweats. Then shaking her hand—Heaven knew he'd shaken hundreds of hands, but when his palm touched hers, it felt different, and he panicked. Like a lad attending his first cotillion and forgetting everything he'd learned. She rattled him. Similar to what he felt in the presence of an unmarried woman he found desirable.

And she was desirable—correction: *had been*—until they spoke, until he saw through her attentions to his aunt and her friendship with Arel. Whether it was securing an inheritance through companionship or marriage, she was in Belle Haven for personal gain.

He removed his cap, ran a hand through his hair, then plopped it back on. "It's . . ." He cleared his throat. "I—"

His mind went blank.

Miss Varrs said nothing, just waited with an unveiled look on her face as if she were truly interested in his explanation. Truth be told, her curiosity was disconcerting, scrambling his thoughts again. So much so, he focused on her line in the water as he sought to remember what he'd been about to say. The only people he had ever spoken of his ailment with were Aunt Priscilla and Uncle Harold, the former not agreeing with the latter for him to seek trepanation to remove any demons lurking in his skull.

Her fishing pole dipped, water rippling around it, but she gave it no notice.

He *could* be honest with her.

Now, it was a disconcerting thought. Why tell her? She wouldn't laugh, he knew for certain. How he knew *that* was as perplexing as the inclination to be forthright and risk embarrassing himself further. After what he'd said to her in his aunt's parlor—

Never again did he want to experience the humiliation of telling a woman she looked lumpy instead of lovely, as he had to Mrs. Fannie O'Brian upon her leaving her widow's weeds. Or when he was reading the teams for Belle Haven's annual summer croquet tournament and mispronounced Arel Dewey's Christian name to where it sounded like Owl instead of Arel. The unfortunate twisting of his words, instead of earning a laugh and a *you're so adorable*, always caused ladies to flee and avoid him henceforth.

Zenus winced at the tingling sweeping up the back of his neck and across his face. Talk, but don't look into her eyes.

"During the last eight years, I've often suffered from the disease of faltering speech around unmarried women, resulting in hours of mortification for both the lady and myself." It wasn't so painful. He nodded to her fishing rod. "You've hooked a fish."

She held onto the rod and reel with both hands to keep it steady, yet maintain her attention on him. "I am still the lady I was earlier, and your tongue isn't tied."

The fish on her hook increased its fight, the water splashing onto the dock.

Still, she ignored it.

"Yes, but you're no longer—" He clenched his own fishing rod to keep from grabbing her frantic bobbing one. They were wasting time. "Aunt Priscilla wants fish for breakfast. If you aren't going to reel it in, then might I do it?"

"No longer what?" she asked somewhat briskly.

"Potential," he murmured before he realized what he'd admitted to. Zenus grit his teeth for what felt the thirteenth time since meeting her. Nubs, nubs his teeth would be. "The fish—"

She jerked on her pole and turned the reel two clicks, yet the fish still fought. "Potential what, Mr. Dane?"

"Miss Varrs, you know *exactly* what I mean."

"Then say it, least I presume incorrectly."

"Marriage potential," he spat out. "Now would you—"

"Certainly. And just so we are clear . . ." She lifted the rod and simultaneously reeled in a fish. As quickly as she had with the first one, she leaned down, scooped it into her cotton net, and removed the hook with pliers taken from her apron pocket. Instead of releasing it, she grabbed it by its mouth, opened the basket with her other hand, and dumped it in. "You, sir, are not *potential* either."

7

Mr. Dane had the intelligence to keep his mouth shut for the remaining time they'd fished and during the walk home. Rather impressive, albeit a surprise. Complimenting him, even if only in her mind, soured her thoughts.

Mary cocked her head to the side, observing him as she held their fishing rods and as he unlatched the waist-high front gate to the Linwood estate. He swung it open. The iron gate creaked. Napoleon's sudden impassioned barks broke the silence surrounding them, drawing Mr. Dane's attention for a brief moment. Then he looked at her most intently. His lips were a perplexing parallel to his dark brows, which, unlike his aunt's, didn't have a single arc in them. Even in the twilight, the faint bristles on his face enhanced the strong angle of his jaw.

While he'd spoken fairly in saying she was no Venus, she'd wager he drew more stares than she did on any good day.

She imagined Holly Jane Ferris was making a list of her best flirts and flatteries to use during the rest of the week while Mr. Dane served as his aunt's host and errand boy. Quilt embroidering output would decrease whenever he entered the parlor. For the sake of Lydia Puryear's bride's chest, it would not do, not do at all. What he needed to do was take his lemony Astor cologne and leave town and come back once the quilting bee was over.

Better yet, come back after she left Belle Haven.

But how to convince him to leave?

"You look serious, Miss Varrs."

"I—" She gave her head a little shake. "Napoleon has not barked like this before," she said, moving past the gate and onto the bricked path. She stopped and waited for him.

"I'd say it is due to my arrival." Mr. Dane followed, closing the gate before reclaiming the rods from her. "A more logical reason is he is male, thus possessive and protective of the female in his care."

Mary fell into step beside him. "Of me?"

She hadn't meant to sound astonished, but she was nothing more to Napoleon than a nanny, maid, cook, valet, and upon four unpleasant occasions, including this morning, an apothecary.

"Sir, I have yet to meet an English bulldog as gentle and agreeable as Napoleon. More likely he is protecting the home he holds most dear and refuses to leave."

Mr. Dane stared straight ahead, not looking at her directly, as he had for most of the night. "In the presence of a lady, a gentleman does as a gentleman should. Even canine ones." His tone held sincerity, not sycophancy, and her chest felt hollow, achy, discomforted.

Not all gentlemen did as a gentleman should.

Some stole, with no remorse, things they had no right to take.

Some used women for their own gain.

Mary fingered the pliers in her fishing apron's pocket, the pair Edward had given her upon their engagement. The ones she had wanted to hurl at him yet lacked the courage to do so. She glanced at the star-sprinkled night sky. So much for Mr. Dane minding his aunt's sunset curfew. Yet from the torchlight and soft fiddling streaming from the back of Mrs. Osbourne's house, she suspected Mrs. Osbourne and her quilting bee attendees weren't going to mind a curfew either.

She hadn't had to ask Mr. Dane to escort her home. Nor had he asked. He merely did. And she'd known he would. Just as she'd known he'd carry their poles, her net, and his filled basket of fish she'd caught. The assurance of his actions grated on her nerves.

Her feelings for him were less clouded when she was blind to his virtues of chivalry and fortitude—when she saw his beauty as only skin deep.

Zenus Dane was a gentleman. It galled her to admit it.

Gallantry aside, it did not necessitate she declare him a likeable man.

Nonetheless, he had confessed his most shameful secret, something only a less-than-arrogant—certainly not a roguish—man would do. His unpleasant admission she wasn't marriage potential chipped at her pride, but the truth was, her snappish retort—

Mary sighed.

Was there a time she behaved more poorly? No.

She should apologize to Mr. Dane for her sour look. Knew it. Knowing, alas, did not enhance the want-to.

"Is there a problem?" he asked as they neared the covered porch.

"No."

"Yet you are scowling."

Mary sighed again. "It's nothing."

He stopped at the front steps. He handed over her fishing rod and net, his gaze somewhere near her shoulder. "Thank you . . . for all the fish."

She nodded then glanced to the window left of the door where Napoleon had ceased barking. His nose plastered against the pane. "Thank you for seeing me home."

Mr. Dane looked to his aunt's house, but didn't make a move to leave. Nor did he appear interested in adding an *I had a delightful evening* platitude.

No offense taken, for she had not had a delightful evening with him either.

"Good night." Mary hurried up the front steps.

As she opened the door, her gaze caught on another ivory envelope on the wicker table on the porch. Napoleon bounded down the stairs to Mr. Dane. As before, her name was scrawled in the center. Mary laid her pole and net on the table and picked up the envelope, removing the card inside.

My dear Miss Varrs,

Due to my housekeeper's continued illness and my need to focus on your botanical illustrations as well as my nephew's quilt design, your presence is requested to assist with breakfast and dinner preparations during the Quilting Bee. Please arrive each weekday morning over the next two weeks promptly at 6:30. Breakfast will be served at 8, with quilting immediately following the meal. Lunch, as always, is potluck.

Sincerely,

Priscilla Dane Osbourne

"How delightful," Mary muttered, reinserting the card in the envelope.

"What is Aunt Priscilla requesting of you now?"

"Breakfast preparations."

"Better you than me."

Mary turned her head enough to see Mr. Dane. Napoleon stood at his heel in best show dog (though he was not one) form. "You have not tasted my cooking."

There's that, his look said.

She plopped on a wicker chair.

She'd be a fool to think this would be the last addition to Mrs. Osbourne's terms. Mrs. Osbourne could, however, accomplish more if she had only one person to help at a time. Mr. Dane had time on his side. She had eleven days. Well, then now. Instead of thinking about convincing him to leave, she needed to just do it.

"Mr. Dane," she said, standing and reclaiming her fishing pole and net, "clearly your aunt cannot do it all." She took a side step to the opened front door. "Return to Philadelphia and see to your mill. You need to meet with the insurance company anyway. Come back in ten days after Mrs. Osbourne has finished assisting me, and then she can attend, with no distractions, to your quilt pattern. It is the wisest course of action for all."

His foot rested on the bottom step, his hand on the right-side stair rail. "Why ten days?"

"Why does it matter?"

"Because I want to know," he said frankly. "Why are you avoiding the question?" He looked at her as if she hid deathly secrets. Worse, as if he knew the truth and was waiting for her confession.

Her grips tightened on the pole and net. "I am not avoiding anything."

He quirked a brow. "You're avoiding the truth about why you're in Belle Haven."

"Why I'm—" She cut herself off, realizing he suspected her reasons. Her eyes widened. "Hallo, do you think I am up to something nefarious?"

He made a face. "Are you?"

Mary flinched, and thus died the little bit of admiration she felt for him over his gallantry in walking her home. "My tomato study needs to be in the mail by next Wednesday—ten days—to make the application deadline."

"The deadline for what?"

She let out a furious exhale. "For employment."

"For employment where?" He sounded—and—looked utterly fascinated by what she would say next. Which was why she wouldn't say a thing. The man was clearly used to getting what he wanted, and she wasn't about to appease him.

Mary patted her thigh and made a *ppt ppt* with her lips for Napoleon to come. He stayed next to Mr. Dane, confirming her suspicion his barking had been due to Mr. Dane's arrival. She'd feel betrayed, or a smidgeon rejected, but in light of the persnickety dog's easily distressed bowels and his aversion to taking elixir, she'd be quite content should he choose to forever stay with Mr. Dane.

One corner of Mr. Dane's mouth twitched upward, which she truly hoped was not a sign he was enjoying himself over her inability to command Napoleon.

"You're avoiding the truth," he repeated.

She threw him a startled glance. "Why do you say so? I have nothing to hide." She merely had things she didn't want anyone to know, and she wanted to be left alone. Why couldn't he understand?

"Then answer the question, Miss Varrs."

She squared her shoulders. "I am applying to be a research assistant at the Virginia Agricultural Experiment Station in Blacksburg. It is the only position currently available for a female botanist." Thanks to her father's adjunct professorship. "So you see I have the more pressing need for help."

He shrugged as if he wasn't impressed. "I need this quilt design to stay in business."

"Yes, but you have a month," she put in earnestly, "maybe longer, if you work your silver-tongued charm on the bankers. This is my *only* chance."

"Silver-tongued charm?" He laughed. "Were you not listening to what I confessed at the dock?"

"Yes. *And* I heard you speak to your aunt," she said, halting the interruption she saw forming on his lips. "She never shares her designs, yet agreed to make a new one for you, even though she has a quilting bee this week and next and agreed to draw for me."

"Because I begged!" Despite his tone, he looked more amused rather than irritated with her. "Begged, Miss Varrs. Past tense of beg, which means to earnestly or humbly ask for something."

She stared at him. Hard. "There is no charm in mocking me."

He smiled a little. "But there is enjoyment."

Mary chose to ignore his comment. "Mr. Dane," she said in all seriousness, "once you've settled things with the insurance company, you will know the true state of your financial affairs. If necessary, beg the creditors for leniency. It behooves them to work with a reputable businessman. Unless I've judged you wrong."

He looked vaguely affronted.

She allowed herself a slight smile at hitting a nerve.

He adjusted his cap, and she wondered if he realized he did so whenever he needed time to think.

"I employ forty-eight workers. Most women with children. Losing their jobs means"—he glanced heavenward—"at least eighty

86

children going to bed hungry." His eyes met hers directly, and Mary froze.

Whatever else he said, if he even spoke, she did not hear. There was something in his pale eyes, something friendly, close. Inviting. It pulled at her, sliding across her skin, creating gooseflesh, leaving her off-balance. She wanted to be an arm's length from him. Not her at the door and him at the bottom of the stairs. Not apart.

Not alone.

She shivered. How awful. She didn't even like him.

But it was dark. And the music was soft in the distance and the breeze across the nearby shrubs fragrant and sweet . . . and . . . and they were alone. Yes, in the front of Linwood House, on a porch properly open to viewing from any of the three houses across the street or the two on either side, where anyone could come upon them. With a dog their chaperone. Nothing risqué and yet—

Alone.

"You said?" she blurted.

"Said?" Before she could respond, he looked away from her. Crossed his arms. He leaned against the stair railing, breaking the strangeness of moment. "I said I see how your singular job is the more pressing need. Children don't need to eat before going to bed anyway."

"Please be serious," she retorted, and felt a might less light-headed, a bit more like herself. She didn't want to be close to him. Or to anyone. Not for several more years at least.

She may not have a choice, though. Not with the allowance from Prince Ercole dwindling and the pressures from her mother increasing.

She continued, "It benefits you none to spend a week in Belle Haven attending to your aunt's whims. Go, do what you have to do for your business then come back."

The music next door ended.

While voices rose, Mary couldn't distinguish what was being said.

Mr. Dane held silent. His lips tightened as he looked down at Napoleon then checked his pocket watch.

"Luck would have it we both need my aunt's help." His grip tight around his watch, he looked her direction, yet his displeased gaze seemed more on the opened door behind her. "While we cannot change our circumstances, we can choose to make the best of them."

"How sanguine of you," she said.

He gave her a lopsided smile. "Optimism is the first necessary ingredient for success."

"Oh, is it?"

He didn't climb the steps, nor did he continue to lean against the railing. He just stood there. His eyes turned positively pleased with himself. "Don't lament the obstacles is the second."

"Indeed." Why was she smiling? Worse, now as she realized it, why couldn't she stop?

"You're laughing at me."

"Doing so is not in my character. I am, however, not surprised *you* created rules for success." Not giving him time to respond, she pursed her lips and again made the *ppt ppt* kissing sound the Linwoods had said Napoleon responded to. "Let's go, Napoleon. Time for bed."

He stayed at his contented spot next to his preferred human.

Mr. Dane looked across the yard, then at Napoleon, then back at her. "I've always believed the unbearableness *or* endurableness of a circumstance depends on a person's attitude. As long as we fulfill the terms Aunt Priscilla requests of us, then she will help us obtain what we both want." Something in his tone made her think he was referring to more than the quilt pattern.

Mary leaned against the stair railing. "You are not the one conscripted to eight hours of quilting in a parlor full of chatty women." True, it hadn't been as insufferable as she'd expected, but facing the deluge of questions during dinner had been more than she anticipated. She hadn't experienced this many hours of socializing since attending Wellons & Whitacre School for Young Ladies in Brighton. Thankfully, Arel Dewey wasn't a quilter.

See, she could find the best of the situation.

Mr. Dane repocketed his watch. "I'd much prefer quilting next to Holly Jane Ferris than being the man she intends for her future husband."

He had a point there.

"Mr. Dane, you are a true optimist."

"A compliment, Miss Varrs?"

She paused—just for a moment—just long enough to appreciate the amity in his expression. "Would you receive it better were I to say it was begrudgingly given?"

A tiny wrinkle formed between his brows. "I do believe I would."

"Then begrudgingly given it was."

And the amity was gone. "Be of good cheer, Miss Varrs. In four days, you will be done with me. Do know if you are up to something nefarious, I will stop you." So saying, he whistled, then motioned to the front door with an "inside."

Napoleon climbed the steps and walked past her without a glance in her direction. He disappeared into the house's darkness, leaving nothing but the sound of his needing-filed nails clicking on polished floorboards.

Mary closed her gapping mouth. He did not just say . . . *if she was up to something nefarious.*

"Mr. Dane, what did you mean by—?" She looked back down the steps to where he was no longer standing.

Instead of explaining himself, instead of staying to ensure she was safely inside—though she had nothing to worry about in Belle Haven—he left her. Alone. On the porch while he walked across the yard to his aunt's property, toward where buggies were already rolling down the drive. Without even the smallest or most awkward of goodbyes. Not the ideal end to a conversation, but with the American oddity named Zenus Dane, how could she do anything *but* make the best of him? If there ever was to be a study done on a person, it should be him.

He paused and looked over his shoulder in her direction.

Mary lifted her hand to wave cheerio. Thinking the better of it, she removed her hat pin and hat, turned, and walked inside, softly closing the door behind her. For four days, she would have to trust

Mr. Dane wouldn't be up to anything nefarious for his benefit and her loss. Life as Edward Argent's fiancée, however, had taught her no one could be trusted.

Stop focusing on four days. Two days was all that mattered. Because she had only to endure two days with him before Arel Dewey returned to cause her usual distractions.

Who knew she would actually look forward to seeing Arel—Miss Dewey again.

⸎

"What do you think you are doing?" demanded Aunt Priscilla the moment she walked into the kitchen, slamming the door behind her.

"I'm preparing the fish so you don't have to." Zenus tossed another bone-free fillet into the bowl of ice. He then flipped the fish over and sliced the fillet from the other side.

She drew in a harsh breath through her nostrils. "No."

No? She didn't want the fish filleted? Of all the wasted—

Mouth tight, Zenus tossed the second fillet into the ice bowl and the remains into the bucket in the sink. This wasn't the first time she sent him fishing for no other reason than to get him out of the house. If he found out she sent him to the dock for the sole purpose of spending time with Miss Varrs—

He clenched the knife until he could speak calmly. The last woman on earth he wanted to be match-made with was Mary Varrs.

He looked away from the cutting board to where Aunt Priscilla stood in the center of the room. "Did you want the fish filleted or not? I'm almost done."

"Of course," she bit off. "They're for breakfast." Her eyes narrowed, hands resting on hips, warning of the lecture to come. "The girl is not for you."

"What girl?"

"Miss Varrs."

"Miss Varrs?" Laughter burst from his chest. "I should hope not. I've never met a more patronizing woman in my life." He grabbed another fish from the basket, laid it on the wooden board, and with one swift whack, chopped off its head. "I pity any man who marries her."

He filleted the fish then started on another. Four more to go and then he could call the evening quits. Best guess it was a quarter to ten. Zenus grabbed another fish. Whack. Slice. Check for bones. Toss. He worked his way through the remaining ones while Aunt Priscilla stood lost in her thoughts. By the time he grabbed the last fish from the basket, Aunt Priscilla pulled out a chair from the kitchen table, the legs scraping across the wooden floor.

She sat and said, "Where were you tonight?"

A pointless question if there ever was one. "I was at the dock, fishing." He held the tail down then slid the knife along the backbone. "Per your orders."

"When I went to the Linwoods to deliver my note, she wasn't home." Her fingers strummed against the table. "Was she with you?"

He didn't bother to question to whom *she* referred. "Why does it matter?" he asked, checking the filet for bones and finding none.

"So you don't deny she was?"

Zenus tossed the last fillet in the bowl of ice and scraped the remains into the bucket. "Why should I deny it?" He soaped and rinsed his hands, then grabbed a lime wedge he'd precut to rid the fish smell from his skin. He turned to face her, rubbing his hands with the lime. "Aunt Priscilla, what does it matter if I fished with Miss Varrs?"

"She is too smart to be limited to society's—especially your—expectations of what a wife should be," she lectured in the suffrage stance he'd never known her to reveal to anyone but him and Uncle Harold. "I will not have you interfering in her future."

"Interfering in her—?" He tossed the lime into the bucket of fish remains, rinsed his hands, and toweled dry. "Let me be clear, I don't like your neighbor. I have no interest in courting her."

"Good."

He paused, waiting for her to say more.

When she didn't, he watched her carefully. "Did you know she would be at the dock?"

"I wouldn't have sent you if I had," she snapped. "She said she had a book to read."

Her gaze never wavered, never gave a hint she was lying.

"So . . . we're in agreement," he said. "You aren't doing any back-handed matchmaking by telling me not to court her in hopes I will do the opposite?"

She grimaced as if he'd placed the bucket of rank fish remains under her nose. "Heavens no! Zenus Rhodes Dane, there is no one more ill-suited for Mary Varrs than you."

"I appreciate the compliment."

"It wasn't intended as such."

She stood, walked to him, her expression growing soft. "My dear sweet boy," she said, cradling his cheeks in her palms. "I agreed to help you woo Arel, and help you I will. You can be confident of it. The good Lord brought Miss Varrs to Belle Haven to assist Arel in finding the true purpose for which God created her. They are good for each other, and Arel will be good for you."

"Then why at Christmas wouldn't you agree to help me court her?"

Her hands lowered to his shoulders "Because you weren't ready, but now you are."

He hesitated, watching her warily. "What changed your mind?"

"You did."

"Me? I'm the same man I was in December."

"The stodgy and predictable Zenus would have never taken out a risky loan." She smacked the sides of his arms. "What we have, my boy, is an improvement!"

Zenus blinked then rubbed his eyes, trying to make sense of it all. She was still smiling, so he gave his head a good shake. Even blinked a second time. She continued to look elated. Like her cat at Thanksgiving.

He stared at her for a moment, then said, "Have you lost your senses? What about dropping out of college a semester before grad-uation, taking the inheritance from my parents, and buying a textile mill? It's not risky enough for you?"

A *pffft* rolled off her lips. "It was *before* you became stodgy and predictable."

He had no response.

She watched him, her eyes deadly serious. "Sean and Clara's elopement changed you from the high-spirited boy I knew."

More like naive boy.

"You had your failings," she said dismissively. "Any young man who loses both his parents at age seventeen is prone to adventurous choices."

No need to sugarcoat his behavior by calling it adventurous.

"I'm not excusing what I knew was wrong." Her voice grew quieter. "Whether taking out a loan was the wise thing or not doesn't matter either. You took a risk. I'm overjoyed because it's the first spark of life I've seen in you in years."

Zenus stared absently at the wall across the room. Lips pursed, he nipped at the inside of his cheek. No telling how exuberant she would be if he told her about his mail-order bride courtship and subsequent rejection.

She gripped both of his hands. "Zenus, look at me."

He did.

"Sometimes a man is so desperate to prove his loyalty to God he stops living. He lives in fear of being a stumbling block to anyone. He forgets Jesus made him free." Her eyes softened, and the corners of her lips curved, reminding him of all times she'd shown adolescent Zenus a grace he didn't deserve. "At Christmas I refused to help you court Arel because . . ." She sighed. "Arel is a dinghy so easily influenced by the tide. She needs an anchor to enable her to drift, yet will keep her from becoming lost in the sea. I feared your routine would sink, not anchor, her."

"And now?" he grumbled.

"You're letting go of your self-imposed shackles and growing a chain. Not the best metaphor, but you understand." She kissed his cheek. "Now off to bed. You have a busy day tomorrow."

"The fish—"

"I'll clean this up." She motioned to the back stairs. "Go on."

Zenus removed his apron, taking his time as he watched her watch him, waiting for some sign she was playing him false. Nothing but sincerity radiated from her features, her stance.

With no reason to stay and question her further, he grabbed his suit coat from the back of a kitchen chair then headed upstairs to his room.

She saw him as a boat sinker. A dead weight.

An ache grew in his chest as he stopped at his bedroom door. Hand gripped the knob, not turning. Hadn't he realized it about himself?

He had risked everything—his business, his home, his savings—on the purchase of newfangled looms expected to double his yearly production output. All because he'd told God on January 1, 1891, at precisely four minutes into the new year, he wanted to stop playing life safe. "Grow your flocks" was the response. He metaphorically bet all his money on God instead of trusting man's wisdom and keeping a nest egg "in case things don't pan out," as Sean had advised. He hated comparing taking a step of faith to gambling, but with God on a man's side, the odds should be favorable.

Last Friday's storm hadn't been favorable.

Last Friday's flood had been outside the odds. A once-in-a-century.

Convincing Miss Varrs to leave was futile. Despite what she said about her tomato study and job application, she was hiding something. For Arel's sake, he had to keep Miss Varrs from her. For Mr. Dewey's sake, he had to keep Miss Varrs from him. For Aunt Priscilla's sake, he had to keep Miss Varrs from wheedling her way into an inheritance.

For his own sake . . . well, he needed to stop noticing the curve of her neck. To stop wondering what caused the sadness in her eyes. To just stop thinking about her at all. Take his thoughts captive—it's what he had to do regarding Mary Varrs.

He rested his forehead against the door. "Jesus, I know this is all going to work out for my good. Eventually. Why do I feel like another flood is coming?"

8

The next morning

She deprived him of sleep. Two hours, to be exact.

Zenus dropped the last egg-battered fish into the same cast iron pan his aunt had used to wake him up before the crack of dawn. The batter crackled and grease splattered on the apron he wore over his black waistcoat. In Aunt Priscilla's opinion, his ability to properly fillet fish and experience cooking over a campfire qualified him to be the executive chef for her breakfast preparations. If he closed his eyes, he could still hear the ringing of the cast iron from when she'd pounded it sooner than he'd planned on waking.

He couldn't close his eyes. If he did, he'd fall asleep.

"Joy," he muttered.

The odd reaction he'd had to Miss Varrs upon looking into her hazel eyes, thankfully, had dissipated overnight. He'd looked at her directly several times this morning and not been adversely affected. He could count it a joy, too. Much could be said for spending an hour last night meditating on Scripture and praying against the anger he'd felt toward her. Didn't mean he woke up believing she was nothing more than a botanist with no greedy aspirations. A gentleman protected those under his watch.

Using the back of his hand, he wiped his moist forehead then checked the time—almost seven and a half. He returned his pocket watch to his waistcoat. They needed to hurry. The Eleven would be arriving soon.

Zenus nudged the fish around in the oil. Once the ladies were quilting, he would pay a visit to Mr. Dewey. When a man courted a woman, he needed to court her father, too. And while he was there, he'd find out if Mr. Dewey was aware of his daughter's and Miss Varrs's acquaintance. A wise man always had a plan.

"Aunt Priscilla," he called, while keeping his eye on the frying fish, "what's left to be done?"

When she didn't answer, he glanced to the empty table where she'd been slicing peaches earlier. Her filled bowl remained, along with a basket of sliced bread and corn muffins and the platters of sausages and boiled eggs he and Miss Varrs had cooked earlier under her direction.

A silent and compliant worker she was. Never questioned. Never offered other ideas as he had, all of which Aunt Priscilla rejected.

"Miss Varrs?" he prodded.

At the counter opposite him, she stood frowning. The notecard containing her job list from Aunt Priscilla in one hand. A box of Quaker Oats in the other. Her mid-calf-length brown split-skirt and white pin-striped shirt with red scarf tie looked more suited to a bicycle tour of Paris than his aunt's kitchen. He suspected being different than the norm came naturally to her.

She didn't answer.

Zenus flipped the fish to cook on the other side, and bubbles immediately rose in the oil. In a louder voice he said, "Miss Varrs, do you know where my aunt went?"

She waved the oat box toward the door leading out to the patio.

"What did she want out there?" he asked as she set the box on the counter next to the kettle in which she should have already been cooking the oatmeal.

She still didn't answer.

Zenus drew his lips tight. Trying to draw a response from her was like casting a lure in a lake filled with three fish. The odds of hooking one were slim to none. Still, the anger he had yesterday would not resurface. He refused to allow it. She would not bring out the worst in him. Since they were duty-bound to prepare breakfasts for the remainder of the week, the least they could do is come to an agreed-upon cordiality.

"Miss Varrs," he said in a genial tone, "I know you don't enjoy having to work with me, but I would appreciate it if you at least respond when I ask you a question."

She shook her head slowly, as if she wasn't listening to him. "This doesn't make sense," she muttered, turning the job card over.

"Miss Varrs!"

Her gaze jerked to him. "Yes?"

"My aunt," he blurted.

Eyes widened, face paled. "Is something wrong?"

At the sheer panic in her expression, he released his steaming frustration he had built up. He smiled somewhat, his irritation lessening. "My apologies for yelling. I am looking for my aunt. Where did my aunt go?"

Her shoulders sagged, hands covered her heart. "You had me worried there. She went to Linwood House," she said sweetly. "I'd made marmalade from the bergamot oranges I brought from Florida, and she wished to try some."

"Marmalade?"

She nodded.

Zenus glanced to the pantry where he knew his aunt had myriad jars of her own marmalades, jams, and jellies. The sly woman had better not being trying to match him with Miss Varrs. A little alone time here. A little tender moment there. Poof. They were in love.

That was *not* going to happen.

He forked the fish from the oil, mounding it on the paper-lined platter. He then turned off the burner and tossed the fork into the kitchen sink. Rattle. Clank.

"Mr. Dane, you seem—" Miss Varrs fell silent. Again.

He turned back to her. "I seem what?"

Her head tilted, and she gave him an odd look.

"Go ahead," he ground out, "say it." He waited for her to speak.

And waited.

And waited more.

Zenus clenched his palms to keep from dragging his hands through his hair. What was going on in her pretty head? He wanted to know. Had to know. Did she wonder why he looked flustered? He certainly felt flustered. Skin damp. Pulse erratic. Did she want to know why he'd practically bitten her head off? Simple answer: Her predilection to silence was like a spur in his heel. In both heels.

He groaned loudly. "Why can't you spew words like every other normal woman on the face of this planet?" he snipped, and she didn't even flinch. "I was on my knees last night begging God to help me conquer this . . . this . . . uggh. I don't even know how to describe it. You're like a . . . a . . . a dark cloud hovering"—he tapped the sides of his head—"in here. An enigma. Contagion. Driving me mad with your silence. Say something. Say anything. I know you don't like me. I know it. I *feel* it. I am sure I deserve it after what I said to you yesterday. Can we please just put aside our differences and work together for Aunt Priscilla's sake?"

Her lips parted. "You—"

Nothing else came forth, as if she couldn't decide to take offense because he had accused her of having ill feelings for him or to lie and deny how right he was. The muscles in her face moved, enough to let him know she was thinking and wasn't sure how to answer. Or even if a lady should respond to the fool. Amid his verbal volcanic eruption he'd known he should stop, but couldn't. This time because his tongue was loosened not tied.

He groaned inwardly, shame drawing every last bit of warmth from his cheeks. Why couldn't he keep his mouth closed around her? He excelled in proving he was the fool.

"Yes, Miss Varrs?" he said weakly.

"Mr. Dane, I would like to put aside our differences." The brokenness in her tone crushed him.

He hadn't meant to hurt her. He was tired. Frustrated. Even his housekeeper knew not to talk to him until after he'd had his second cup of coffee. And none of this was her fault. Yet Miss Varrs stood there like she was to blame for it all. She wasn't. He was.

"I'm sorry," he rushed out. "I've never spoken to a lady like that. I shouldn't have—"

"Shhh." Her hand moved in a dismissive wave. "Say nothing more. Please."

He nodded, because there was something in her voice, in her eyes, something meek and fearful. Something—could it be?—so familiar because he'd seen it in the mirror for years following Clara and Sean's elopement. Rejection.

One corner of her mouth indented in what he presumed was an attempt to smile. She turned away, resuming her perusal of the job notecard, her eyelids blinking rapidly.

He immediately retrieved his handkerchief from his suit coat draped on a kitchen chair. In four strides, he offered it to her. "Here."

"It's not necessary. I'm quite—"

"No, you're not."

For the longest moment, she stared at his offering. Her eyes still glistened. Then her jaw shifted. Lips pursed. Nose sniffed. She took it from him and dabbed her eyes.

"Thank you," she said softly.

"We should get back to work."

Nodding, she turned back to the job notecard, and he walked back to the stove to collect the platter of fish. He carried it to the table.

Somewhere under the other food dishes had to be his job note-card from Aunt Priscilla. But after moving each dish and not finding it, he gave up and walked to the screened back door. The morning sky held several clouds. The cool, springtime air blowing from the Atlantic to the Chesapeake didn't smell like rain, yet it lulled. Peaceful. Relaxing. The cardinals in the nearby tree chirped their morning joy, lulling him even more.

He yawned. This afternoon he'd take a nap.

"She must have taken it with her," he murmured. He widened his eyes, stretching them to wake, yet he yawned again. "I need more coffee."

If he were home, he'd be finishing the day's newspaper and his second cup of coffee. Then he'd begin the thirty-minute walk to the mill. He liked his schedule. He missed his schedule. It gave order to his life. He liked order. Aunt Priscilla chastised him for living according to a schedule, yet created a detailed list of what he—why enlist him anyway?—and Miss Varrs needed to prepare each morning for the course of her quilting bee . . . for two weeks! He wasn't staying two weeks. Why couldn't she understand? Four more days was all he was giving her to draw his quilt and help him begin courting Arel.

He had to return to Philly on Saturday. His Sunday school boys were counting on him being there. And he had the mill repairs to oversee. His life was—

"I need medium meal."

Zenus jumped, startled to hear Miss Varrs's voice so close to his ear. How had she managed to walk across the kitchen without him hearing?

He turned, and she was right there next to him, holding the notecard up to his nose. Instead of his aunt's handwriting on the card, all he saw was Miss Varrs watching his face. She looked puzzled. And vexed because she was puzzled. And more than a little appealing when she repeated with her melodic accent, "Oatmeal, Mr. Dane. Not oat flakes."

"There's a difference?" he said, his voice rougher than he would have liked, but at least his tongue managed to stay untied. She smelled of cinnamon, which was peculiar because they had yet to use any spices this morning.

"Of course, there is a difference." She lowered the notecard. "Once the outer husk of the oat has been removed, the groat"—he must have looked confused because she corrected with—"the *kernel* can take one of three paths. One: steamed, then rolled into jumbo oat flakes. Two: cut in half to be eaten as is, known as pinhead, or steamed and rolled to make ordinary oat flakes. Or three: ground into oatmeal."

Zenus nodded, because it seemed an appropriate action to fill in for the lack of thoughts in his mind.

She released a huff of breath. "If I am going to make porridge, I will make it the proper way. My way. Regardless what you Americans think. Your aunt gave me rolled oats. The recipe calls for rolled oats. I will not use rolled oats." She blinked. "Well?"

Zenus glanced to the box of Quaker Oats he was fairly certain was the same kind his housekeeper used to make his breakfast porridge. "They'll be fine," he offered optimistically.

She blinked again.

"I have them every morning with twelve raisins."

She looked at him with some confusion.

"I like oatmeal," he explained in honesty. "With raisins."

"Every morning?"

He nodded.

"Why?"

"I'm loyal," he said, and realized how true that was. That was why he'd loved Clara Reade Gallagher far longer than he should have, even after her rejection. But the love brought grief upon her death, and the grief opened his heart to God. "Trust me, Miss Varrs, the rolled oats will be fine."

She stepped forward, eased up on her tip-toes, putting their eyes at even level, which sent his heart racing and his feet wanting to flee. Worse, his hands wanted something quite the opposite. Hands to the side, hands to the side.

"Fine?" she said, the coffee on her breath heavy and inviting. "*Fine?*"

Zenus swallowed. "Oats are oats." He tried to smile and knew he failed miserably.

She looked at him as if he'd spoken a blasphemy. "Don't be daft." She then dropped down on her heels. "Since you wish for me to speak, I shall say rolled oat flakes make for a tasteless and pappy porridge. I will not disgrace my Scottish ancestors by preparing pappy porridge."

"Pappy—?" His lips paused on the *p* in porridge.

He was *not* going to laugh. But it was bubbling up. He could feel the tickle, so he clamped his mouth shut . . . except the bubble kept growing, as did the tickle, and his face felt rather warm, and her glare didn't look the least bit intimidating. Self-preservation his goal, he held his breath. But the bubble sent air through his nose sounding like a pathetic snort.

"Do not laugh at me," she warned. "Porridge is not a laughing matter."

Clearly, the British took their porridge seriously.

Zenus drew in a slow breath and another, until he could manage to say, "How 'bout I look in the pantry for oatmeal?"

"Excellent idea." She smiled, and it tingled through him.

She wasn't beautiful, not like Arel's dainty perfection. But the confidence she bore about what she liked, even if it was only oatmeal mush—heaven help him, it was alluring and intimidating. He didn't know anyone like her. And since he knew of the barely there scar above her lip, he could not stop staring at it. His fingers flinched, itching to touch her.

"My cooking skills are limited," she assured him, "but I know porridge."

He started at the sound of her voice, jerking his gaze back to her eyes.

"I, uhh, bet you do," he muttered. She also knew fishing, excelled at it. He imagined she studied whatever subject fascinated her until she became an expert at it. "Aunt Priscilla should—" His mind went blank at what he'd been about to say. Not now. Not when they had developed a comfortable ease between them.

Her head tilted again, and she looked at him, frowning. She moistened her bottom lip. Not like Holly Jane had as she handed him a dinner plate. No, her action seemed more contemplative and unconscious than coquettish.

Say something. Anything.

"I, uhh, like porridge." Brilliant.

It jolted her. "Porridge, yes." Her smile sent another tingle through him. "Trust me, Mr. Dane, if you like the monstrosity you call 'oatmeal,' you will love the real thing."

She whirled around and, with a "we don't need this," discarded the notecard on the table of food, where it landed against the chair holding his suit coat. With a determined tap-tap-tap of her heeled boots across the floor, she claimed the kettle and moved it to the stove.

Minutes later, Zenus followed Miss Varrs's methodical directions of toasting the medium ground oatmeal to give it a nutty flavor while she heated to boiling the liquid—a specific 1:3 ratio of oats to liquid. Because, as she informed him, a 1:2 is too gluey and 1:4 is too loose. Even the liquid must be a precise 1:2 of milk to water.

"They must all be measured exactly," she explained.

Zenus looked from the kettle to Miss Varrs. Who knew *intentional* and *exact* would best describe her? "Now what do we do?"

"Add the oats." Wooden spoon in right hand and a handful of toasted oats in left, Miss Varrs scattered the oats, the meal falling effortlessly into the liquid. "They should be sprinkled in a steady rain from the left hand," she said, her voice as velvet as she worked, "while stirring sunwise with the right."

Her focus never left the kettle. His never left the elegant line of her neck or the wisps of hair grazing her skin. Lissome and alluring.

"And never," she said, her voice even softer, "heat the oats with the liquid in the pan."

"I didn't know you could turn cooking into a science experiment," he murmured, mesmerized by the soft bumps of her spine, by the bronzing of her skin growing lighter as it neared the hairline. It was the type of neck a man would enjoy draping a necklace around merely for the purpose of having an excuse to kiss it after he affixed the clasp.

At the soft and recognizable squeak of someone on the back porch, he jerked his gaze away. Aunt Priscilla opened the screened door with what looked to be two jars of green-colored marmalade in her hands. She stepped inside the kitchen, drawing the screen door closed. He held a finger up to his mouth and mouthed a *shhh*, then pointed to the food they'd finished preparing. Aunt Priscilla gave a cursory glance at the table. Her gaze shifted from Zenus to Mary then back to him, and her chin hardened, eyes narrowed. He could feel her silent warning. *Back away.*

He didn't need to be told. He knew.

He nodded and took a step back. "Miss Varrs, since you have the porridge under control, I will—"

"Wait." She grabbed his apron, stilling him. "Application is the next step in the scientific study. Hands please."

Zenus tossed his aunt an apologetic look and then held his hands out.

Miss Varrs poured the last of the toasted oats in his palm, his skin prickling where hers lightly touched. Then she covered his other hand with hers and directed him to grip the wooden spoon in it. "When you stir, you are to be brisk, not forceful," she instructed, moving in sync with him. She released her hold. "Now, the gentle rain. Go on."

Zenus let the oats flutter from his left hand while he stirred with his right.

"Sunwise only," she whispered.

"Why can't I stir counter-clockwise?" he whispered back.

"My Scottish grandmother used to say anti-clockwise will"— her voice took on a lilt—"encourage the devil into yer breakfast. Ye dinna want that now, do ye?" She smiled at him, and he felt himself smiling back . . . until he remembered his aunt was watching.

Aunt Priscilla cleared her throat. "Zenus, I believe the food could be taken to the sideboard. I saw the Ferrises and Mrs. Scarborough arriving when I was walking back from the Linwoods'. And set the Royal Doulton china out, too."

"Yes, ma'am."

Zenus moved away from the stove, but not before seeing a lovely blush steal across Miss Varrs's cheeks. Potential, all right.

Just not for him.

9

Two days later

I need your help."

Mrs. Osbourne's voice cut into the silence of the night as they strolled at a leisurely pace toward Mary's temporary home. Both their white blouses glowed bright in the moonlight enhancing the dark rings under the older woman's eyes. Three days into her quilting bee and she looked tired, her gray-sprinkled chignon loosened, her posture not as straight.

Mary opened the creaky gate to the Linwoods' back yard. "What can I do for you?"

With a weary sigh, Mrs. Osbourne passed through. "If I know Arel Dewey—and I do—she will show up tomorrow morning, bright and early, on your doorstep to share about her rally."

A likely possibility.

"And when you aren't home," Mrs. Osbourne continued, "she will come here to see if I know where you are. Between your illustrations and Zenus's quilt design, I can't afford the distraction Arel is."

Mary nodded. She fully understood, yet she was looking forward to Miss Dewey's distractibility. Had been. Until this moment, she'd not given one thought today to Miss Dewey, or her imminent return. Mary was drained from another day of quilting and talking and an evening of serving dinner and cleaning the kitchen while she watched the dancing through the windows. Nor had she wanted to join in. Where Mr. Dane had managed to hide a second night from Holly Jane Ferris, she had no idea. She suspected he left with the Reverend and Mrs. Jaeger for choir rehearsal. After overhearing Mrs. Osbourne rave about how he participated in the Philadelphia Literary Club on Tuesdays and was a member of the choir at his home church, it made sense he'd be somewhere singing on Wednesday night.

The man, like her father, was a product of tradition and routine. *I'm loyal.*

His words danced across her mind, leaving a curve to her lips.

She rather applauded him, though, for disappearing. Mrs. Ferris the Younger had been in high form tonight. Had Mr. Dane been outside, the besotted widow certainly would have claimed all his dances. Mary had not wished to dance with him. But had Mr. Dane been there, and had she not had to clean the kitchen, and had Holly Jane Ferris not . . .

Good heavens, it'd been so many years since she danced, she likely wouldn't have remembered the steps anyway. So it all worked out for good. And considering what Mrs. Osbourne was sacrificing to help her, she couldn't deny any request the dear woman made.

She closed the gate with another grinding creak then motioned Mrs. Osbourne toward a stone bench near the back of the house.

"What do you need from me?" she asked, clasping her hands behind her back as they walked.

Mrs. Osbourne offered a smile, but it wasn't a real smile considering the troubled look in her eyes. "After we've prepared breakfast tomorrow, I'm sending Zenus to the strawberry auction. I need you to accompany him—"

"What?"

"—and keep him gone until lunch. Preferably longer."

Mary blinked. Of all the things Mrs. Osbourne could have asked her, she would've never wagered on this. She'd been to the strawberry auction numerous times since arriving two months ago. Buying strawberries was not so difficult a city-raised man like Mr. Dane couldn't accomplish it on his own. She, simply, did not wish to go. With him. Anywhere.

"Why must *I* do this?" She elected not to be bothered by the whininess in her tone.

"You two worked well preparing breakfast and serving dinner these last two days."

"Yes but . . ."

It was the very the heart of her opposition—the recollection of how well they *had* worked together after he had his verbal explosion and she finally accepted he needed her to talk to him. Comfortable. Easy. Like they'd known each other for years.

Lord have mercy, where had this frightening thought come from?

From her heart. From her memory. She could still feel the warmth of his skin as she'd showed him how to stir the porridge. Or when he whispered his thanks the morning after she gave him his properly prepared porridge with the twelve raisins he liked. Then he looked at her and—

Her heart tumbled and clenched as it had then, a quite familiar feeling, undeniable. Troubling. And one she had not felt for over two years. Attraction.

She let out a little sigh.

"You don't care for my nephew," Mrs. Osbourne stated.

Mary stopped cold. Not care? She neither cared nor not cared for the man. He was nothing more than a practical stranger with whom she felt an intense physical draw. Not illogical. The survival of a species often depended on how attractive the male was. Such as the *Betta splendens* displaying its flared opercula. Or the *Panthera leo*. The darker and fuller the mane, the healthier the lion, thus more desirable to lionesses. Or the *Passerina ciris*—the most beautiful North American bird. While the Painted Bunting's dark blue head, green back, red rump, and underparts made it alluring, it also coaxed females with its irresistible song.

She did not have to do a study on Zenus Dane to know he had been given a glorious exterior by God to attract females because of the occasional discordancy of his "song." And she wasn't immune. At times when his eyes met hers, she felt as if his hands were on her waist pulling her close.

Her cheeks heating, she countered with, "Your nephew is of no consequence to me. I'm supposed to do my share of quilting. I cannot if I am gone. After seeing how Mrs. Scarborough did a padded appliqué on the quilt top this morning, I thought I might try an embroidered overlaid appliqué consisting of birds, rabbits, and foliage. I've done one before." Years ago. Not as if it were a concern. Embroidering, after all, was much like riding a bike.

Mrs. Osbourne watched her for a long moment, not stumbling a bit as they walked. "Taking Zenus away for the day is more vital work. When Arel discovers you are at the auction, she will seek you out."

Mary opened her mouth to argue then closed it. She cast her gaze to the grass under her feet, the hem of her skirt skimming the strands. The Belle Havenian most fascinated—oh, let's say it, obsessed—with her was Miss Dewey. She'd never given much thought to being someone's mentor, but sometimes it felt as if Miss Dewey had created a paradigm of womanly perfection in her mind as to who Mary was, and it had little in common with whom Mary actually was.

She, supposedly, embodied the "new feminine ideal" Miss Dewey raved about. Unsexed. Living an unattached life, independent of a man and the chains of matrimony.

Mary didn't wish to be a "new feminine ideal" any more than she wanted to become the "lady" Headmistress Whitacre had believed repetitive hand smacks would turn her into. Nor did she even wish to be the "Exalted Women of Proverbs" the revivalist in Florida had preached about. All were too exhausting a standard to live up to. Neither did she wish to be "unsexed" or applauded for being this way by people thinking she'd be proud of the compliment. She wasn't proud of what Miss Dewey believed about her or having the mayor accuse her of being a socialist, unionist, Darwinist, or spy. Or even Mr. Dane considering her a dark cloud. It hurt.

Unbidden tears burned in her eyes.

She wanted marriage and a family. Someday, God willing. But not one where she obliged her philandering mate as her parents did.

Mary blinked to stop the faucet her eyes had become since she received her father's letter regarding the need for botanical illustrations. She'd prided herself on restraining any and all emotional outbursts. These tears—Now. Again. Ugh. Why?

She removed the Mr. Dane's handkerchief from its spot tucked in behind her belt, dabbing her eyes, steadying her breath.

"Miss Dewey thinks highly of me," she admitted as they reached the bench.

They took a seat next to each other.

"If I may be so bold to ask," Mrs. Osbourne said softly, "how does it make you feel?"

"Honored." She said it, but what she felt was—

Her heart tightened in her chest. Pain. Pressure.

Mary looked to the blue-painted back door behind which she knew Napoleon waited for her to return. So many other women Arel Dewey could—should—take on as role models. Women who truly impacted their world. Women like Queen Elizabeth, Joan of Arc, Sojourner Truth, Harriet Beecher Stowe, Florence Nightingale, and, her favorite, Elizabeth Blackwell for being the first woman awarded a medical degree. Mary's decision to enroll in University College London came after hearing a rousing speech by Miss Blackwell eight years ago in her—and Mary's—birth town of Bristol.

Those women, and many more, should be honored by Miss Dewey. Not her. She had done nothing deserving of admiration.

"Unworthy," she whispered, shaking her head.

Mrs. Osbourne didn't look surprised. She turned from Mary and focused on the garden next to them, a frown spreading across her features. "The suffrage words Arel espouses are her newest cause."

Mary nodded and waited for Mrs. Osbourne to continue.

"For her act of sacrifice during Lent this year," Mrs. Osbourne said, still focused on the garden, "she convinced her father to allow her to give a portion of her inheritance to Methodist, Mennonite, and Baptist missionaries, for them to start reservation missions to the natives in Oklahoma."

An honorable cause.

"Last summer she advocated for the rights of match girls."

Equally honorable.

"The year before she began drinking naught but lemonade and tea in her temperance stance." She gave Mary a little nudge with her elbow. "Coffee, to her, is the poor man's whiskey."

Before Mary could recover from her surprise over this pronouncement, Mrs. Osbourne turned on the bench to face her and said, "Arel refuses to shop at the mercantile until Mr. Hayes ceases selling corsets and furs. The first is punishment to the wearer; the latter is criminal to the unwilling provider."

"Miss Dewey is"—she searched for the right word—"zealous."

"Yes, she is." Mrs. Osbourne sounded . . . well, it was more than accepting. Proud perhaps? A dulcet sigh eased from her chest and she said, "Arel is what many women wish they had the freedom to be. She needs to see a strong, stable man will anchor her, be a completion, not a limitation. So you understand now why it is I need you to volunteer to go to the strawberry auction with my nephew."

"No," Mary answered, shaking her head, "I don't."

Unless—

She stiffened. She felt her eyes widen, mouth agape like a fish's.

Arel Dewey and Zenus Dane together. As in a couple? Married? It would be like trying to take a leisurely cruise down the river while sharing a canoe with a discordant orchestra and a hungry wolverine. He was wrong for her. *Wrong.*

American social rules restricted married women. Miss Dewey's liberty was in her single state. Her immediate future lay beyond managing a household and birthing children. By the simple lever of her own personality, Miss Dewey could transform herself from a simple American heiress to an influential lobbyist, if she so desired. If someone guided her properly. And if she didn't marry right away. She needed an education first. She needed to see there was life beyond the Commonwealth, beyond society's archaic view of women.

Horrified, she turned on the bench to face Mrs. Osbourne directly. "Do you wish to match Miss Dewey with your nephew?" The words came out before she could stop them, and her cheeks warmed.

110

Mrs. Osbourne smiled. "Yes, yes, I do."

"But do you not *see* how they are ill-suited?"

"One's weaknesses are the other's strengths," she answer, "and once you see them together, you—" Mrs. Osbourne frowned. Eyes narrowed. She leaned forward. Her hand rested over Mary's, her blue eyes searching for some hidden truth. "Do you have warm feelings for my nephew?"

Mary jerked her hand free. "No. NO." She did not hide one ounce of her mortification.

Yet, Mrs. Osbourne's appraisal continued.

Mary's cheeks felt aflame. If only she could hide under the bench. "It's not like that," she said, shaking her head. "You shocked me is all. Miss Dewey is"—she raised her shoulder and release a squeak—"and he is"—she held her hands up like bear claws and growled. "He is not a fit husband for her. Miss Dewey does not need marriage to complete her, nor should any woman—*any*—be made to feel it should." Realizing how high-pitched and insipid she sounded, she clamped her mouth shut.

Who was this rambling, exaggerative, emotional waterfall of a person she was turning into? Reserved and composed—it's what she wanted to return to being. She didn't want to say something, anything, merely to fill the silence, despite Mr. Dane's request. Doing so didn't make her a better person. It made her—she cringed—like an American.

"Miss Varrs, our views on marriage are not dissimilar," said Mrs. Osbourne. "My nephew needs someone like Arel who will push him out of his status quo."

"Why? Mr. Dane is—" No, she would not defend the man to his aunt no matter how compelled she felt to do so.

Mary faced forward on the bench, her hands in her lap. "Marriage should be for love and companionship. When entered into for personal gain or hopes of changing the other," she said, aware of the bitterness creeping into her tone and unable to stop it, "it never ends well." But end it does. Or it becomes obliging.

Several moments passed in silence.

"Arel wishes to be your friend." Mrs. Osbourne covered Mary's balled fists with her own hands, giving them a little squeeze. "I am convinced God led you to Belle Haven for Arel's sake. You are good for her, and I believe she is good for you, too."

Mary shrugged. Not a ladylike response, but better than a curled upper lip or a five-point discourse on why Mrs. Osbourne was wrong.

Mrs. Osbourne stood, leaving an empty spot on the bench. "Mary, look at me."

She did.

"I am not asking you to match-make them," she said frankly. "The sparks are there. Love will happen on its own, as it always does. What I need you to do is give them a reason to be at the same place together. Tomorrow, and until Zenus leaves." She paused. Fingers plucked the side of her black skirt. "I don't know how, but he managed with you to overcome his problem with faltering speech. If you can keep him calm, Zenus won't say something mortifying to Arel."

Mary couldn't help but nod in agreement. "This is not your means of secretively matching your nephew with me?" she asked with more bite to her words than she intended.

Mrs. Osbourne's shoulder slumped. "He, too, questioned my motives. I can see how I deserve the suspicion, and the answer is— it is not." She waved at the air before her. "No offense taken. Zenus's happiness is and has always been paramount to me. I also desire the best for you and Arel. The world is before you, and Zenus wants nothing more than life in Philadelphia. You are, to be frank, too much of an achiever for a man like him."

"It does not feel like a compliment," she grumbled.

"It is." She leaned down, cradling Mary's face in her hands, and placed a soft kiss on her forehead. "Mary, I am so proud of what you have accomplished thus far in your life." She released her hold, stood straight. "I also appreciate you helping me match Zenus and Arel. In gratitude, I will not add any more terms to our agreement."

"I did not give my answer to accompanying Mr. Dane to the strawberry auction."

"Sleep well." Mrs. Osbourne raised a hand in the air and waved, walking away. "Wear comfortable shoes, dearie."

Mary didn't wave back.

Arel Dewey did not deserve to have her life manipulated by a woman who, even if she did have her best interest at heart, could not see the future, could not know she knew best. Nor did Mr. Dane deserve it either.

You are good for her.

Was she? Mary rubbed her palms against each other, circling them as she mulled her neighbor's words. What good thing had she done for Miss Dewey? Nothing. Although she had been invited to the rally because Miss Dewey viewed her as a mentor. Mentor? She straightened on the bench. What if God truly did orchestrate her coming to Belle Haven, so she could influence Miss Dewey's life? Maybe.

She sat up a little straighter. Maybe, just maybe the influence Miss Dewey already acknowledged meant Mary's duty was to convince Miss Dewey to forego marriage until after she had earned a college degree. Until she came into her own.

A slow grin spread across Mary's face, filling her with purpose.

Arel Dewey needed a mentor's help.

She gave her thighs a quick smack. "And help her I will." For Miss Dewey's sake. As well as Mr. Dane's.

10

"Zenus, I need you to go to the strawberry auction."

As he leaned against the kitchen counter, Zenus waited for Aunt Priscilla to say more. She always had *more to say* in the mornings. And her *mores* were never pleasant.

She set the pan of muffins on the table next to the food they'd finished preparing. "Did you hear me?" she asked, lifting a muffin from the tin.

Zenus took the spoon and bowl of porridge Miss Varrs offered him and noted the twelve raisins again in the center. She'd added fresh cream and butter. Two days in a row now. What more could a man ask for than a woman who obliged his routine? He could have fallen in love right then and there. Instead of allowing his gaze to follow Miss Varrs—whose fitted green riding habit was the same shade of the lawn he was to mow—he kept his eyes on his aunt. No sense giving her another reason to suspect he had romantic inclinations for her neighbor.

Not as if he couldn't still see Miss Varrs in his peripheral view.

She would make a good wife for someone like . . . like Sean. The man constantly changed transcriptionists and secretaries. He'd like a non-traditional, yet elegant woman like Mary Varrs. Aimee would like her, too. Miss Varrs was a nice woman.

She stopped abruptly. With an "oh," she held a hand to her mouth as if she just remembered something. Then she did an about face, changing course from going to the stove to going to the hutch on the other side of the kitchen, crossing his line of sight. He couldn't look at his aunt now without seeing her. She knelt. Whatever she was searching for wasn't in the bottom cabinet.

"Yes, I heard you," he said in a manner-of-fact tone. "I don't know how to pick strawberries."

"It's not difficult," answered Aunt Priscilla without looking up from the tin of muffins she was emptying into a wooden bowl. She adjusted the pile. "Your uncle used to go with me to buy them. Such a sweet man to . . ."

Whatever else she said, he didn't hear because Miss Varrs stood and opened the hutch's top doors, stretching with the grace of a dancer to reach a bowl on the top shelf. The length of her arms and the alluring curve of—

"Well?" Aunt Priscilla demanded.

Zenus met her gaze. By the chilled look she was giving him, he knew a lecture was forming, beginning with *Rule number one: Miss Varrs is not to be noticed, studied, and certainly not ogled.*

A fitting lecture, if there ever was one.

Food, not figure. He dipped his spoon into the porridge, scooping one raisin, giving the raisin his entire focus. "Then you should go. I can stay here and manage your quilting ladies." He moved the spoon closer to his mouth. "A few minutes away from the house would be good for you," he said before taking the bite. The porridge teased his tongue, not too sweet, not too salty. Just right. Now since he had tasted Miss Varrs's porridge, he was done with the monstrosity his housekeeper made for him.

The cabinet doors closed with a thud.

Miss Varrs flicked her nail against the crystal bowl. *Cling.* Her lips curved, and he couldn't stop his own from mimicking the action.

"Zeee-nus," Aunt Priscilla groaned, drawing his attention. "I don't need time away. I *need* strawberries."

"I'm not stopping you from getting them," he snipped back. Eyes on her. Eyes on her.

"Errand boys run errands." She snatched the bowl of muffins off the table. "I don't understand why you are fussing about this. We had an arrangement. Buying strawberries is not a difficult task. Why can't you trust I have your best interest at heart?"

Miss Varrs walked past him again in her path to the stove, cradling the crystal bowl against her stomach as if were a child in her womb. The sway of her hips—

Breakfast. Focus on the breakfast. Zenus scooped another spoonful of porridge. "Aunt Priscilla, if it matters so much to you, I'll go . . ."

"Thank you."

" . . . tomorrow," he finished as Miss Varrs scooped the remaining porridge into the serving bowl, her spoon scraping against the sides of the kettle, emptying it. Plop. Scrape. Plop. He grinned. Nothing beguiling in her action at all. Finally. He looked to his aunt. "Today there are more pressing things on my list." He withdrew the notecard he had slid between his shirt and the waistband of his trousers, holding it up. "Correction, your list."

Aunt Priscilla arched her brow.

Zenus returned the notecard to its secure spot. He then ate another spoonful of porridge, taking his leisurely time to swallow. "You can look at me all you want. Last night I had an epiphany." He spooned another raisin. "Improved men don't succumb to their aunt's manipulations."

Aunt Priscilla gasped.

A curve touched Miss Varrs's lips, then disappeared. She dropped the wooden spoon in the kettle with a clang. Her gaze shifted from the filled porridge bowl to him. "Mr. Dane, what is so pressing you cannot assist your aunt?"

"The lawn needs to be mowed," he said between bites of porridge. He'd already oiled and sharpened the push-mower's blades. "For tonight's croquet tournament."

She slowly nodded. "I see." She picked up a cloth and began wiping down the counter. "You should go."

116

"Go where?" Holly Jane Ferris said breathlessly, passing through the kitchen's propped open door with her three-pie basket in one hand and a twine-tied bundle of asparagus in the other.

Zenus groaned under his breath.

The red day dress she wore couldn't have been less suited to a quilting bee. But she wore the dress, he knew, because Aunt Priscilla had shared yesterday at lunch red was his favorite color. Proving how little his aunt knew him. He liked green. Thus the olive-striped waistcoat he wore. He could count it joy he'd left clothes at her house due to his hasty Christmas retreat.

Holly Jane stopped in the center of the kitchen and posed like Mona Lisa posed before da Vinci. There was no other word for the way she stood with her shoulders back and plump lips in a seductive pout. He wasn't sure how she'd managed to make her black hair even glossier, but it was, and her heady Oriental perfume—

He took another bite of porridge to put a pleasing taste in his mouth. A man needed to be the pursuer, not the pursued.

"Well?" Holly Jane said impatiently. "Go where?"

Miss Varrs stopped wiping the counter. She looked to his aunt. Panicked. Aunt Priscilla looked to her. Panicked. If he didn't know better, he'd think they were in cahoots. Zenus gave his head a shake. A ridiculous notion. Still, in unison, they turned to him, each silently begging him to answer Holly Jane. Not happening. She wasn't—nor ever would be—his anything to solve.

Zenus resumed eating. He had a lawn to mow and a book of poetry to finish reading to ready his mind for courting Arel tonight. She'd show up for the evening quilting bee festivities, he knew for sure. No one liked a party like Arel Dewey.

Compliments, must find compliments.

"Mrs. Osbourne?" Holly Jane prompted.

"Strawberry auction," answered Aunt Priscilla. Crisply.

A smile broke out over Holly Jane's face as a squeal of delight erupted from her mouth. "Why didn't you say so? I love the auction. We shall take my buggy." She held the basket and bundle of asparagus out to Miss Varrs and, in the same tone Zenus had heard her speak to lower class workers, ordered, "Mary, put these in the cellar, and see they are served with dinner. Seven exact slices per pie."

Seven? Zenus dropped his spoon in the empty bowl. *Chink.*

"Oh," Holly Jane continued, "and steam the asparagus later for lunch with one-fourth a teaspoon of salt and one pat of butter. No more. No less."

Zenus looked at her and saw red.

Aunt Priscilla stood speechless, which was fine with him because he had enough of Holly Jane's machinations.

"Holly Jane," he snapped, "it is—"

"So generous of you," Miss Varrs finished sweetly. She hurried over to take the pie basket and asparagus. "My cooking skills need all the assistance they can receive." She sniffed the asparagus. "These smell wonderful. In how much water should I steam them?"

Holly Jane looked startled. "Three cups."

"Bring to a boil with the salt and butter?" Miss Varrs asked, smiling. "Or do I add the salt and butter after steamed?"

Holly Jane blinked. "With."

Miss Varrs rested the asparagus on the counter. "And steam for ten minutes?"

"Eight is best," she clarified, the haughtiness in her tone lightening.

"Splendid." With both hands, Miss Varrs held the basket to her chest. "Mrs. Ferris, would you be so kind as to do me a favor?"

Although her eyes had a bit of a narrow to them, Holly Jane said, "Of course."

"I had thought to attend Saturday's auction, but—" Still not glancing at Aunt Priscilla or him, Miss Varrs stepped closer to Holly Jane and spoke conspiratorially. "Since Mrs. Osbourne needs strawberries today, and with Mr. Dane needing to hurry back so he can mow the lawn, would you mind ever so much if"—she cringed—"I accompanied Mr. Dane instead? I desperately need strawberries for the canning I do for the Linwoods, and I failed to exercise Mrs. Linwood's mare enough this morning. Makes perfect sense to accomplish both things at once."

"But I—"

"Holly Jane," Aunt Priscilla warned, along with arched brow of disapproval.

"I suppose not," she answered.

"Oh, thank you." Miss Varrs backpedaled to the door leading to the kitchen. "I'll go put your pies in the cellar. And I will be sure to bring you a jar of strawberry-tomato jam to show my appreciation of your kindness." She repeated "thank you," as she stepped outside to the cellar.

Holly Jane stood awkwardly as if she wasn't sure what just happened or how she should feel about it.

Zenus covered up his smile by drinking his coffee. Mary Varrs was one surprising woman. Considering how well she managed Holly Jane, he'd wager she'd have some excellent advice in helping him charm Arel Dewey. He just needed to figure out a way to ask her without embarrassing himself or looking desperate.

———

Amid the noise from the train whistle and people conducting business on the street, Zenus rode to the left of Miss Varrs down the main thoroughfare to the railroad station. Back straight and serene, she held regal form on Mrs. Linwood's sidesaddle. Trotting. Galloping. Sedate pace. Nothing broke her relaxed composure. Even her top hat sat perfectly level despite the moderate Atlantic breeze.

He nodded at the numerous pedestrians on the boardwalk parallel to them. Did every man on the street need to observe his riding partner as if she were Diana the Huntress? The absence of layers of petticoats under her too fitted green riding habit allowed for the curvature of her leg to be noticed. Ogled.

They should have taken a buggy.

Zenus eased Mr. Linwood's gelding closer to her mare.

Walking—would not attract unnecessary attention. Yes, they should walk.

Zenus looked for an empty hitching post amid the wagons already lined up. He found one up ahead near the church, next to a lamppost with a cluster of seagulls waiting for a stray strawberry to fall from a crate. He'd seen Mrs. Linwood ride her mare about town. But even with her fashionable riding habit, he doubted she ever drew the admiring and curious—even wary—looks Miss Varrs garnered. Her English elegance was out of place in Belle Haven. What did anyone have to be suspicious about?

All the evidence pointed to her being nothing more than what she'd admitted: an English botanist temporarily staying in Belle Haven as she finished a tomato study. No money-grubbing motives. He'd been a fool to suspect otherwise.

"Tell me about this study you're doing," he said, breaking the comfortable silence between them since leaving Aunt Priscilla's house.

"Was doing." Her nervous gaze shifted from one curious pedestrian to the next.

"Your study," he pressed.

"Yes, my . . . umm, I typed the conclusion last . . . uhh, night."

They paused at the intersection for a trio of wagons to roll past.

"Does knowing people are watching make you tense?"

She looked to him, slight frown on her features, and a heap of worry in her eyes. "They see me riding with you. It is enough, trust me, to make them wonder, and wondering leads to talking and talking leads to all sorts of assuming and concluding. If I had a sterling reputation no one would suspect me of anything, but I do not, even though I am, for all practical purposes, still a stranger."

Zenus shifted in the saddle. "Belle Haven is not London society."

Her brows rose. "Indeed." She gently tapped the whip against the mare's right flank, spurring it into motion.

Zenus nudged his gelding. "You think little of the Belle Havenians."

"Oh no," she answered without pause. "Some here are gracious and welcoming, like your aunt. However, some believe I am a Darwinist, unionist. Last Sunday, the mayor accused me of being a spy."

A spy? Zenus adjusted his grip on the reins, the leather squeaking against the leather of his gloves. "Meet their gazes and smile."

"What?"

"Do it," he seethed. Then to lead her, he demonstrated, looking at Mr. Hamilton as the postmaster stood outside the Post Office. "Morning," Zenus called out with dip of his head as they rode past. In the corner of his eye, he watched Miss Varrs nod, smile, wave even.

They continued until they were past the bulk of the pedestrian crowd.

Zenus said, "About your study, you were saying?"

She slowly released the breath, he hadn't realized she'd held. "It is complete, save for the botanical illustrations your aunt is sketching." Her gaze lowered to the reins threaded through her kidskin-gloved hands. "Mr. Dane, you need not continue to pretend interest in my study to distract me from my qualms at being watched. I am fine."

"I'm not pretending."

She turned to look at him, hesitation and doubt in her eyes. "You really wish to know?"

"I do."

Her eyes held his, assessing, taking measure of his words, character. Did she see an honest man? Not a flatterer. Not a rogue. But a good man. Reliable. He wanted her to see deep into his soul, to know she could count on him. To see he would be a friend, if she would have him. And he would do what he could to help her obtain the research position she desired.

A faint expression of gratitude seemed to flit across her face.

She turned away, refocusing on the road. "I compared the top four seeds in each variety, as well as the hybrids I developed. Then I tested for yield and taste."

She created new seeds? Stunned, yet impressed, Zenus rode up to the post. He dismounted, looped his reins over the hitch, and waited for her to ride up to him.

He took the reins from her and tied her horse next to his. "How did your seeds fare?"

"As expected."

He stepped forward to help her dismount. "Just *as expected*?"

Her head tilted then, and she met his gaze, her hazel eyes finding his in an oddly intimate manner. As if they were the only two people on the street. As if she had a secret she could no longer hold back from sharing. And he knew exactly what she would do next— smile. Disconcerting, yes, because she wasn't Arel Dewey whom he had known for years, yet it felt natural. Easy. Right.

Her smile bloomed. Little bursts of joy danced along the back of his neck.

"Exceedingly well, actually." Her eyes were wide and sparkling. "My hope is to expand my tomato germplasm if I secure the position in Blacksburg."

"You will."

"You say it as if you know with confidence it will occur."

Did he? He gave her a lop-sided grin. "Miss Varrs, I have deduced you are a woman with determination exceeded only by your passion."

An enchanting blush stole across her cheeks.

He liked it. He liked how when she was relaxed, she released the restraints on her emotions—let them run free. He also liked how she could focus so intently on a task she ignored all distractions, something he had never been able to do.

He continued with, "You will achieve whatever you set your mind out to do, because you've predetermined you will not settle for anything less than success. Is it a fair assessment?"

She nodded. Not an insecure *if you say so* nod. Not an arrogant *of course* nod, either. It was factual. Exact. Just like her.

"Being intentional," he said, "is a quality more people should possess."

She looked at him strangely, as if she were debating whether to believe or doubt his sincerity.

"Shall we?" He lifted his hands to assist her dismount.

She shifted her leg over the pommel and leaned down, placing her gloved hands on his shoulders. His hands curved around her waist, lifted her to the ground. And he froze, fully aware she was in his arms. No, not in his arms, per se. She was standing before him, with him holding her close, twelve inches at least, but wanting to pull her closer. Her eyes, so lovely with the flecks of brown amid the green, met his with startling directness, unwavering, nervous, yet unafraid. She trusted him. *Him.* Even after all the mortifying things he said to her. Even when he didn't deserve her trust. Something flared within him.

His heart lurched dangerously, breath skipped.

Say something.

Anything!

He couldn't think of anything. He couldn't move. He couldn't seem to take his eyes off the barely there scar, the little spot on the right side of her top lip. A kissable spot, if a man were inclined. And he was. Inclined. Obliged. Desperate.

A little rush of breath passed over her lips.

A sigh of pleasure? Anticipation? He didn't know.

He moistened his lips.

Her hands slid from his shoulders to his chest, lingering, as if she couldn't pull away. Magical. Magnetic. Her eyes held a longing he recognized, because he'd felt it all morning. Tried to ignore it, to ignore her, but she wasn't ignorable. He wanted to know her more. Beyond knowing she had a scientific mind, cooked delectable porridge, and had the graciousness to manage condescending women, he wanted to know her hopes, fears, and opinions. He wanted her in his life. And the intensity of it all scared him. Filled him. Confused him.

"What are you doing to me?" he said softly.

She jerked her hands away. "I'm n-n-not sure what you mean," she said with a bit of a waver in her voice and looking positively ill. She brushed past him to step on the boardwalk.

He wasn't too sure himself what he meant. Or what he'd intended. What he did know with confidence was letting her run away, ignore him, wasn't an option.

In two seconds he was next to her, matching pace as they—as she—hurried around people and toward the loud voices coming from the auction tent two blocks away.

"What was *that*?"

"What was what, Mr. Dane?" The cool, detached Miss Varrs was back. She stretched her neck to see around those ahead of them. "The bidding has already begun. Does it not amaze you how loud the auctioneers can be? Then when the train whistles . . ."

"Miss Varrs."

She kept walking.

Zenus grabbed her arm, stopping her. He waited until the pedestrians behind them passed by. Even though no one was near, he lowered his voice. "Mary, don't tell me you didn't feel it, too."

For an endless moment, they stared each other down.

"You imagined whatever it is you think you felt," she said with a dismissive wave.

He crossed his arms over his chest. "I know what I felt."

Her shoulder lifted, shrugged. Conveyed *it is of no consequence.*

"You don't need to be embarrassed over what you feel for me," he reasoned. "I know it's shocking. And sudden. I'm shocked, especially considering three days ago I—"

"Stop, Hercules, before you begin an unnecessary quest. I am *not* here because I feel any . . . any . . ." Her hands waved wildly. "Any of *what* you imagined." She looked at her hands in the air, winced, jerked them down to her side. "Do you understand?"

"Felt, Mary, felt," he insisted. Grinning. Emotions only heightened her beauty. "Not imagined. You felt it, too."

She growled through clenched teeth. "Let me be clear." Her voice deepened, peeved. "Last night after you shirked your duties and deserted me to clean the kitchen alone—"

"Wait right there," he cut in heatedly. "I didn't shirk anything. Aunt Priscilla suggested I go listen to choir rehearsal."

"You did not *have* to go."

"You would I had stayed and let Holly Jane have her way with me?"

"I would rather you honor your obligations."

He leaned forward. Since she didn't back away, it encouraged him. "Obligations such as . . . cleaning with you. And now, we are here, together, by your orchestration. Me with you."

"Mr.—"

"My name is Zenus, and you, Mary, should admit you are as attracted to me as I am to you."

Her mouth opened. Closed. Clamped. She looked away, her breath ragged and sharp. He could hear her thoughts: *Not proper, not proper at all.*

He had about given up she would respond when she said, "Last night your aunt insisted I accompany you to the auction for the sole purpose of ensuring Arel Dewey will follow me here so she will not be a distraction to the quilters. Mrs. Osbourne wants me to ensure you say nothing mortifying, being her objective is to match you with Miss Dewey." Mary held up an elegant hand. "Shh. Let me finish. I shan't permit it to occur. You will not make her a fit husband. I intend to show Miss Dewey an option she has never considered, yet should do—attend college."

Zenus could feel the blood draining from his face.

Not make a fit husband. What else did he have to do to prove he would make the ideal mate? He didn't earn, in the last eight years, eight perfect attendance pins from the church because he couldn't stay faithful. He was loyal. And patient. And adjustable.

Lips tight, Zenus looked to the boarded wall beside them to keep from saying something mortifying to both of them.

She clasped her hands together. "I do apologize for breaking it to you in this manner. The news of your aunt's matchmaking is clearly disturbing. If you wish to return—"

"I'm not disturbed by *that*," he bit off. "I know she's matchmaking."

She gave him a hard look. "You know?" The volume of her words drew several looks.

With a growl under his breath, Zenus pulled her into the shaded alleyway. "Not everyone needs to hear this discussion."

"Yet you had no qualms when the discussion fixated on me."

Something in her tone caught his attention, and he met her gaze, the sadness, just before the detached façade recovered her features.

"Point taken. I'm sorry," he said sincerely. Why couldn't he ever say the right thing to this woman? "I asked my aunt for her assistance in this matter."

"Why?" She could have sounded· less disgusted; his pride would have preferred it.

Zenus tipped his cap back on his head. "Because I wanted—want to marry Miss Dewey."

He did, didn't he?

She paused so long he didn't think she would respond, as she stared at him, looked at him as if he had said the most absurd thing. Why was it so inconceivable to her he would want to marry Arel Dewey? She was perfection. Hair the color of . . . of yellow. And with a personality like a . . . a pleasing female. What red-blooded American male—correction, man from any nationality—wouldn't want to marry Arel Dewey?

Much to his surprise, Mary said, "Why? Seriously, Mr. Dane, why? She dislikes you."

His teeth grit. "You don't know it's true."

The pretty little head of hers bobbed. Incessantly. Like an annoying woodpecker.

"I rather do," she said, sounding quite certain. "But what I do not know"—she stepped forward until they were close, close enough he could taste the coffee on her breath—"is how you want to marry Miss Dewey, yet claim you feel something for me?"

He flinched.

"Zenus Dane, is your heart so fickle?"

11

Mary waited, gave him a chance to respond. She had been harsh. Too harsh. But his words hurt. Actions hurt. She hurt.

He stared straight ahead, not looking at her, not looking like he was focused on anything.

She let her eyes fall to his lips. Had he intended on kissing her? There, as they'd stood between the horses? Though he had made no movement, it had felt like it. She'd felt it. Considered it. Wasn't sure then—or even now—if she'd wanted it. For all Edward Argent had been, he was, by and by, a flirt, stealing kisses whenever he could. Why she fell for him she didn't know, couldn't remember. Mr. Dane was, simply, absent of artifice. It explained his verbal stumbles around women and his not proper *what was that*? The art of flirtation and flattery did not come natural to him. He said what he thought, what he felt, even when those thoughts and feelings were a cornucopia of confusion. Refreshing.

Frightening.

When he was near her, she felt . . .

She felt desirable and interesting. As if she were free to express her opinions and beliefs without fear of reprisal because he wanted to hear her speak, say something, say anything, because he enjoyed talking with her. But he couldn't truly mean *anything*. He couldn't. He could not—did not—enjoy talking with her. Men who wanted to marry Arel Dewey of America did not find Mary Varrs of England fascinating. Women like Arel could kiss a man and it not mean anything. Not Mary. While she wasn't one of those English girls who would approach the altar for the first time in her virginal life actually touching the elbow of a man, kissing—no, the mere thought of kissing a man meant something.

Meant—

Her heart felt as if someone had corseted it to restrain the frantic beating. Good heavens, she was quite capable of falling in love with him.

It would not do, not do at all.

She took several necessary steps back to put space between them. "We should go," she offered.

He nodded.

She didn't move. *I'm sorry* teetered on the edge of her tongue. He was a good man, anyone could see it. Anyone except Arel Dewey. He'd make a fine husband, a wonderful husband someday, but not for Arel. She was too flighty. She'd never remember how to make his oatmeal properly, nor would she sit still long enough to discuss a book with him, let alone read one. Arel, fishing? Never.

He pointed to the boardwalk. "The strawberries await."

"Of course." She fell into step with him, nothing but the sound of their shoes on the pavement as they headed at a leisurely pace toward the white-tented produce exchange at the end of the block. She glanced at him over her shoulder. "I am sorr—"

"Don't," he ordered, still staring straight ahead.

She waited for him to say more, but he didn't seem inclined to further elucidation. So she offered a safer topic. "Have you ever had tomato-strawberry jam?" she said cheerily.

He gave a little shrug. "Can't say I have. If it tastes anything like your porridge, I'm sure I'll love it."

Mary didn't smile over his compliment, but she did feel one tingle dance its way throughout her body.

"The seeds you developed," he said, "will you patent them?"

"One cannot patent plants or animals derived from conventional breeding."

He turned his head, enough for her to see genuine curiosity in his eyes. "But you could sell your seeds, if you wanted to?"

Mary bit her lip. She'd never considered doing anything with her seeds other than using them in her own garden. "I could," she admitted, feeling a bit more encouraged by his genial tone, "but I do not see any merit in selling them. Your Department of Agriculture devotes one-third of its budget to collecting and distributing seeds across the country."

"Doesn't that limit the private seed trade?"

"According to the American Seed Trade Association, it does."

The corner of his mouth lifted, brows drew together. "There's an American Seed Trade Association?"

She chuckled. "Yes. Since 1883. You Americans seem to enjoy creating organizations, associations, and clubs."

His hands covered his heart. "You wound me."

"I doubt it." She watched him through the corner of her eye, enjoying the feeling of renewed ease between them. "Mr. Dane, perhaps someday your government will permit the patenting of life forms on the basis of their genetic coding. Some people play chess for a hobby. I cross-pollinate. It makes me an odd fish, I know."

His head nodded, gaze returned forward. "My name is Zenus, and what you think, Mary, isn't always true."

Not more than what he thought he felt for her was true. Once Arel arrived in all her morning glory, he would know it for sure.

"Perhaps," she muttered, still watching him, waiting for an indication she was right.

"You're not odd," he said firmly. "You're an original."

"Do put it in a letter to Headmistress Whit—"

His arm snuck around her waist, pulling her to his side, stealing her breath. Mary struggled to find her voice amid the fluttering of her heart. If he kissed her right now, here, she would not . . . she could not . . . she might . . . she—

He dropped his hold and stepped back.

"Morning, Erstwhile," he said, a cool edge to his tone.

The mayor? Mary spun around, face warming. Goodness, if Mr. Dane hadn't pulled her out of the way, she would have walked right into the man.

"Morning, Dane," said Mayor Erstwhile. His eyes—beady and as disapproving as ever—shifted to Mary. He tipped his hat. "Miss Varrs."

"Mr. Erstwhile," she said with a slight dip of her head.

"You've been missed at the café."

She had? "I, uhh . . ."

Mr. Dane's hand grazed against her back. She straightened her spine, drew in a breath as his hand pulled away, hearing his words in her mind.

Meet his gaze and smile.

She raised her chin. "I have been attending Mrs. Osbourne's quilting bee."

"Ah, yes, I did hear . . ." His words trailed off, yet his glare stayed steady.

Mr. Dane moved forward; his thigh bumped the side of her leg. He lifted her hand and placed it on his arm. "We best not miss the bidding." He nodded to the mayor. "Erstwhile."

They had taken two steps when—

"Oh, Miss Varrs."

Mr. Dane's arm tensed under her fingers.

Mary looked over her shoulder at the mayor. "Yes?"

He slid a hand between the buttons of his waistcoat. "Hamilton mentioned a letter arrived for you. Postpaid . . ." his pause lingered, stretched, ". . . from Italy."

Mother.

Or—

Alarm rippled through Mary. Had the prince waxed the envelope? Used his seal? Franked it with stamps bearing the Caetani coat of arms? If anyone found out . . . if they knew . . . oh dear, oh dear, oh dear. Please let it be from Mum.

She used a smile to restrain the panic from showing on her face. "Thank you for letting me know. Good day to you."

He stared at her for a lengthy moment, his eyes growing in beadiness. More beadily? Beadier? Was it even a word?

He said, "To you, too," and walked away.

Mary started to move her hand from Mr. Dane's arm, but he tucked his arm against his side. He resumed walking, weaving them through the crowd, responding to those acknowledging him. "Excuse us. Pardon us. Morning. Good to see you again, too."

Mary held onto his elbow with both hands.

They stopped under the auction tent. As she dropped her hold, Mr. Dane began examining the next set of crates to be auctioned.

"Are you not going to ask from whom the letter is?" Mary said.

"No." He patted the crate on his left. "How about this one?"

Mary gave it a cursory glance. Berries red. Good-sized. Fresh-smelling and identical to all the other crates on the table. "It'll do." She narrowed her gaze up him. "Do you not wish to know?"

"Curiosity is native to all." He grabbed her hand, threading his gloved fingers through hers, and then drew to a shade tree, to await the bidding. Standing to her side, he released her hand and folded his arms across his chest. And he said nothing more. Just stood there in his black suit with his cap cocked jauntily over his dark hair, shielding his eyes from the morning sun. Beautiful yet aloof. Like Mr. Darcy standing back and watching the Bennett sisters dance.

It wasn't as if he didn't care what others thought of him. It likely never dawned on him he was supposed to care. Just like Prince Ercole.

Her mother would love him.

Mary moistened her lips as the bidding began on the next set of crates.

Why didn't he inquire about the letter? Any other person in Belle Haven would. The letter was from her mother, most likely. She would have no qualms with him knowing, but if it were from Prince Ercole inquiring about the return on his investment—

Come July 1, she would be researching in Blacksburg, or sitting in an Italian *castello*. Wife or *cortigiana onesta*. At least, her mother and Prince Ercole had the graciousness to allow her to choose. Not that she had the choice of husbands. Yet only as courtesan—not a wife—she could have a career simultaneous to her companionship obligations. And Mr. Dane wanted to know how she felt about him. She didn't have the luxury of permitting any romantic seeds to grow in her heart.

She rubbed her palm against the one he'd held, yet even through the kidskin of her glove, the feel of his tender grip remained. "You exasperate me," she murmured.

"Good to know our feelings are mutual."

Mr. Dane's pockets were lighter. Mary's too. After what had to be an hour of bidding, losing, and bidding more, two crates of prime strawberries were to be delivered to Aunt Priscilla's house. Mary strolled with Zenus down the boardwalk back toward the church. Arel Dewey had yet to arrive, and a letter from her mother was likely waiting at the Linwoods. Still, Mary sighed, contented. Tomorrow's worries were for tomorrow, or at least later today.

She stole a glance at Mr. Dane's profile, strong jaw, lips perplexingly parallel to his brows. He wasn't just watching where they were walking; he was looking for someone. Arel most likely. Because he wanted to marry her.

Mary turned away, flinching at the strange ping in her chest. He wouldn't make a fit husband for Arel. But if *she* were looking for a husband, she would like a man like him.

"Of course, I also had tests within tests," she blurted to escape her own thoughts. "In my study."

Mr. Dane stepped closer, his hand grazing hers from the slight movement of their arms as they walked. "Such as . . . ?"

Mary fingered her skirt, unsure of where to place her hands without drawing attention to the fact. The only subtle option was to put distance between them, which meant stepping in the path of an open door from one of the businesses. She couldn't do it. It'd be dangerous and unwise. Besides, it wasn't as if he meant anything by the action. People bumped each other all the time. Accidental touch. Meaningless.

There it was again, the swipe of his glove against hers, like a breath across skin. Her neck, shoulders, and the little spot between her shoulder blades tingled.

Be rational. Focus on words, not him.

"The, uhh, rates of growth were related to nutrients and sunshine," she said, "which I, umm, used to develop cultivators to create more meat on the tomato, sweetness, firmness, and—"

Another touch. Tingle. Rush of breath from her lungs, and her heart began to race, beating erratically in her chest.

She cleared her throat. It was dry, utterly parched, despite the strawberries she'd tasted. My goodness, what had she been talking about? Her study, yes. Details. Speak what she knew. Don't focus on him.

"Also," she continued, "for each variety I—"

Another touch, this time the slight lift to his little finger could never be construed as accidental. And the tingle traveled down her spine, tickling her in odd places, pinking her cheeks.

"—uhh, I gave fertilizer at specific times to see how the, umm, plant responded."

"Is there something wrong?"

"No. *No*," she repeated for no good reason. Her voice sounded all creaky and rough. "All is, uh, well."

He held a hand out, stopping her. "You sound distracted. Is it the letter?"

His eyes met hers, concerned and tender, and she almost looked away.

Meet his gaze and smile.

She did. Just a little smile, because too much would look suspicious and insincere, like she was hiding something. Such as, how utterly distracted she was by him. Oh good gracious, it was nothing more than a female's natural response to the close proximity of a healthy male. She had nothing to be nervous about, nothing.

"I just—I, umm—" Looking at him and thinking at the same time weren't possible. She clasped her hands together behind her back and resumed walking. Focus on science, on the study. Focus on the ground. "Incidentals were noted such as signs of disease or insect damage." Excellent. She had perfected the monotonous drone of a college professor. "Testing for resistance would be another"— she spared a glance at him—"why are you doing this?"

"Doing what?" he said, keeping pace and smiling.

"Acting like you are enjoying the discussion."

He turned his head to look at her, his eyes as blue and light and unclouded as the morning sky. Slowly he said, "Why wouldn't I be?"

His voice was soft, sincere, and it stole a beat of her heart.

At this moment, she realized she was holding her breath, realized they had stopped walking and were not alone on the street. Wagons rolled pass. Horses and riders. Bicyclists. Anyone could see them. Anyone could notice.

But she could not look away, simply could not take her eyes off him, even as he said, "Mary, you glow when you talk all sciencey."

Glow? Thankfully, the brim of her hat shielded the blush that must be coloring her cheeks. "Sciencey is not a word."

He shrugged, as if he couldn't be bothered with something as trivial as a word's nonexistence. "Glowing, what's the sciencey word for it?" he asked matter-of-factly.

Mary opened her mouth then closed it. For aught she knew, there wasn't a scientific name, only slang. "Our ancestors saw glowing mushrooms on rotting wood and called it fox-fire." She resumed walking, at ease with talking with him. Up ahead were the church and the hitching post where their horses waited. "The ethereal and eerie glow of insects fluttering about—"

"Ah, fireflies."

He was smiling again, which made her smile, too.

"Prince Ercole likes telling stories of Italian seafarers, both enraptured and frightened by the sea turning milk white in a ship's wake and glowing as if from within. They call it sea-fire."

Mary felt herself warming inside, amused, wistful for magical life in the sea and sky. She had loved listening to his stories. For years, she'd dreamed of mermaids and fairies who would take her away to enchanted lands. They weren't real. At twenty-eight, she was too old to continue believing in faerie tales, but joy remained in pretending all was good, right, and heavenly in the world.

She stopped walking and leaned toward Zenus. "He says his underwater excavators have seen sea creatures glow blue and green. Countless jellyfish, squid, fish, and even certain coral. Can you imagine?"

"They glow colors? Not just yellow?"

She nodded. "Who knows what creatures exist in the seas. Every year more and more species are being discovered."

"You're glowing again," he said. "Mary-fire, in your eyes."

This time Mary didn't look away. "Whether it is botany or ocean wonders, this world God created is fascinating," she admitted, sparkles of joy raising the hair on her arms. "So much to learn and see, how can it not create a fire inside someone?"

"Don't you want marriage and children?"

Of course she did, but—

Her smiled died. "My father says I would have to choose." Not so according to Mother and Prince Ercole, but they said a lot of things she found difficult to believe. How much freedom could one have being a *cortigiana onesta*? She did not see how being treated more-or-less equal to women of the nobility made being a courtesan any more appealing, despite what her mother said.

Mr. Dane slowly nodded. "It makes sense."

"It does?" she said in surprise. She'd expected him to disagree. "How so?"

"Most of my mill workers are mothers raising their families alone."

Mary nipped at her bottom lip. Having a job plus raising a child— children—on one's own. . . . Those poor exhausted women. What burden they must bear. Alone. Like her father had borne, until her brothers left for Eton and she was shipped off to Italy to her mother. Ministering to those workers should be someone's next cause.

"My female workers, they—"

"Yes?" she pressed, watching, wondering what was troubling him.

His brow furrowed as if the realization crossed his mind for the first time. "They all look tired. It must be tough being a parent alone. Our church should begin a ministry to them."

Mary's eyes widened.

"What?" Mr. Dane asked.

She shook her head, unsure of what to make of it. They couldn't have been thinking alike because it would mean . . . well, *could* mean they were . . . of the same mind. No, people didn't have "connections" no matter what Mother claimed. A person did not have a kindred spirit. He wasn't supposed to connect—to have sparks— with her any more than with Arel Dewey.

Yet she couldn't keep from saying, "I had just been thinking the same."

He didn't move as he watched her. "We must be two strips cut from the same cloth."

"Yes," she said, hesitant, lowering her gaze, "I suppose." But she didn't suppose. They couldn't share thoughts. They couldn't believe the same. Couldn't.

He wrapped her hand around the crook of his arm, his gloved hand resting atop hers. "We should return. Aunt Priscilla will have new lists and . . . Mary?"

At the whisper of her name, she looked up. She'd intended to meet his eyes, stopped at his lips.

"I am not sure . . ." he was saying.

"Not sure about what?" She sounded breathy, nervous. "I should—we should . . ."

Somehow, his face was closer. "Who is Prince Ercole?"

Her eyes widened, mortified. How could she have let his name slip? She'd been so careful about what she shared. With Mr. Dane, she hadn't felt the need to stay guarded—a wonderful, awful, foolish feeling.

"Mary!" a feminine voice called out. "Miss Mary Varrs!"

Mary turned around in unison with Mr. Dane.

Arel Dewey rode toward them, waving wildly with one hand, gripping her shaking bicycle with the other, narrowly missing a wagon heading to the auction like most of the street traffic. Something was different about her. With her brown tailored jacket, navy bloomers, and straw hat perched atop her blonde hair, she looked—

"Like me," Mary whispered, and covered her mouth with her hand.

"Yes, I do."

She turned sharply to him. Blinked. "What?"

"I see it now," he rushed out, grabbing the sides of her arms, "how much I like you. When you mentioned Prince Ercole—I know he's a prince and I'm not, and women expect—" He groaned. "This isn't coming out right. Yes, you could say my heart is fickle because I wanted to marry Arel before I arrived in Belle Haven, even up to an hour ago I thought I did. I now see her and whatever I thought I felt isn't there. It is with you. If you feel anything for me—"

"Oh, Maaare-reee!"

Mary jerked her gaze to Arel, who cut off a pushcart, causing the man's crate of strawberries to spill to the ground. He yelled. She didn't even look back. While she gripped the handles with both hands, she had no better control over the wobbly bicycle.

"It's Arel," Arel called in a sing-songy voice, "Arel Dewey."

"Anything for me," Mr. Dane insisted, his breath warm against her ear, "tell me now."

Did she? Mary looked to him, their faces inches apart. Her heart lurched, flipped. What she felt for him was . . . was beyond *anything*. And even more inconsequential. If she didn't obtain the position at the Experiment Station, she had to return to Italy. It was the arrangement she'd agreed to. She did not have the luxury of falling in love, nor of being honest with him about what was in her heart.

"Mr. Dane," she said weakly, "there is nothing between us."

He looked as if he were in pain, or perchance she imagined it because it was what she felt. She needed to leave. She took a step.

His arm slid around her, drawing her close, holding her firm, keeping her from fleeing. "My name is Zenus, and you, Mary, only say this because what you feel frightens—"

"No," she cut in. She pushed him back. "I'm sure I—"

"Mary!" Arel screeched.

"Don't look at her," he said, tight, low, "look at me."

Her eyes met his, her pulse pounding between her ears, her breath catching.

"You feel it, too," he said.

What she felt was the beat of his heart against her palms.

Mary jerked her hands away. "I cannot," she whispered, unable to find the strength for another lie. "The prince paid for it all. Paid for me."

"They don't own you." His voice was rough. "*No one* can own you."

Mary just stared at him in shock. Breathless. Did he not understand how the world worked? Debts always had to be paid.

"Oh, Zenus," she sighed. "Please understand—"

"I do. Finally." His sigh, unlike hers, was desperate. "You need to understand, too."

His free hand cupped her face, thumb tracing her bottom lip before his lips, soft and tentative, touched hers, sealing away her gasp. She heard her name, again, somewhere, in the distance. His eyes closed as he focused on her lips, on the kiss. The contact was electric. The tiny brush of his lips tinged by the strawberries they'd tasted, the barest touch of his tongue, asking, wishing, hoping for a response.

Mary didn't move. Didn't close her eyes. Didn't respond.

Dare she?

Even as Zenus kissed her, achingly gentle, she could feel the tremble of his fingers against her chin, feel the pounding of his heart in his chest. This wasn't his first kiss, either. No eager, unskilled forcing. No awkward, jerky pounding of mouth against mouth. He kissed her with reverence and awe, with restrained passion yearning to be released. With love.

Her fingers tingled with a need to cling to him and to respond.

She breathed deep, the lemon, sandalwood, and petitgrain scent of his cologne reminding her of nights sitting by the hearth with her father and listening to him read a botany journal. Comfort. Home. And disappointment.

Mary forced her arms to stay at her side. Maybe the prince didn't own her, but neither was she free.

He drew back, just enough for her to see his troubled expression.

Her eyes blurred. "I am sorry. I cannot . . ." *love you.*

12

At the same moment

A "Noooo!" pierced the air.

Zenus didn't release Mary as he looked over her shoulder to the owner of the scream.

Arel stopped peddling and, in one fluid motion, lowered her bicycle, dropping it as she stepped to the ground. The bicycle landed with a thud, wheels spinning like his thoughts, his pulse, drawing the attention of the passersby on the street. She ran to them. Raced.

"Zenus Dane, get your lecherous paws off my friend!"

Arel slapped at his arms until he let go of Mary. She shoved him back. Then with the backs of her hands, she wiped the perspiration along her face, down her neck, and then dried her hands on the peplum of her jacket. She released a loud breath.

"Now we have an end to that—" Arel smiled at Mary, all innocence and light. "We missed you at the rally."

"Nice to see you too, Arel," Zenus muttered. He should go. He should leave Mary with Arel and attend to whatever it was he wanted to attend to. He couldn't. Whatever the aftermath of their kiss, he would not desert her to face it alone. He offered a token, "You're looking well."

Her owlish eyes settled on him. "Say no more to me," Arel ordered. "You've caused enough damage today."

Mary's gaze shifted from Arel to him then back to Arel, panicked, paling. As if it finally dawned on her people had seen him kiss her. "I did not intend—"

"I know," Arel cut in. "I know. Zenus can be so"—she patted, dismissively, the air in front of him numerous times—"ugh." Arel then released a loud breath. "Oh, Mary, my dear, dear Mary, the rally was so inspiring. Shall we go to the café and have a glass of lemonade while I tell you all about it? You look parched." She wrapped Mary's arm around hers and tried nudging her into walking.

Mary didn't move. "I could use a drink. Miss Dewey, would—"

"Mare-ree, how many times must I tell you to call me Arel? We're sisters. Two peas in a pod." She smiled and chirped like a bird at sunrise.

Zenus rolled his eyes. He didn't remember Arel being so young and annoying.

Mary's lips pursed for a moment, like they did when she was debating her options and the outcomes for each. Then she said, "Mr. Dane, if you don't mind."

He released a pent-up breath. "Not at all. I'd rather you call me Zenus. Formalities no longer necessary among friends. Arel, Mary, Zenus. Zenus, Mary, Arel. Isn't this how it's supposed to go?" He smiled. A slight—and smug—uplift of the corners of his mouth. Couldn't help it. So, this was what it felt like to say something glib, and with a sardonic edge, at exactly the right moment.

Arel's eyes narrowed. One brow lifted as she looked at him suspiciously. He suspected her thoughts went something along the line of *I'm not sure what you said, but I think I should be suspicious, so I'm going to look like it in hopes you confess.*

Mary's chin lifted. She just looked at him, expression blank, but, oh, he knew her thoughts: *This is not the time for you to be witty.*

She made his smile grow.

"Now we have it settled," he said, "I would be honored to escort you two lovely ladies to the café. For lemonade. Even lunch. My treat."

Mary's lips parted, yet she paused, no words coming forth, as if she wasn't quite sure what to answer or do. She had to go with

Arel—he knew for certain because she'd admitted Aunt Priscilla wanted her to keep Arel away from the quilting bee. And Arel had enough good breeding not to refuse his gentlemanly offer.

He kept his gaze on Mary's face, motioned toward the café. "Ladies, shall we?"

Silence.

The Belle Havenians watching them finally resumed their business.

Arel gave Mary a look of desperation clearly begging, *Tell him no.*

"I suppose," Mary murmured.

"Excellent," said Zenus with great cheer. He motioned again toward the café.

Arel patted Mary's arm. "Don't fret over who we may see, for I shall curb any slight to your reputation due to his thoughtless impunity. Everyone in Belle Haven knows what Zenus is, so they will believe you are innocent."

Mary gave her a confused look. "And what is he?"

"Rake, flirt, philanderer," Arel said without pause. "Dallier with the fairer sex."

Mary glanced over at him with surprise. "Is that what they believe about you?"

He had been a fool to think anything he could've said would have endeared Arel to him. Mary had been right: Arel didn't like him. Defending himself to her wasn't worth the effort.

"You don't believe Arel?"

"Are you asking if I believe you are a rake," Mary said, because the woman he knew her to be preferred a precise question, "or do I believe people believe it about you?"

"Both. Either." He shrugged. Society's views of him weren't his conscience.

Arel looked heavenward and groaned, "Oh, why does it matter?"

Mary stood utterly still, her arms straight to her side.

Zenus said nothing. Her head tilted, her hazel eyes without a hint of unease over him watching her study him. Unlike Arel, she didn't have any creases around her mouth. She needed to smile more. She needed a *reason* to smile more and to laugh and—

Now wasn't this peculiar. He'd never heard her laugh.

He wanted to hear it. And he wanted to hear her laugh with children, their children, in their home, as they sat by the fire reading, and laughing, and loving each other. Until death did them part.

His head was nodding, hand tapping against his thigh. This had promise. This could work. She didn't kiss him back because . . . she felt nothing for him. No, she didn't kiss him back, because she wasn't able to let go of all she'd been taught to be. It made perfect sense. Once he got her to let go of her proper English lady restraint, whatever was holding her back from loving him would break. He would break it. No matter how long it took.

Because he was loyal. And patient. And adjustable.

And she was the one for him.

Ironic —it took a Philadelphia flood for him to find her.

"Well, Mary," he prodded, "what are your results from your study of my character?"

She let out a *hmph*. She touched Arel's shoulder. "The man before me is not a rake," she said to Arel before looking back to him. "Nevertheless, I will not put it past some Belle Havenians to believe the worst about you."

Their eyes met and held. There it was again—the understanding of each other, the connection. She was aware of it, too.

"A compliment?" he asked, grinning.

Her mouth moved into a lop-sided smile. "Yes, but it was begrudgingly given."

Zenus chuckled. He didn't know what Mary had done to him, but their kiss had changed him. He wasn't bound to the past. He didn't just feel it; he knew it in his soul. He would tell her everything. About Clara—about his parents and—

"Stop this, Zenus, stop this right now," Arel demanded, turning Mary to face her. "He is trying to charm you with those eyes he thinks are pretty, and our friendship requires I issue a warning. He kissed Holly Jane. Last summer. Three people told me. When her husband had only been buried"—her voice lowered with disgust—"an hour. And it was not the only time. I also heard someone found them kissing when she was married. Some say Bartholomew isn't his father's son."

Mary looked at Arel. "Is this the basis of your animosity toward him? Gossip and rumors?"

"Yes, but—"

"Bartholomew Ferris isn't mine, but the rest is all true," Zenus admitted, because Mary needed to know about him and Holly Jane. He vowed not to allow a repeat of last summer's kiss, thus his quest to not be alone in the same room with Holly Jane, the initiator for each incidence of impropriety between them. With Holly Jane, a man should never underestimate her determination to get what she wanted. A noble trait . . . if the "what she wanted" for the last eleven years wasn't him. Every refusal he gave her only heightened her resolve.

"I see, yes, I see," Mary drew out, clearly having taken to heart his request she say anything versus allowing awkward silence to linger.

"Regardless, he is still a rake by admission," Arel put in, showing herself to be more of a flibbertigibbet than the perfection he'd cast her to be in his mind.

Mary turned her attention to Arel. "Would a rake or a gallant man accept culpability for kisses initiated by the female?"

"What?" Arel's eyes went even more owlish. "Why do you assume the best of his actions?"

Zenus's lips came together to ask his own why, in hopes, as in vain as they may be, of her confessing she believed the best because she loved him. Before he could speak, Mary curled her hand around Arel's fist and softly said, "I assume the best of his actions because Zenus has yet to show himself false. But mostly because, even though I am guilty at times of judging unfairly, I would want the assumption of the best done for me. And I would hope you would want it done for you, too."

Arel stared at their joined hands, and then, slightly, she nodded.

Mary wrapped Arel's arm around hers. "Off to the café we go," she said, drawing Arel into a pleasant stroll. "We will drink a pitcher of lemonade if need be, and you are going to tell us every little detail of your trip, because I promised Mrs. Osbourne I would keep you from disturbing her quilting bee. And ensure that, I will."

"What will you do about Zenus?" Arel asked as they walked away.

Fitting question. Zenus waited to for her response.

Mary looked at him over her shoulder. "Come along, sir. You did offer our pleasure to be at your expense."

"I have a better story for you." Mary stopped at the path connecting the Linwoods' backyard to Osbourne property, feeling refreshed by lemonade and a morning's leisure in the Bumblebee Café. She looked to Arel, standing beside her bicycle, and to Zenus, curiosity alight in their eyes. Nothing like a hearty conversation about a man's verbal follies to bring together friends. Seeing Zenus laugh at himself rather impressed her. And when he'd humbly and sweetly apologized to Arel over calling her Owl—

Mary gave her head a shake to clear her thoughts. The ache in her chest remained.

"When I lived in Florida," she said with solemn seriousness, "I attended a revival service. You've seen them, the ones with the large white tents."

"I've been to one," Arel said, smiling.

"One came through Philly last month," Zenus added. "I liked how the singing lasted longer than the preaching. It's my kind of worship service."

"Me too." Mary unlatched the gate, moving her boot between the gate and fence to keep it open. "In the spirit of Jonathan Edwards and George Whitfield, the revivalist was preaching"—she raised her arms, circled her hands, deepened her voice —"a great oratory of God's love and care for us, His sheep. I was on the edge of my seat, truly I was, awed at words I'd read in Scripture, but never heard spoken with such passion and authority." She lowered her hands.

"Then the lady next to me giggled. According to the revivalist, Jesus was not a loving shepherd, but a shoving leopard."

Silence.

Then from Arel: "No, he didn't."

From Zenus: A chuckle and an, "Oh no, he did."

Mary smiled, her lips twisting with pleasure over their enjoyment of her story. "Dare I confess I heard not another word of the sermon in quest to restrain my own giggles. So you see, Zenus, even the most gilded tongue blunders upon occasion."

He nodded, still chuckling. "So they do." He drew in a breath and smiled. "We should probably see to the luncheon remains, and you have quilting duties and I still have a lawn to mow. Aunt Priscilla's list and all."

She opened the gate. "Do go on without me. I have something I must attend to first."

His gaze shifted to the Linwoods' back door. "The letter?"

Mary gave what she hoped looked to be an apathetic shrug. "One never knows what important news dear ol' Mum has to share."

He hesitated.

Of course, he had to be wondering if any mentions of Prince Ercole were in the letter. Or how Prince Ercole was connected to her. Or even if the letter was from the prince instead of her mother. How to ask without imposing on her privacy. How to ask when they were nothing more than friends. Friends, though, did not kiss friends. And the beautiful man named Zenus Dane had kissed her. Mary. Because he desired *her*.

Her heart literally jumped in her chest.

"Oh, go on," Arel said with a one-handed shove of Zenus to the gate. "Don't you know a *please leave* when you hear one?"

Uncertainty flashed in his eyes.

Mary offered a small shrug of her lips to imply agreement. Eventually they would have to discuss his kiss. For now, it could wait.

"Leave," Arel urged.

"All right, all right." With his gaze never leaving Mary's face, he passed by. His gloved hand brushing against hers. Not the least bit accidental.

Mary sighed. Doing so was the easiest and least telling response.

Zenus left, but not without a lingering backward glance.

Once he was beyond earshot, Arel said, "He favors you."

"Yes, well . . ."

"I am so sorry," Arel continued, her hands tightening around the handles of her bicycle. "Once Zenus gets something in his mind, he is unwavering. A dog with a bone. If Mrs. Osbourne does a croquet tournament this year during her quilting bee, relinquish any hope of playing with the green ball. Zenus only plays green. The rest of us are limited to luck of the draw."

Mary strolled along the sun-brightened path to the Linwoods' back door while Arel led her bicycle, rattling from the damage caused when she dropped it in the street earlier. It wasn't merely the letter Mary needed to attend to.

"Arel, I must be candid, even if what I say may distress you."

Arel smiled. "Sisters are always honest with one another, because we care enough to desire the best for one other."

"Why do you call me sister? You have two older ones."

"But I had no say in the matter." Her voice took on a familiar sprightliness, where all was right in Arel Dewey's world. "You are *my* choice."

Mary moistened her lips to disguise her smile. The six years difference in their ages seemed inconsequential. She removed her riding hat to give her hands something to do while she mulled how to break the news to Arel. A blunt and direct approach seemed the wisest.

She took a deep breath then blurted, "Mrs. Osbourne wants to match-make you and Zenus, and she asked me to assist."

Arel blinked. Twice. Then a third time. Her mouth opened, closed, and opened again to finally utter: "Why would she want to?"

Because her nephew asked her to. No, she would not heap embarrassment upon Zenus over his former infatuation with Arel.

"Because," Mary answered, "Mrs. Osbourne believes your *joie de vivre*—joy for life—is what Zenus needs, and his reliability and maturity will help ground you."

"She thinks I'm flighty?"

"Are you?"

They walked in silence for several moments.

Arel rested her bicycle against the garden fence. When she looked to Mary, her eyes were hard and hurt. "Maybe I am flighty, but I don't want to marry, because then I will lose the liberties I have. My sisters are burdened with restrictions and responsibilities, and shamed into submission to men who lord their authority, while forgetting their duty to love their wives as Christ loved the Church. I don't want such a life. I want to be like you."

"And how is my life?" Mary asked, strangely amused.

"Forever free."

The laughter burst forth before she could stop it. "You think I am free?"

"Why yes!" Arel waved her hands as she spoke. "You can live where you want. Dress like you want. Use your money on whatever you want. Spend as much time with your friends as you want. Do, think, read what you want without the encumbrance of a husband demanding you serve him food whenever he wants it. How is it not free?"

If life were only so simple.

Mary motioned to her. "Come with me."

13

Arel C. Dewey had a naive understanding of freedom and an even more naive understanding of Mary.

Without looking over her shoulder to see if Arel followed, Mary hurried to the Linwoods' house. She darted inside, tossing her riding hat into the first chair she passed, and evaded Napoleon as she transversed the hallway on her path to the front door. Three pieces of mail delivered through the letter slot lay on the wooden floor. She collected them, depositing the two for the Linwoods on the foyer hutch with their other mail.

Her letter, with the Italian postmark. Thankfully no distinguishable stamps. And in her mother's handwriting . . .

> To Miss Mary Varrs
>
> At Linwood House
>
> Belle Haven, in the Province of
>
> Virginia
>
> United States of America

"Who's the letter from?" Arel asked as Mary broke the seal and unfolded the lettersheet.

"My mother."

Mary scanned the contents. Exactly as she expected.

She handed it to Arel. "Read this."

"Oh I couldn't," said Arel, head shaking. "It's your private mail."

"Read it," Mary ordered.

Arel took the lettersheet and began to read, walking with Mary and Napoleon into the parlor. They sat on the stiff-backed velvet settee, Napoleon at Mary's feet. Back and forth, Arel's eyes scanned the writing.

She gasped in delight. "This is wonderful news! Your mother has found a wealthy benefactor—Monsignor Franco Moretti—who will support your research and provide an allowance for your worldly comforts." Arel rested the letter in her lap, smiling. "I'm so happy for you. Why are you shaking your head?"

"Do you know what a *cortigiana onesta* is?"

"No, but it sounds pretty."

Her innocence was truly astounding.

"Courtesan."

Without making a sound, Arel slowly covered her mouth and stared.

And stared.

And stared.

Mary took the lettersheet from Arel and refolded it. "Sixteen years ago my mother and an Italian prince fell in love. She left her husband and three children to become his *cortigiana onesta*. Mother's benefactor, Prince Ercole, paid for me to attend university, when none of my blood relations would, even against both my parents' wishes. He financed my tomato study. If I don't show a return on his investment in my education—in me—I agreed to return to Italy."

Arel's lips pursed. Several seconds passed before she managed to say, "To become a courtesan?"

The resigned breath escaped her lungs before she could stop it. "If my mother has her way. She believes a woman has more freedom as mistress than wife. Prince Ercole—" Her voice caught.

Two years living as his darling "daughter." Two years hearing him—not her mother—daily tell her she was loved. Two years of feeling like she had a real family before the Marquess of Iddesdowne demanded his only granddaughter be put in the Wellons & Whitacre

149

School for Young Ladies in Brighton because she needed "improving." Because she was tall and ungainly. Because she enjoyed casting a lure as much as a bicycle tour about Paris. Mostly, because she didn't partake in tea parties and socials, embroidering, or anything her grandsire deemed ladylike. The only heated words she'd ever heard between Mother and Prince Ercole were the ones said when Mother had insisted upon sending her back to England.

She's fifteen, Kate. She needs a father, she needs me.

But you are not *her father!*

And after Edward's theft and dissolution of their engagement, who offered her refuge? Who consoled her during her grief? Prince Ercole. The man—with four legitimate sons and an invalid wife— was more a parent to her than her own mother and father. He, not her flesh-and-blood family, was supposed to be the villain in her life.

Little lamb, you are my daughter, in my heart. Why can you not accept I give to you out of love?

Tears welled in her eyes, her throat tightening. Mary blinked repeatedly. Why was it so hard for her to believe he—or anyone— could cherish her?

Napoleon lay down. With a guttural explosion of breath, he rested his head on the toes of her left boot.

Mary withdrew Zenus's handkerchief from the inner pocket of her riding jacket and wiped the tears from her eyes. She sniffed. She looked to Arel, who was teary-eyed, too. "The prince has found several suitors he has deemed worthy for me to marry. Unless I can find employment in my chosen career field, I have to return. My allowance is almost at an end."

"I have money," Arel offered.

"'Neither a borrower or a lender be. For a loan oft loses both itself and friend.'"

Arel's face went blank.

"Shakespeare."

"Oh. I've never read him."

"Even more reason why you need university."

They sat for a good and long minute. Arel with her face all scrunched as she pondered Mary's words. Mary metaphorically putting her overpowering feelings in a box, tying a brick around said box, and dumping it in the ocean. She didn't expect her emotional outbursts of late to stay contained, but she chose to be optimistic. It was, after all, the first necessary ingredient to success.

Mary dabbed at her eyes with the handkerchief. "Prince Ercole insisted the allowance was a gift," she resumed explaining, "but I now feel obligated to please him and do what he and my mother want. I don't feel like I am free to oppose them. Were I to take money from you, I would feel the same. Do you understand?"

Arel nodded. "A little." Her gaze fell to the handkerchief Mary held. "Sometimes I feel like there is more going on than I know."

Mary clasped Arel's hands, drawing her attention. "You are a bright girl with a grand future ahead of you if you choose wisely. I used to believe marriage was a woman's only future until the prince gave me the encouragement and financial means to attend university. Marriage is not slavery, Arel, not when you find someone you love and who loves you back. Go to college first. Expand your horizons."

Arel thought. She shrugged. "I don't know where to go."

"I compiled information on numerous mixed-sex colleges when I was seeking a professorship in America. I can help you find a school."

"Near where you will be?"

"If it is what you would like," Mary said, feeling oddly pleased. "I could tutor you, if need be."

Arel's gaze shifted to the letter, the saffron-colored paper bright against the green of Mary's riding skirt. "I want to help you with your . . ."

"Plight?" Mary supplied.

Arel nodded.

Arel was right, there was more going on she didn't know. Since attending the quilting bee, Mary had shared more about herself than anywhere during her tomato study. From this point on, she was going to be unveiled with Arel, no matter what Arel asked. Friends were that way.

"My grandsire is the Marquess of Iddesdowne."

Arel's eyes widened. "And it makes you?"

"Nothing significant," Mary answered with a sad shake of her head. "He is land-poor, and my grandmother does not have the courtesy to die so he may marry an American heiress. Nor can my mother divorce my father. My father, Lord John Varrs, is currently serving as an adjunct professor at Virginia A&M, where I have opportunity for employment."

"To do what?"

"Be his research assistant."

"But I thought you wanted to be a professor?"

"This will give me a credential."

"Why do you want to work for him when he hasn't shown you any support?"

"It is my only option," Mary says brusquely. "Even at all-girls' colleges, the botany professors are male."

Arel slowly nodded. "So you choose to be subservient to a man, albeit your father, because it is your 'only' option for financial independence?"

"Yes," Mary snapped.

Who was Arel to lecture her? She had two degrees from the University College, London—botany and biology. What did Arel have? An American birth certificate. A flimsy piece of paper giving Arel Dewey more liberty than two sheets certifying a *magna cum laude* education. Good heavens, it was wrong. Life was wrong. And unfair and . . .

Mary thought she might be sick.

This time her eyes didn't blur. "It is not my preference either, Arel, but it is the least pride-sacrificing choice. And it's only for a year. Once I have the experience working in academia and find someone on the faculty to champion me other than my father, professorship opportunities will become available. I have to do something. I cannot return to Italy."

"No," Arel said softly, "I don't want you to have to."

"My hopes rest upon the botanical illustrations Mrs. Osbourne is drawing for me while I quilt during her bee."

Arel said, "So I should leave you alone until the bee ends?"

"Yes—no." Mary paused, nipping at her bottom lip. "Per Mrs. Osbourne's requirements for helping me, she expects me to aid her in matching you and Zenus. I am to ensure you two spend time together, so you may fall in love."

"It will never happen." Arel leaned forward a bit, and her face took on a lofty expression. "Ever."

"Nevertheless, it does not lessen my quandary." Mary neatly folded the handkerchief. She wasn't going to begrudge the obstacles. She merely couldn't see a workable solution. "If I do not comply as she has requested, I risk losing her willingness to give me aid," she explained, twisting the handkerchief again. "And I have no time to find someone to finish the drawings. Neither can I do what she's asked, for you and Zenus are ill-suited."

Arel's hand covered Mary's, stilling her from twisting the kerchief more. "Ill-suited is an understatement."

Arel growled, "This is not good," then walked to the unlit hearth and examined several Linwood family photographs on the mantel. "Tsk tsk." Head shake. She moved to a window, drew the heavy curtains back, sighing. Then: "Hmph." She released the curtains and, with her hands together at her middle back, she leaned against the wall. Her gaze settled on Mary. Intent. Watchful.

Curious.

Mary didn't look away. Yet her chest felt hollow, throat tight. Arel was a bright girl. Zenus saw Mary-fire—the glow in her eyes when she spoke of things about which she was passionate. If he did, wouldn't Arel have noticed a glow when Mary spoke of Zenus? It had to be there. It felt like it was there.

It warmed her cheeks even now.

Mary focused on the handkerchief she'd been strangling. She smoothed it on her lap, the fold of each crease earning a shake of her head. Left. Then over. Once more. Until the initials RZD were on the exact top of the square. Then, with precise care, she laid the handkerchief atop the letter and sat them both on the coffee table.

There had to be a solution to benefit all.

The last time she reached out for help, she was conscripted into joining a quilting bee. In four days her life had gone topsy-turvy. When people offered to help her without her asking, her life turned for the worse, too. She allowed Prince Ercole to convince her to do a

153

tomato study to take her around the world. She allowed Edward to steal her fertilizer study. She allowed her mother to think she was willing to become a courtesan. She allowed her parents, grandsire, even Prince Ercole to send her to the Wellons & Whitacre School for Young Ladies. She even allowed Headmistress Whitacre to belittle her in front of her classmates. If she looked back at her life, every major tragedy befalling her was because she allowed people to manage her.

She was an *allower*.

What had she ever done for herself against everyone's judgment? Nothing. Because she wanted people to like her, to love her. To choose her.

I want to be different, Lord. I want to stop allowing this desire to be liked and loved control my choices. But I'm afraid of what will happen.

"I don't want to be alone," she muttered.

Reaching down, she scratched Napoleon behind his ears then stroked his smooth fur. Not to comfort him, but for her own need to feel connected. Even if only to a dog.

"You're a good boy."

He grunted, sighed, snuggled against her leg.

Mary straightened and looked to Arel, who was now staring as if she'd had a bit of enlightenment too.

"What is it?" she asked.

"Zenus favors you." Said too matter-of-factly to be a surprising bit of news. Arel placed her hands over her heart, speaking with compassion. "Oh, Mary, and I know how uncomfortable it is, having numerous times myself been on the receiving end of emotions not reciprocated." She tugged at the front of her jacket. "But it is not the case with you, is it?"

All sorts of denials teetered on the edge of Mary's tongue.

She sat, shaking her head, saying nothing.

"Oh, Mary, Mary, Mare-ree," Arel sighed dramatically. "This is an inconvenience, to be sure. Zenus? He's so stodgy and mundane."

"Stodgy? He is not—"

"No, no, no," Arel cut in. "I'll hear none of this. Love makes people say, think, and do things they never would were they not afflicted. Once you've had time to recover, you will see I am correct."

"Love is not a contagion."

Arel looked down her nose at Mary. "Really?" She raised one finger. "Shh. I shall support you unreservedly, whatever you choose to do regarding your"—her vexed gaze shifted for a second to the letter—"employment options, for I have chosen you to be my sister. So, I must be candid, even though what I have to say will distress you." Little lines tightened around her lips. "And you will be distressed."

Mary swallowed.

Arel walked forward, each step increasing the pounding in Mary's chest as she reached the coffee table. "If you," she said in a low voice, "do not tell Priscilla Dane Osbourne today—this afternoon—to stop matchmaking her nephew to girls ill-suited for him, then I will have words with her. Words! Dare I say, I will not be as pleasant as you."

"No." Mary jumped to her feet, causing Napoleon to bark. "I cannot risk losing her willingness to draw my illustrations. Napoleon, hush. Shh. My application—my future—depends on them."

Arel just stared.

"No," Mary repeated. "She will suspect I have feelings for her nephew."

"But you do," Arel snipped.

"Well . . . but—but . . . it's not—" she sputtered. Her lips pursed, and she growled. "Why are you doing this? I have no intention of acting upon any feelings."

"Irrelevant!"

Napoleon barked.

"Shh," they said in unison.

Arel leaned forward, patting her chest. "This is about me. Me! I will not have the woman manipulating my life."

"I do not wish to have her do it to me either."

"Then, because I am a generous sort, I shall give you until tomorrow night to talk to her, or I will tell her you warned me of her plan." In the blink of an eye, her anger vanished. Arel squeaked, smiling, shrugging her shoulders. She turned on her heels and strode from the parlor. "Until later."

She was mad. Mad, mad, mad as an English hatter.

Mary sank to the settee, sighing, the only sound in the room. Now what was she to do?

14

Precisely twenty-two hours, eighteen minutes later

Arel Dewey was a flirt who put even Holly Jane Ferris to shame. Peals of laughter ebbed though the opened parlor windows.

With a frustrated puff of breath, Mary jabbed her needle into the quilt top, jerked the thread through with a pop. She wasn't going to wonder about what was going on outside. Wasn't going to give another thought to what Arel and Zenus were talking about as he trimmed the lawn for the croquet tournament his aunt had rescheduled for tonight. If she listened closely—though she not was trying to—she could hear the clickity-click of the push mower and the occasional scrap of the blade against a rock hidden in the grass.

They were probably chatting about the moderate weather, lack of humidity, or the bird's nest in the dogwood nearest Mrs. Osbourne's front door. They had known each other for years. Were friends. Friendly.

Mary pulled her green thread taut then pierced the needle through the plush velvet scrap atop the muslin. With Arel out there, it revealed more of her self-absorptive nature. A man didn't need a woman talking to him while he mowed the yard. Then there was the promise Arel had made to stay away from the quilting bee during the day, as to not be a distraction.

Mary paused on the thought. She *had* asked Arel to stay away, hadn't she? She couldn't remember. With all said yesterday, how could she possibly be expected to remember? And then there was the kiss—

She didn't care a whit what Arel and Zenus were discussing. Because she didn't.

What mattered was fulfilling her obligation to quilt.

As the other quilters made small talk, Mary continued to focus on her stitching. Jab and jerk. Pop. Stab and pull. Pop. Ensure the stitches were even, nicely done, and repeat. All in all, it'd been a productive week: the quilt top a little more than halfway finished, her illustrations coming together quicker than anticipated . . .

What would they have to talk about anyway? They had little in common. Zenus liked to sing. Arel didn't. Zenus read the newspapers, journals, and books. Arel read suffrage pamphlets. Then there was the fact Arel had been quite clear yesterday in her unfavorable feelings toward Zenus, and Zenus had kissed Mary.

Laughter drifted through the opened windows.

Arel's laughter. Zenus's, too.

Mary knotted off her thread, then cut and threaded a new piece. Jab and jerk. Pop. Stab and pull. Pop. And repeat. Why flirt with Zenus? It made no sense. Unless—

She nipped at her bottom lip. Could it be intentional? To make a point. *Until you confront Mrs. Osbourne, I shall flirt with the man you have feelings for, so I can incite jealousy in you.* Yes, she could hear Arel saying it.

Sadly for Arel, her plan wasn't going to work. Mary wasn't jealous in the slightest. True, she should have talked to Mrs. Osbourne yesterday afternoon upon returning to the quilting bee. Or last night during the evening activities. Or this morning during breakfast preparations. Delaying made the doing harder. It made logical sense to put off the "talk" until Mrs. Osbourne had more of the illustrations finished. Then, when Mrs. Osbourne, in her anger and disappointment in Mary, stopped work on the illustrations, then at least Mary would have four of the five completed. She could manage submitting only four drawings.

Oh, to be sure, she did not want talk to Mrs. Osbourne any more than she wanted to talk with Zenus about the kiss and how they had no future together. If she closed her eyes, she could still feel the tingle—

A throat cleared.

Mary looked up.

In her spot near the hearth, Mrs. Osbourne gazed out the opened window instead of drawing. She flicked the pencil between her fingers. A satisfied curve on her lips.

More laughter.

"Of all the—" Holly Jane dug through the basket of scraps in her lap, muttering under her breath. She tossed one atop the quilt. Slapped two more down.

"Holly Jane," Mrs. Scarborough said, "is something bothering you?"

"Why do you ask?" Holly Jane snipped.

The eyes of every quilter centered on Holly Jane. Then they looked to the person next to them, no one saying anything.

Holly Jane grabbed a handful of scraps from her basket then dropped it to the ground. "Mary seems a little tense. Why don't you ask if something is bothering her?" She stood. "It's warm outside, and I'm sure Arel and Zenus could use some lemonade."

As Holly Jane left the parlor, all eyes, confused and curious, looked to Mary, stealing the breath from her lungs.

Desperate for a new topic, she leaned over the quilt to speak to the quilter on the opposite end. "Mrs. Marvin, did you not say earlier this week the new Singer you ordered was to arrive today?"

Mrs. Marvin's smile brightened her face to where she looked like a curly-haired sun. "Oh, Mary, I was wondering if anyone would remember! Yes, on the afternoon train."

Mary said, "How wonderf—"

"It has gold Peacock Tail decals," Mrs. Marvin continued, "and comes in a paneled box for ease of transport." She put down—actually put down—her needle. "Of course, it is attached on a bentwood case, which I've already informed my son he must immediately mount onto my treadle table so I may sew the moment the bee ends. I'm sure he is doing it as we speak. You must all come over tomorrow and see it."

"Deborah," Mrs. Turner said, "did you get one with a double spool attachment?"

And with her question began a slew of incomplete sentences and interruptions, rushing from one question about her new machine to opinions if the Singer 12 was a better model than the Singer 13, opening a floodgate of words leaving Mary looking from one quilter to another in order to catch every detail.

Mary couldn't stop sighing in relief.

These ladies and their joy for sewing were what she needed this gloomy morning. Everything would work out for her good, no matter what happened once she spoke with Mrs. Osbourne, and even with Zenus. She chose to be optimistic.

After all, things couldn't get worse.

—∞—

Zenus stopped laughing the moment Arel's gaze shifted from the push mower she was failing to use correctly around an oak tree . . . to the horse and buggy stopping at Aunt Priscilla's drive. An unfamiliar bouquet-bearing man descended, and the driver whipped the horse into motion.

"Who do you think he is?" asked Arel.

Zenus watched the man carefully. "I thought you might know."

"We need to correct this constant wrong thinking of yours." She tapped the push mower's handles. Her chin rose, eyes narrowed suspiciously. "It's one fancy ensemble he's wearing."

"Uh-huh."

"He looks shifty."

Not much color to the stranger's skin. Whoever he was, he spent most of his time indoors. His black-and-white-vertical-striped suit coat and white trousers unwrinkled. White bowtie aristocratic and unruffled. Bowler centered perfectly atop his head. Even the way his shoes didn't make a sound as he walked across the gravel drive seemed shifty.

Despite his agreement with Arel, Zenus said, "What's the difference between his suit and my brown one?"

Arel reached out and gripped his forearm, yet her gaze stayed fixated on the new arrival. "Trust me," she said with deadly calm, "my instincts about people are never wrong."

Zenus rolled his eyes. Despite his apology for his misspeak, she had yet to admit wrong in her assumption of his rakish behavior. Arel and her anti-love stance had the power to come between him and Mary. Whatever was necessary—even if it meant entertaining Arel's whim to learn how to mow—he would win her support. But it didn't mean he had to trust her.

He took the mower from her and leaned it against the tree. "Let's go see who this mysterious man is."

Like adventurers on a joint mission, they fell into an even stride across the part of the lawn he'd finished trimming. Sprigs of grass clung to the bottom of Zenus's trousers and her white skirt.

"Zenus, I think—" Arel's words died.

"Don't hold back on my account."

Arel sighed loudly. "You need to let me do the talking. All the talking."

Zenus turned his head enough to see her, even though with their height difference and the straw hat she wore, he saw nothing more than the side of her pert little jaw. Mary was right: She needed to experience college. She needed to learn she didn't know everything. She needed to learn discretion.

He said, "Why should I?"

"Because I know how to be subtle in figuring out why he is here."

"I don't?"

This time she growled. "Why must you persist in questioning my reasons?"

"Answer the question."

"Subtlety isn't in your nature," she practically spat.

"Isn't in—"

"Do not take offense," she hastily added. "Some would find it refreshing."

"Mary would," he said and couldn't stop his grin.

Arel's upper lip curled, confirming his suspicion she and Mary had discussed him—and Mary's feelings for him—yesterday before Mary had returned to the quilting bee.

"Don't argue with me, Zenus," she said as they approached the front porch. "I know how to manage men like him." She spoke as if she were nine years older than him, not younger.

"You expect him to not be candid?"

"Shifty men shift."

"Ah, yes, the whole *in their nature* bit."

"Precisely. Trust me to manage him," she ordered, and he still felt no more inclination to trust her.

They said nothing more until they reached Aunt Priscilla's front porch. With Arel on his right, Zenus stood to where they would block the stranger's path up the steps. Not as if he suspected the man of ill intentions. It was just—the man's hair was the fairest shade of blond Zenus could think of ever seeing. From a distance, the man's proud stance had made him seem taller, not the several inches shorter than Zenus that he was. The arrogance in his eyes, the swagger in his walk—

The man did indeed look shifty.

He stopped before them. Tipped his hat to Arel. "Good morning," he said and sounded like he came from somewhere up north. New York? Boston? He also looked to be somewhere near Zenus's age.

"Welcome to Belle Haven," Arel answered, reaching a hand forward to shake his hand, which the man obliged without moving his gaze away from Zenus. If his action bothered Arel, she gave no sign. Her voice remained chipper. "Arel, Arel Dewey." She pointed to Zenus. "And this gentleman is Mr. Zenus Dane of Philadelphia, nephew to the owner of this estate."

"It's a pleasure to meet you." The man firmly shook Zenus's hand, his blue-gray eyes never leaving Zenus's. "Mention of you was made at the train station."

"Of me?" Arel squealed in delight. "Ooh, what was said?"

"Of Dane," the man clarified.

"Of Zenus?"

"Indeed," Zenus said in a matter-of-fact tone. From the puzzlement on the man's face, it was clearly not the answer he was anticipating.

The man looked at Zenus, then at Arel, then back at Zenus. "It was complimentary, of course."

Arel snorted. Proving Zenus's actions this morning had done little to endear him to her. They might be on the same adventure, but they weren't working in tandem.

The man shifted the bouquet from his left hand to his right, his brow furrowing. He cleared his throat. "I was told at the train station I could find Miss Mary Varrs here."

Zenus glanced at Arel, who, for a brief second, had a flicker of panic in her eyes. She didn't know what to do, what to say. For the first time in his presence, she was flummoxed.

He turned back to the man, folding his arms across his chest.

The awkward silence continued until Zenus took pity on the other two and said, "She's quilting. Doesn't want visitors."

The man's blink lasted two unbelievably long seconds. "Mary Varrs is quilting? By choice?"

Zenus nodded, even though the reason she was quilting was out of obligation, not choice. How this man knew Mary well enough to know quilting wasn't her forte made him uneasy.

Arel turned a blinding smile upon the man. Zenus went on alert. She was up to something. Worse, there was no stopping Arel Dewey once she set her mind on something.

She shielded her mouth with a hand and giggled. "What Zenus means to say," she said, twisting a loosened strand of hair near her ear, "is during Mrs. Osbourne's quilting bee, she insists the ladies aren't disturbed. Finishing Lydia Puryear's bride's quilt in time, mind you, is most pressing." She looked at him with sad, sad eyes nothing short of sincere.

But he knew she wasn't. Arel Dewey was, if anything, a manager of men, at least in her perspective.

"Oh," she continued with a pout to her lips, "I do hope this isn't an inconvenience, Mr.—?"

"I see." Again his gaze never left Zenus as he spoke.

Arel looked at him with a curious expression. "Is there a message I could pass along to Mary, Mr.—?"

He didn't supply an answer.

Arel trudged on by batting her lashes and covering her heart with the tips of her fingers. "We—well, she and I—are the closest of friends. Sisters, for all practical purposes."

The man finally broke his gaze away from Zenus and gave his undivided attention to Arel. "Mary considers you a sister?"

She nodded. Her head tilted in a coquettish manner. "You may speak to me as if you were speaking to her."

The man turned his own charming smile upon Arel. "Your kindness is most appreciated, Miss—?"

"Dewey, Arel Dewey. And your name is—?"

He gave her the bouquet. "I would be honored if you would take these inside to Mary along with a request she spare me a few moments of her time. The intimate words I have to say to her, every gentleman knows, should come from his own lips. She is my future."

Zenus gave the man a bored stare, disbelieving the insinuating undercurrent in his words. "Arel, take the flowers inside and tell Mary she has a visitor."

"With a proposal she will want to hear," the man clarified.

Arel didn't move.

Zenus leaned forward and tilted his head enough to get a view of her face. Good heavens, she looked like she might gag. The words love, proposals, and marriage were profanities to her, and his uneasiness grew. He could head off the upcoming verbal explosion, but why? He distrusted the stranger far more than Arel.

Arel's eyes narrowed, every last bit of friendliness in her demeanor gone. She shoved the bouquet into his chest. A few loose petals fluttered to the ground. "Listen here, Mr. Whoever-You-Are, my friend Mary isn't interested at all in what you have to say. She has a future not including you, or any man, and I know this because we discussed it yesterday morning at almost this very hour."

The man shrugged. "It's for Mary to decide." His mouth curved into a smug grin, and he motioned to the porch steps. "Go tell her I'm here."

163

"No," Arel snapped back. "I don't need to bring Mary out here to decide, because I know what her decision would be. She trusts me to do what's best for her. Friends do so. Zenus, tell him."

The man looked unimpressed with her outburst of loyalty.

With the tip of his finger, Zenus eased his cap back. "Are you staying in town?"

"At the hotel."

Arel coughed a breath. "Why does —"

Zenus grabbed her arm, the action enough to warn her to silence. "You should go," he said to the man. "I'll inform Mary—"

"What?" Holly Jane cut in. "No need to be inhospitable."

Zenus caught the man's open-mouthed expression before turning in unison with Arel, his heart skipping a beat out of dread. Holly Jane stood at the top of the steps holding two glasses of lemonade. How long had she been standing there?

She started down the steps, bringing her heady Oriental perfume with her. "Tonight we are having a croquet tournament. You are most welcome to attend." She handed one glass to Arel, the other to Zenus. "Here you go, darling."

Darling? She'd ruined any hope he'd had with Clara. He wouldn't allow her to come between him and Mary. He gave Holly Jane a cold stare. "Thank you for the drink, but you need to return to your quilting. I have this under control."

Her hand rested on his arm, lingering, caressing. "Of course, darling. You know I live to please you." Then she turned to the man. "I'm Mrs. Holly Jane Ferris, a widow," she said shaking his hand. "Zenus and I are . . ." Her words trailed off, letting the man interpret whatever he wished and increasing Zenus's irritation with her. "A pleasure meeting you. Mr.—?"

Again, he didn't supply his name. His gaze flickered south of her face before he met her eyes. "It's a pleasure meeting you."

"Dinner is at six," Holly Jane continued, "with the tournament beginning around seven." She took the bouquet from him. "I'll give these to Mary and inform her of your arrival. But she is quilting, so I cannot promise she will leave the Bee even to speak to a dear friend from her past, which I am correct to assume you are?"

He looked at her admiringly, too admiringly in Zenus's estimation. "You are correct, ma'am."

"You will be waiting for her at the hotel?" she inquired.

He nodded. "All weekend."

Her lips curved. "I will ensure Mary receives the news."

"I owe you a debt of gratitude," he said, not looking away from Holly Jane, not bothered they were the only two talking.

Arel grunted.

Zenus drank his lemonade.

Holly Jane smiled, said, "My pleasure," and headed inside with an even greater sway to her hips than usual.

The man cleared his throat, then looked to where the push mower rested. "Dane, I'll leave you to finish your task."

Zenus acknowledged the man's words with a slight nod.

Arel snarled.

Neither said anything as they watched the man walk away.

"What do you think he wanted?" Arel said once the man was beyond hearing.

Zenus turned to look at her. "I thought you were going to figure it out."

She gave him a slant-eyed glare. "I told you he was shifty. Are you going to tell Mary?"

"You mean warn her?"

She nodded.

He drank the last of the tart lemonade while he collected his thoughts. "Holly Jane will tell her."

Her eyes widened. "You must actually like Holly Jane to believe the best of her motives. When did you become her *darling*?"

In Holly Jane's eyes, eleven years ago.

"Trust me," he said with deadly calm, "my interest in Holly Jane Ferris is nonexistent. Her flirtation with the stranger was intended to make me jealous. You, of all people, should know jealousy is a powerful motivator."

Her face paled.

"If he is of any consequence," Zenus put in, "Mary will seek him out."

"If she doesn't?"

Zenus sat his empty cup on a porch step. "As long as she isn't concerned, we shouldn't be either. Don't worry a problem into existence."

She made no response as he headed back to the push mower. His words were as sour on his tongue as the lemonade. He didn't like the stranger. And his gut told him Mary wasn't the only female the man had his sights on. Coming to Holly Jane's aid—he didn't want to have to do it. But he would, if need be.

Surely she had enough wisdom, like Mary, to avoid shifty men.

15

You disappoint me."

Mary ignored Arel as she nudged the remains of the coconut cream pie around on the china plate. After enduring numerous stolen glances at Zenus all throughout dinner, and each time noticing him immediately turning away when their gazes had met, she wanted—no, needed—a few moments alone with her thoughts.

Arel, in typical Arel-form, which was oblivious to everyone else's wishes but her own, slid into the dining room chair next to her. "We are the only ones in the house in case you were concerned about someone listening in. Except Zenus. He is in the kitchen cleaning."

Mary ignored her.

"Have it your way," Arel murmured. "Looks like I have something to say to Mrs. Osbourne."

Arel moved to stand, and Mary grabbed her arm stopping her. "Wait. Please. Mrs. Osbourne only began the fourth illustration today." She looked about the dimly lit dining room. Indeed, they were alone. Still, she leaned forward, lowering her voice. "She will be livid with me—livid—when she learns I warned you of her matchmaking and, thusly, will fault me for the desolation of a possible courtship between you and Zenus."

Arel gave her a peeved look. "Oh, please, Mary. The courtship would have never occurred even if—"

"Then why demand I confess?" Mary cut in, with an impolite bite in her voice.

Arel's brows rose. "My, my. Someone is testy tonight."

"You are being unreasonable."

"You are being a coward."

"I am no—" Mary cut herself off at the knowing gleam in Arel's brown eyes.

Truth be told, she was a coward when it came to standing up for herself, because she feared losing a relationship. It's why she allowed people to manipulate her life. Including Arel. Oh, for heaven's sake, why had she not realized it until now? Arel's estimation of being a friend meant pushing Mary into a corner under the guise of "doing it for Mary's own good." Because Arel "cared enough" to not let her stay a coward, an allower. There was no benefit in telling Mrs. Osbourne she has warned Arel, except Arel getting what she wanted. Arel would never be happy unless she got what she wanted. Not this time.

Instead of doing something because other people thought it would be for her good, from now on, Mary was going to make the decision for herself. It felt so liberating just thinking it.

"Where is Mrs. Osbourne now?" she asked.

Arel had the decency to school her smug grin. "Outside, organizing players for the croquet tournament. Shall I sign us up?"

"Yes." Then, as an afterthought, Mary added, "I want the orange ball."

"When did a particular color matter to you?"

"It doesn't. If I do not choose one," she said, "you will choose for me." As long as she allowed people to make decisions for her, she would never be free.

Arel looked at her strangely. "What has come over you?"

Mary stood, smiling in delight over this new empowerment she felt. "Me. I've come over me." She picked up her plate, as Arel stood, and pointed it to the kitchen. "I am going in there to have a word with Zenus so he understands exactly where we are—aren't." She winced then continued with: "You will go out front and wait for me to join you for the tournament."

"Are you going to confess to Mrs. Osbourne?"

Mary didn't hide her smug grin like Arel had. "Not unless she asks me about it. You hate her manipulating your life, yet you, my friend, are doing the same to me. I shan't stand for it, Arel. Never again. Not from you, not from anyone."

"But—but—I—"

Mary cradled Arel's cheek. "You can be vexed all you like, but your disappointment in me will not change how I feel about you. No matter what happens, it will all work out." She hoped. She waited as Arel collected her thoughts.

Arel finally said, "Orange?"

"Yes. It is my favorite color." Mary turned on her heels and headed to the side door, leaving in the opposite direction from Arel.

Zenus was at the sink drying a crystal bowl when she walked through the propped-open door to the kitchen.

She stopped in the middle of the room, beside the table holding the clean dishes, a good four feet from him. Beyond the length of his arms. Where she still felt safe.

No, no, it wasn't right. Or fair.

She didn't trust *herself* to be any closer, because what she felt for him didn't feel safe. It felt too much. Electric. More than she could bear. Or at least she felt this way when she was near him. When he wasn't around, the whirlwind of emotions seemed imagined, until she thought about him. Thus, she'd try not to think about him. It— this beginning of love she had for him—had to stay in the tightly bound box where she'd placed it. Until she secured a professorship, and thereby fulfilling what Prince Ercole asked of her, she did not have time for love and marriage.

Mary waited for Zenus to acknowledge her presence, to speak.

He didn't.

Since he wasn't aware of her, she gave into the inclination to admire his posture, to memorize the way his finely tailored coat stretched across his broad shoulders, a slight movement of his shoulder blade as he dried the bowl. He did more at his mill than sit behind a desk and lift a pencil and an accounting book. Yet with all his strength, he took delicate care with his aunt's china and crystal.

Something caught in her throat. Last night they had worked together while Mrs. Osbourne entertained her fellow quilters outside amid the dancing. They had worked side-by-side washing and drying and not saying anything. But she'd wanted to. She'd wanted to say she had felt the same as he had there beside the horses. She wanted to beg him not to return to Philadelphia. She wanted to lay her head on his shoulder, in the crook of his neck, and rest as he held her close and told her it was all right to feel happy.

She wanted too much. With him. Forever.

He had no reason to stay in Belle Haven over the weekend. If she wanted to speak to him, wisdom said now was her chance, albeit in a well-lit kitchen with the windows and door to outside open. Where anyone could walk in.

She touched the spot on her chest, right above her heart, where she ached. For him. For her. For what couldn't be. At least couldn't be yet. If he truly cared about her, he would give her time. Maybe a year. Or two. And then if they still felt the same, they could begin to court and—

His arm stopped moving, towel lowering. Yet his gaze stayed on the window over the washbasin. "Should I keep pretending I don't know you're here?" he softly asked.

"I didn't realize you heard me."

"I can feel your presence whenever you are near. It's rather disconcerting."

"Oh. Would you rather I leave?"

"No," he said, without looking at her. "Are you sure you want to stay? You've been avoiding me since the auction."

"I—" She hesitated.

Why do this? Why not walk away and leave things unsaid? It would be easier for both—well, for her at least. Taking control over her life and her decisions included this moment. Included saying what she—no, what they both needed her to say.

She rested the plate on the kitchen table then, with more confidence, said, "I need to speak to you."

He sat the crystal bowl on the counter, leaving the towel inside, turned to face her. "I'm all ears." He leaned back against the sink.

"I want a professorship," she said quickly before she lost her gumption, "in America, at a mixed-sex college like University College London from where I received my degrees."

He nodded. "Do you have a particular college in mind?"

"One which doesn't segregate genders in separate buildings. Oberlin, Hillsdale, Franklin, Otterbein, although it would not have to be a private or religious-affiliated institution." She stood breathlessly still and watched him. "Waynesburg, Westminster, and Saint Joseph's are three I lean toward in Pennsylvania."

He grinned, and her stomach did its little flip. She should not be here, in this kitchen, with him. Alone.

"Have you considered the University of Pennsylvania?" he said, his voice husky. "It is within walking distance from my mill."

"They are beyond my reach."

"They hired a woman three years ago."

"Yes, I know about her. She was a teaching fellow, and she had a doctorate."

"Then get a doctorate."

"I am female," she said, and it truly was enough of a response. However the practical reasons prompted her to add, "I have no means to attend the University of Zurich. No university in America offers a doctorate program for women." She could ask Prince Ercole for an additional allowance, but why put herself in further debt to him?

Before she had a chance to second-guess her actions, Mary closed the distance between them. "This job as a research assistant at the Experiment Station will give me a credential in academia. I must work there a year before I can pursue becoming a teaching fellow or, more preferably, a professorship." She paused. "Before I have time in my life for more than my career."

His eyes clouded with confusion. "What are you saying?"

He was not making this easy on her. But why should he? After he had been so honest with her after leaving the strawberry auction, and after she rejected him, he shouldn't make this easy on her.

Mary moistened her lips and started over. "What I feel for you— it shakes my soul." She shook her head, not quite looking at him.

"It frightens me," she whispered. She drew in a steadying breath. "It entices me, but I cannot pursue my feelings until I have honored the agreement I made with Prince Ercole. A return on his investment in me in the form of a teaching position at a mixed-sex college or university. He wants me to achieve my dream to become a professor."

"Are you in love with him?" His tone was rough.

She shook her head. "He is my mother's benefactor, and the only man who been a true father to me. I do love him, though not as I love—" Her voice choked.

Not from embarrassment. Not from shame in being open. Nor in fear.

Her voice had choked because of the overwhelming pounding in her chest, the swelling in her heart. She felt light, happy, radiant. And free.

She smiled.

He smiled back and chuckled. "I'm still not sure what you are telling me—"

"Oh, good heavens." Mary laughed, and then space between them melted away, by her choice. Hers.

She wove her fingers through his dark hair and kissed him with passion, with everything in her neatly tied box that wasn't so neatly tied anymore. His arms wrapped around her, holding her close. His lips tasted of coconut and vanilla, of sweetness and hope. She needed him in her life, supporting her, wanting, loving, and desiring the best for her and for them both. Together. No more wasted years. No more being alone.

He pulled back, enough for their gazes to meet, for her to see the questioning in his eyes, to feel the ragged rasp of his breath on her skin, the tingle of her swollen lips. Did she want this?

Mary nodded.

"I love you," he said quietly.

The words stole what little breath remained in her lungs. So she nodded again, unable to do anything else.

"Mary," he said it as a caress. "I will make this—us—work." And his lips found hers again, this time less urgent, less burning. Soft. Achingly gentle and reverent.

I love you. She wanted to scream it from the top of her lungs. How could she love him? How could she know for sure? She had known Edward for five months before he'd proposed, before he'd shocked her senseless with her first kiss. The kiss, looking back, seemed so chaste. The kiss had felt nothing like the touch of Zenus's lips against hers. She'd thought herself in love. Five months was a bit more time to know one's heart than five days, even though she knew more about Zenus than she'd ever known about Edward.

She stood on her tiptoes, grabbed the back of his head, and deepened the kiss in desperation, breathing in the scent of his cologne. No matter what came tomorrow, this man—his kiss—was what she wanted emblazoned in her memory. Not Edward. She wanted him as gone from her mind as he was from her life.

Zenus broke the kiss, and a tiny rasp of air rushed over her lips.

"I think," he said, breathing hard, with a quaver to his voice, "we should go play croquet."

Mary smoothed the back of his hair as she willed her hands to stop trembling. "Yes, it would be wise." She took a step back.

But he stopped her, gripped her shoulders, and looked serious despite his smile. "Apply for the research assistant position, and we'll figure out what to do about us after you get the job." He kissed her forehead. "This will work out. Optimism is—"

"—the first key to success," she said in unison with him.

He winked and threaded his fingers between hers. "Don't begrudge the obstacles either."

Filled with hope she never expected to have about the future, Mary walked with Zenus through the house and out onto the front porch. They had a good two hours before darkness descended. They stopped at the first step. In the middle of the sheared lawn milled the quilters and their spouses, Arel was face to face with Mrs. Osbourne and in a low, heated discussion bringing color to both their faces, and off to the side was Holly Jane Ferris and—

Mary froze, as a wave of nausea hit, literally chilling her at the sight. Her skin lost every last bit of warmth it had from kissing Zenus.

Oh, dear God, be merciful, let it not be him.

Time slowed, or at least it felt like it did.

Her heart pounded in her chest. It couldn't be him. Couldn't. But she knew it was. Even though she could only see the side of his face, he tried to cover his too-small ears by wearing his flaxen hair looking like it perpetually needed a cut. Overly familiar flirtatious—oh, call it what it was: seductive—gaze, this time being cast upon Holly Jane, who had no idea what type of man was toying with her. No man wore a black-and-white-vertical-striped suit coat with the same cocky arrogance as he did.

Liar. Thief. Betrayer.

What was he doing here? In Belle Haven? In Virginia? In America?

A shiver crept up her back like the flame burning the fuse toward the stick of dynamite. She tensed, clenching the hand Zenus didn't hold, in an effort to restrain the simmering anger. She wasn't supposed to see him again. She wasn't. She'd vowed to kill him if she ever did. She wouldn't actually, but merely screaming the words had provided solace in the moment.

Breathe. Think. Don't panic.

Yet her mind whirled, view blurred. Zurich. A doctorate he'd said he needed to pursue before he could marry. Why wasn't he in Switzerland? He should be in Switzerland. He should be anywhere. Not here. Not in Belle Haven. Not in her life again.

She had to get out. She had to leave. Go. Gogogogogogogo. GO.

She gasped. Her study! All of it was there laid out on the Linwoods' dining table for anyone to see. To take. To steal.

And the house wasn't locked . . .

Belle Haven was safe. No one had needed to lock doors and worry about safety.

With Edward around, one had to.

As if he could hear her thoughts, Edward Argent turned from Holly and, smiling, pointed her way. "Hey, beautiful, you are just the person I came to see."

16

Mary jerked from Zenus's hold, swirling around, reaching for the front door handle. Edward was the last person she wanted to see.

Zenus's hand slapped the door first. "Don't run."

"You do not understand," she seethed. He couldn't. Couldn't know what it was like to love someone and have your love rejected at the same time as having something so precious—something he could never get back—taken from him. Like Edward had done when he stole her study from her.

"I do," he said in a low voice, resting his forehead against the side of her head. "My parents died when I was seventeen. I've been running from their loss ever since. When I finally found a girl who I thought would love me back, I gave her everything, and it wasn't enough for her to marry me. She eloped with my cousin, yet I've spent the last eight years trying to prove my faithfulness to her."

His voice grew hollow. "She's dead. My parents are dead. But I'm alive, for a reason." He turned her to face him. "You're alive, too. No more running from what hurt us. Whoever he is, you will meet his gaze and smile."

Her lips parted, releasing a ragged breath.

She blinked rapidly to rid her eyes of the tears. "Do not leave me alone with him."

"I won't let him hurt you."

"My safety should not be your concern," Mary said with a lethal edge she regretted instantly. "My apologies. I am not angry with you." She placed her fingers over his lips to keep him from saying more. Then she dropped her hand, closed her eyes, and released a slow, agonizing breath.

Oh, God, I am so full of hate right now. I cannot think straight. This is not who I want to be.

"It is not who I am going to be," she murmured.

Mary turned, and with Zenus doing the same, and faced the twenty-two people all staring back at them. Look them in the eyes and smile. So she did. Their gazes were all curious, except Mrs. Osbourne's. She seemed hurt. Later, they could talk. Reason with one another. Right now, she would manage Edward.

Mary lifted the front of her skirt and descended the porch steps. "Edward Argent, I allot you fifteen minutes to speak your piece." She looked over her shoulder to Zenus who stood like a shadow beside her. "Time him."

He pulled out his pocket watch as Edward hurried over to Mary with Holly Jane and a trail of his musk cologne following.

"I came to offer you a job," Edward said as he stopped next before her.

Mary kept her attention on him. "I have no interest."

"You will have." He withdrew an envelope from his coat and, without another word, handed it to her.

Mary took it, turning it over, frowning at the waxed seal. Her father's seal. She looked to Edward. "Why do you have this?"

The man had the decency not to smile. "I needed to find you, so I went to Blacksburg in hopes your father would know where you were. He did. He said you were planning on applying to be his research assistant. I told him I had something better." He nodded to the letter. "It's divine timing, you know. Me arriving in Blacksburg only hours before Lord John got the news. He'd planned on tele-gramming you, but I offered to deliver a message."

For the second time today, her blood chilled. "What news?"

His gaze fell to the letter.

Mary swallowed, then shifted her jaw to pop the sudden pressure in her ears dampening all sound. No difference. She still felt as if she were encapsulated in a glass jar.

Hand trembling, she ripped apart the envelope, withdrew the notecard, let the envelope pieces fall to the ground. A *ching* rang in her ears. True, the sound was only imagined. She was standing on a lawn, not in a glass jar. But, there in her father's block lettering . . .

Mary—

Assistant hired. Sorry.

Lord John

Mary folded the notecard in half, closing off the words. Heart heavy. Mind unable to form a response. Everything—everything— she had worked for . . . gone in two words. *Assistant hired.* Not the most compassion-laden correspondence she had ever received. But at least Lord John had sent it. If her father had cared less for her, he wouldn't have stopped her from submitting her application and losing all the work she had done on her study. Her heart tightened. No tears came. After the last week, she had no more tears to shed. Seventeen days—was all she had to endure in Belle Haven before the Linwoods returned, before she had to return to Italy.

Whispered voices caused her look about the lawn. Everyone looked concerned. For her. And they did because they were her friends.

They accepted her for who she was. They cared.

She tried to smile, but the muscles in her face refused to cooperate. "It saddens me to share the research assistant position, for which I was to apply, has been filled."

Several of the quilters gasped.

Zenus's hand tightened around his watch.

Arel stood stone-faced. Only she knew of the true—and dire— significance of Mary's announcement.

Mary looked back at Edward. "I appreciate you delivering this despite the lateness of the hour."

"I arrived this morning." His confused gaze shifted to Zenus then to Holly Jane. "Neither of you told her?"

Holly Jane lowered her head. In shame? In remorse? In honest compassion over Mary's loss? "I should—I, uhh . . . Excuse me," she mumbled and, with a choked cry, hurried around Edward and past Zenus, dashing into the house.

"Zenus?" Mary prodded.

He shrugged. "I presumed Holly Jane would."

"Don't you find it strange he would presume the best of her motives?" Arel said, running over to them. She stopped next to Mary, grabbed the sides of her arms, fingers pressing into Mary's flesh. "Zenus knows jealousy is a powerful motivator. He's been flirting with you because he and Holly Jane are . . ."

Mary freed herself from Arel's grip. "Are what?"

"Oh, Mary, I'm so sorry." Arel's eyes teared. "I told you he was a rake. She called him darling, and he looked at her all tenderly. He didn't like Holly Jane flirting with Mr. Argent. Said it made him jealous."

Zenus stepped forward. "It is not what I said."

"Ha!" barked Arel. "I heard—"

"Stop," Mary ordered. "Both of you, I do not want to hear another word. I have a more pressing problem." She looked to Edward, trying to find something in his eyes to justify the emotions and tears she had wasted on him.

"I'm sorry." He'd said it with a sincerity she, surprisingly, found believable.

"For what are you sorry?"

He gave her an apologetic look. "Lord John' said the director refused to hire a woman no matter her credentials. It's wrong. What's worse is your father didn't want to hire you either."

And the bias against female accomplishment continued. Would there ever be a day when a woman's feminine virtues weren't emphasized over her ingenuity and intellect?

She offered a sad smile. "Oh, the encumbrance of my gender."

"It isn't with me." Edward stooped to reclaim the envelope remains. He then took from her the folded notecard from her father. "You deserve better than research assistant."

Did she? Yes, but admitting it felt arrogant, prideful, wrong, even though she had the education, skills, and botanical insight to qualify her for more than a lowly research assistant position.

"Your fertilizer study," Edward continued to say, "I knew what groundbreaking research it was, and how academia would not give it honest consideration because you are a woman."

"And it justified stealing it?" Mary snipped, yet not from anger. From exhausted acceptance. Edward would always be Edward. His happiness, like Arel's, was paramount.

"No." He hesitated. Rubbed the back of his neck. "Something good can come from my selfishness. For *both* of us."

Irritated noises came from Zenus and Arel. Then his mouth opened. Arel's did, too.

Mary gave them both a look to remind them to stay silent. She then waited for Edward to elaborate.

"After I earned my doctorate—earned on my own merit—" he said proudly, "I took a job at a research institute in Paris."

"Doing?"

He gave a little shrug she found impossible to read. "Mostly I secure funding for the institute."

Mary nodded. It made sense. Despite all his shortcomings, no one could charm investors and patrons like Edward Argent.

"They've authorized me," he boasted with a renewed twinkle in his eyes, "to hire a director for the new botany department. You, Mary, I want you. Imagine your own lab, greenhouse, and a staff of assistants. Male *and* female."

She studied him for a moment. Working beside him again, even with their relationship being platonic—no job was worth it.

As if he'd read her thoughts, he said, "The most you will see me is at a once-a-month meeting."

Mary pressed her lips together.

"I blundered with you," he admitted. "Forgive me."

She took a moment to stare at him, to assess the sincerity of his repentance. With a man who could charm like he could, one could never know.

"You broke my heart," she said, because she had no reason not to admit it. "You are untrustworthy, dishonorable, and a thief. And a liar. Betrayer. Coward. Deceiver. Irresponsible and reckless. A philanderer."

"Absolutely. All of it, and more."

His acknowledgement halted her retort.

He held his hands out, chuckling. "Ah, Mary, a scoundrel like me deserves all the rebuke you want to toss my way. I also know you are too nice to hate me forever. I had to end our engagement. You are too good and noble and gracious and smart of a woman for me. You deserve better. Besides, you are too impatient to learn to cook. And you are intimidating."

She wanted to slap the outlandish grin off his face. "You said I was decidedly dull," she said, weakly hurling her last accusation at him.

"It's what makes you a fabulous scientist."

She started to say something, but he broke in with: "I need you on my team. Mary, look at me. Right here." He pointed to his eyes—blue-gray, flinty, serious. His voice grew stern, something so unlike him. "I need you to manage the botany research lab. I need your mind, your brilliance. I need you."

Mary nipped at her bottom lip. Should she do it? Her own research lab. Assistants. Paris. The prince and her mother would certainly visit. She could live in their townhouse on the *Place des Vosges*. While it wasn't a professorship, Prince Ercole would find it a suitable achievement. And in a few years, perhaps she could become a guest lecturer at a college. Maybe even a teaching fellow or adjunct professor like her father. Other than an occasional meeting with Edward, she would rarely see him. Her life would still be her own.

How ironic her fertilizer study put Edward in a position where he actually could help her move one step closer to her dream. Even better, in Edward's perspective at least, she would make him look brilliant. In a twisted way, she ought to be thankful Edward Argent was a selfish chap.

What he was offering was the perfect job. Minus Edward.

And minus Zenus.

He would never move to Paris. He would never leave his life here in America. He would never adjust his routine. This decision, whatever she made, had to be what was best for her. In the long term.

Unlike Mum, Mary would not be a fool and give up everything for love.

"Don't do this," Zenus warned, his heart racing in his chest.

Each tick of his watch pounded against his palm. No matter how hard he squeezed, it continued to tick. Time was literally in his hand, and he had no control over it.

Mary's lips pursed like they did when she was thinking, weighing her options, studying a subject. And he could see the choice she was making. Could see he was losing her, just like he had lost Clara when she chose Sean over him. He wanted to reach for her. Grab. Cling. But his hands were shaking, and he couldn't move. So this was what it felt like to be frozen with fear.

"Don't," he begged. "You'd be a fool to work for a man who stole from you, taking credit for what was your work. He did it once. He will do it again."

She let out an irritated snort. "You think I am a dunderhead?"

"Yes, when you trusted him the first time, but you don't have to be one again." No, it's not what he meant. Zenus bit his lip to halt further words from passing forth. She wasn't an idiot. He was. Correct it. Fix it.

He opened his mouth, but Arel spoke first. "You think you know what's best for her, but you don't." She looked to Mary. Her gaze softened "Take the job Mr. Argent is offering. You don't want to return to Italy. You don't have another option." Then she smiled, chirped. "And I could go with you. Attend college in Paris. What an adventure we will have, just the two of us!"

Argent nodded. "You've always wanted a sister. And Miss—?"

"Arel, Arel Dewey," Arel supplied, still grinning.

"Yes," Argent cajoled. "Miss Dewey is perfectly suited to you, and—"

"Don't leave." Zenus cut in, even though in his peripheral view he could see his aunt shaking her head. "I love you, and I think I want to marry you."

Mary's head tilted as she gaped at him. "You think?"

"No. NO." He frantically shook his head. It wasn't what he meant either. Fix it! "I know I want to marry you. Know. Don't choose him. Choose me."

Her gaze faltered.

"Mary," Arel practically whispered, "you don't want what's in Italy. And it isn't as if you are committing to the job forever."

"What's in Italy?" Zenus demanded. What hadn't she told him?

Argent fanned his arm out toward the spectators on the lawn. "See them, Mary. I'd wager they all want you to choose what is best for you."

His gaze returned to Mary, pausing on Zenus long enough for him to catch a shadow of something. Sadness? Regret? The ridiculous grin of Argent's reappeared.

And Argent said, "Love isn't a once-in-a-lifetime event."

"But when you find it," Zenus countered, "you don't let it go."

Mary glanced at him out of the side of her eyes, her expression blank. Not apologetic. Not unsure. Just blank.

"Zenus," she said with little emotion in her voice, "you wish to know what is in Italy?"

"Yes."

"Mary, don't," Arel warned. "They don't need to know."

Mary's lips pursed, tightened, as one did when trying to restrain emotions. "My future is there," she explained, "if I cannot secure employment using my education. My mother's benefactor paid for me to attend university, gave me an allowance for the term of my tomato study. If I cannot find employment, I must return to Italy and either marry a man I do not love or become a courtesan."

"We could marry," he offered again. "Love is enough."

Mary shook her head. "No, it is not. Mum threw away her family for love. I will not become her."

She then looked to Argent. "I shall take the job."

Argent offered her his arm. "Let's have tea and discuss the specifics."

She nodded, yet didn't take his arm. "Arel, please join us."

Without a glance back in Zenus's direction, Mary walked with Argent to the Linwood House. Arel was halfway across the lawn when she looked over her shoulder. Her gaze met his, and slowly, oh so slowly, a grin dawned.

Once again, Arel Dewey had gotten what she wanted: another failed courtship of his. Lydia Puryear, ruined because Arel warned her away. Mary, rejecting his proposal because Arel convinced her that trusting a thief was wiser than marrying a man who loved her. He despised Arel. Almost as much as he loved Mary. She loved him. He knew it, felt it. Why didn't she love him enough? Why wasn't she willing to fight for love?

His pocket watch slid from his palm and landed on the ground with a thud.

"Zenus," Aunt Priscilla called out.

"Not now."

And he walked away.

17

As evening descended on the seventh day of the quilting bee

Tuesday finished. Only three days left before the quilting bee ended. As it had since Saturday morning, rain pattered against the parlor windows, beading, sliding, while music by the esteemed Lovell Brothers filtered down the hallway from the library. Laughter. Joy.

Mary stood at the quilt frame running her fingers along Holly Jane's finished stitches, across what had seemed to be haphazard fabric choices, lingering on the basted scraps. Even under the unflattering orange glow of the lamplight, Holly Jane's quilted section resembled the stained glass windows in the cathedral where Mary had first heard God loved her and desired to give her a new life.

She looked over her shoulder to the empty foyer. The other quilters and their spouses—save for Holly Jane—were enjoying the evening fellowship inside. Billiards. Whist. Pinnacle. Who knew a Virginia reel could be performed in the hallway?

She should rejoin them.

Mary turned back to Holly Jane's basted section of the quilt. Tomorrow, if Holly Jane again didn't show for the bee, her unfinished scraps were to be removed and another quilter had her choice of what fabrics to layer in. Everyone knew she wouldn't show. Since Saturday she'd refused all visitors. Refused to see anyone. Refused to talk. Refused even to listen to Mary's apologies and overtures of friendship. Doing so would only hurt herself the most.

"I should know," Mary murmured.

Her gaze fell to Holly Jane's basket of fabric, embroidery thread, and scissors. She looked back to the quilt top. Threaded needle attached to the last scrap Holly Jane had sewed. Should she?

Another peal of laughter rippled throughout the house like a stone skipping across a lake.

Holly Jane had chosen those particular fabrics and sizes for a purpose. Who were they to change them?

Filled with purpose, Mary slid onto Holly Jane's seat and claimed the needle. Silks, velvets, ribbons, and printed and embroidered fabrics—all combined into a collage of beauty. Beauty? Mary chuckled under her breath. Until now she hadn't been sure if she loved or hated this crazy Bride's Quilt. Order, she liked order and being able to predict results. Nothing about this quilt was predictable. But, if one studied the evidence, facts, details before her . . .

Based on where Holly Jane used feather stitches, French knots on a stalk, and diamond herringbone stitches, she could make logical presumptions on what Holly Jane would have done on this set of basted scraps. And so she stitched.

And stitched.

Then, on a whim, she exchanged the white thread for a green one and began a buttonhole stitch in between the lazy daisy and fly stitch.

"You've created a flower bed," said Mrs. Osbourne sliding onto the seat Mary usually occupied during the bee. "Very clever."

Mary kept embroidering as she said, "Thank you."

Mrs. Osbourne found a threaded needle and began stitching one of Mary's basted scraps. "You could have left Sunday with Arel to the suffrage rally in Annapolis. Why didn't you?"

"You and I had an agreement. I quilt. You draw."

"The illustrations are inconsequential now."

Mary tugged the thread through until she heard the crisp pop. "Yet you continue to draw." She paused embroidering and watched Mrs. Osbourne who started a pinking stitch. "I am sorry for disappointing you and for causing your nephew to leave."

"You didn't make Zenus leave. I did."

"Pardon?"

Mrs. Osbourne sighed yet continued to stitch. "I finished his quilt design in two days. I pretended to work on it to keep him here so I could match him with Arel. After Friday night's—"

"Debacle," offered Mary.

Mrs. Osbourne's mouth twitched. She pulled her thread through with a firm tug, causing the quilt top to bounce. "I realized then my match would never occur even if you had not warned Arel of my plans. Zenus intended on staying in Belle Haven in case you needed assistance with Mr. Argent, but I knew you were able to manage the man on your own. And Zenus needs to not cling. He is quite resistant to change."

Mary nodded, because it seemed a fitting response. But she didn't know why Mrs. Osbourne wanted to change her nephew. He was fine and good and noble as he was.

"Sometimes a man can be too loyal."

She wasn't too sure about it. If Lord John had showed a degree of loyalty to his marriage, maybe Mum's heart wouldn't have been searching for love.

"Mary?"

She looked to Mrs. Osbourne, who was watching her with such sadness in her eyes, and she put down her needle. "Yes?"

Mrs. Osbourne knotted off her thread and cut the needle free. Her bejeweled hand covered the last basted scrap. "I used to make the most orderly of quilts, simple and expected, and I never won any ribbons at the fair." She paused, shifted her jaw, moistened her lips. When she spoke again, her voice quavered. "Then my son, Harry, died in the Ashtabula Bridge Disaster, along with Zenus's parents. Harry was nine. The trip to Ohio was in celebration of Zenus's seventeenth birthday. Sixty-three passengers and Zenus survived."

Mary reached over and covered Mrs. Osbourne's hands with her own. "I am so sorry."

"So am I."

To think what Zenus endured. It was no wonder he clung to what he treasured.

Mrs. Osbourne drew in a deep breath, then let it out, blinking her eyes repeatedly. "Harold was president of his engineering firm there in Baltimore and was just elected onto the Board of Trustees at Johns Hopkins. Quilting was how I grieved. Harry's quilt was a chaotic arrangement of colors and shapes, unlike anything I had sewn before, and something I vowed never to share with anyone."

Her gaze fell to where their hands were clasped together.

"One of my quilting friends stole it."

"What?" literally exploded from Mary's mouth.

"She entered it in the Virginia State Fair and won blue."

Mary relaxed against the back of the chair, folding her arms about her waist, stunned. "With your quilt?"

Mrs. Osbourne nodded. "I had nothing to prove it was mine. I'd never even shown it to my husband."

Oh. She had a point there. After Edward stole her study, she had no means to prove the work was hers, other than being able to describe the study in minute and precise detail.

"Of course, now, I always stitch my name into the quilt."

Mrs. Osbourne picked up her needle, and Mary picked up hers. They both resumed sewing at a leisurely pace, lost in their own thoughts amid the rain, music, and voices from the rest of the house. Smells of fresh baked pies permeated the room.

Mary breathed deep. Peach and apple. "I am glad Mrs. Binkley is feeling better."

"As am I." Her lips curved a bit. "Meals are prepared and served more efficiently. She is not as distracted by your presence as Zenus was."

Mary's cheeks warmed.

"From then on," Mrs. Osbourne went on, "I never made a simple quilt again, and I've won numerous ribbons at local, state, and national fairs."

Mary began adding the three-prong rooster-haired tip to the corner of the diamond herringbone stitch. "What about your friend?"

"She lives on a farm north of Baltimore. We haven't spoken since the day she won blue." Then in a distant tone, as if her thoughts

187

were somewhere else, she said, "Perhaps I shall pay her a visit. No one should be held captive by past mistakes."

"It would be good."

Rain pattered against the window.

The Lovell Brothers changed tunes, beginning with a fiddle solo.

Mrs. Osbourne stared absently at the quilt, the muscles in her face moving as she pondered something. Then her eyes widened. Needle hovered over the fabric scrap. She tapped the cotton with the needle's tip. Once. Twice. The action was so peculiar Mary couldn't help but stare. Mrs. Osbourne looked up with a frown and a serious vertical line between her brows. She kept staring at Mary freakishly. There was no other word to describe her expression.

"What is wrong?" asked Mary, tensing.

"I don't know why I never thought of this before now."

"Thought of what?"

She blurted, "If you had the opportunity to earn a doctorate, would you try for it?"

"Certainly," answered Mary, "as of this year, no American university allows women in their doctorate programs."

"Johns Hopkins does. In a way."

Mary sputtered with laughter at the absurdity of the claim. "No," she said, wagging her head and trying not to laugh again, and not succeeding. "No."

Mrs. Osbourne only nodded.

"No," Mary repeated, losing all amusement. "If they did, I would know about—why look at me this way?"

Mrs. Osbourne turned. She literally turned her body in the seat, eased forward, and, facing Mary, rested her hands contently in her lap. "The university has allowed a few women graduate candidates. They are considered on a case-by-case basis. It is not secretive information, but neither is it propagated."

Mary leaned in, terribly interested, utterly skeptical. "How do you know this?"

"My husband," she said with a shrug. "He and another trustee were avid supporters of admitting women to Hopkins. They called a meeting to discuss the matter, which I remember as being quite heated because Harold spoke of nothing else for days. President Gilman found co-education to be inappropriate. A year later, the trustees did adopt a policy women could attend public and special lectures, and the university would certify the accomplishments of women who offered themselves as candidates for a degree."

She looked at Mary. "So what you need is a champion within the faculty or administration to press your case."

Mary couldn't stop shaking her head. She had considered University of Pennsylvania out of her reach. Johns Hopkins was . . . was . . . even more beyond. The school pioneered the concept of a modern research university. To earn a doctorate from there—merely attending lectures—nothing would make Prince Ercole a more proud father.

The sudden burst of hope she could earn a doctorate bought nothing but pain. Wishing—hoping—for the unobtainable hurt. Her eyes blurred. Better not to have hoped at all.

Yet she could not help asking, "How would it even be possible for me?"

Mrs. Osbourne straightened on her seat. Then she stood and walked to the unlit hearth, gripping it, laughing, muttering, "Oh my." Mary held her breath and restrained the hope inside wishing to be unleashed.

"We would have to end the bee a day early," Mrs. Osbourne said, still focused on the hearth, clearly talking through her thoughts. "And I would have to release Zenus from his obligation to escort me, which he will be delighted to do. I'll send a telegram immediately." She swiveled around and smiled. Her blue eyes twinkled. "Do you believe in providence?"

Mary put down her needle. She wanted to answer, "I do," but did she? Did she really?

Only an omniscient God would have known months ago the need she had for an illustrator. Only a loving God would have orchestrated events to ensure she found a house in Belle Haven instead of one in Onancock or Chincoteague. Only a generous God would have also put Mrs. Osbourne next door. To believe God orchestrated all of it for her benefit did not mean she also had to believe what happened with Edward had been in God's plan for her life. It meant she could believe God provided wisdom, care, and guidance. God worked all things for her good, and—yes, in it—she wholeheartedly did believe.

Mary nodded. "I do believe in God's guidance."

Mrs. Osbourne clapped. "Excellent. Graduation is this weekend. Every year I attend the Faculty and Alumni Brunch on Saturday. I can introduce you to members of the faculty. It will be up to you to woo one of them into championing you."

Mary nervously fiddled with a button on her blouse. Speak to Johns Hopkins professors? Why not also ask her to have tea with Queen Victoria? Her stomach rolled at the mere thought of it.

She moistened her lips, nipping the bottom one. "I would not know what to say. Strangers unnerve me."

"Scientists love research," Mrs. Osbourne reasoned. "Tell them about your tomato study."

"I don't know," Mary hedged, staring at the half-finished line of stitching. Who she was before the quilting bee wouldn't even consider the opportunity. "I gave my word to Edward I would take the job in Paris."

"And you have a month before you are expected to be there. Give this a chance. What would he tell you to do?"

She thought on it for a moment. Edward Argent didn't see gender when he looked at a scientist. He saw skill. He was a fair-minded man. Albeit a selfish, arrogant, philandering one.

Finally she said, "Edward would advise whatever benefitted him the most. Arel does it, too."

Mrs. Osbourne chuckled. "You are a good judge of character. What would Zenus say?"

"He would say—" Mary cut herself off as the tingling began, oddly, in her toes and caught fire inside until every last nerve in her body itched to get up and dance. He would, most assuredly, advise her to be optimistic, as it was the first key to success. Then, not to begrudge the obstacles. But most of all, he would insist—

Mary looked to Mrs. Osbourne and smiled. "What time would we need to leave?"

190

18

Seven months later

Philadelphia

These need to be loaded on the wagon," Zenus yelled over the noise of the mill, slapping a bolt along the storage room's east wall to ensure his foreman heard correctly. "And at the station before the snow starts falling again."

While a crew of laborers began carrying out the bolts, Zenus headed across the bustling mill which was, thankfully, twenty degrees warmer than outside. In the female-dominated spinning room—his favorite part of the mill—older children darted through the mill as they pleased, bringing meals to parents and learning to do factory labor as they played with friends in the factory and listened to their spooler, spinner, and doffer mothers' singing. Their joy bought a smile to his face.

He opened the door to the weaving room, and the sound level soared. Between the twenty-four circular looms, the ceiling fans, and ventilation installations, he understood why his employees had taken to stuffing cotton in their ears. Mill output was on track to hit triple the output of last December. With the demand of quilt kits greater than supply, he needed to find a second warehouse to take the packaging off-site.

Life was good.

He was blessed, even though his ear drums ached.

He stepped inside his office and closed the door with his foot while he removed the cotton from his ears.

"You look miserable," Sean said from where he sat behind Zenus's desk, his shoes propped up on a corner, legs crossed, and half the newspaper lying on his black trousers.

Zenus stuffed the cotton in the pocket of his brown suit coat. "At this rate, I will be deaf before I'm forty." He shifted though the stack of mail on his desk. Orders. Orders. More orders. "What I need is noise suppressors. I'm thinking casings on the looms. Or a sound-absorbing material to . . ." To do what, he wasn't sure. But this had potential. This could work, with a bit of trial and error.

"What you need is a wife," Sean interjected.

Mary's face appeared in his mind's eye.

Bless her, Jesus. Inspire her mind and fill her with love for others.

Zenus dropped the envelopes and looked to his cousin. "I am not interested whoever this potential wife is."

Sean grinned. "You should be. I have the perfect lady for you—Miss Charity Oakes."

"I am fairly certain you told me last week Miss Oakes can't transcribe worth a dime," he said, and Sean began to nod, "refuses to make coffee for you because she abhors the smell, and has killed every plant in the building. Then there was the matter of the small fire in your law library."

"Now you know why I'm asking you to marry her," Sean grumbled. His feet dropped to the ground with a thud. He slapped the paper down on the desk. "She's the worst employee in the history of mankind. I need her gone."

Like all the almost twenty other transcriptionists and secretaries Sean had had in the last five years. Zenus offered, "You could not so subtly suggest she find employment elsewhere."

Sean rested his arms on the desk, leaning forward, and looked at him as if it was the most cold-hearted suggestion in the history of mankind. "She needs the job."

Zenus rested against the wall of cabinets, folding his arms across his chest. "Why are you here harassing me?"

Sean picked up Zenus's half-full coffee cup, sniffed, cringed, and put it back down. "Christmas," he quipped, clearly pleased with the change of topic.

"It's not until Friday. Three days."

"Aimee wants to know if you are coming with us to Belle Haven."

Zenus furrowed his brow to make it appear like he was pondering Sean's quasi question even though he had already decided he wasn't going. Being there would remind him too much of Mary. Aunt Priscilla would be sure to bring Mary into conversation and rave again about how proud she was of Mary pursuing a doctorate at Johns Hopkins University. The bimonthly letters from his aunt were salt in the wound. But he would count it joy Mary wasn't in Paris with the weasel Argent.

He shrugged. "I don't know."

"You don't *know*," Sean said brusquely. "Aunt Priscilla is your only living relative, save for me and Aimee, and you aren't sure if you are going to spend Christmas with her?"

"Yes," Zenus snapped. "I don't know."

With what could have been an oath uttered under his breath, Sean stood. He walked over to where Zenus was still leaning against the cabinets. "There are things a man can't know, such as, is French or Italian the most romantic language? Why God created snakes? Will the sun rise tomorrow? Is his daughter his or his cousin's?"

Zenus straightened, swallowed. Felt the blood drain from his face. He wanted to look away from Sean but couldn't. "How long have you—"

"No, let me finish." Yet Sean went silent for a long moment. His face was pinched, and the shadow in his eyes revealed gravity to his character few except for Zenus had seen. "I do know this: a man must do what is right and loving, even if doing it brings him pain."

Guilt and shame constricted Zenus's lungs, cutting off air. Somehow he managed to speak. "When did Clara tell you?" The words barely came out.

Sean stared at him. Hard. "The morning she asked me to marry her. I had a choice, and I would choose the same again."

"I loved her," Zenus said weakly.

"I did, too." Sean gripped Zenus's shoulder. "You and sixty-three others walked away from a derailment killing ninety-two people. The person you became afterward—" His head shook sadly. "You were lost and in need of a family and desperate for love. You made mistakes. But you don't have to prove your worthiness to be forgiven with earning perfect attendance pins. God isn't going to smite you if you miss Sunday worship."

"It's not why." Zenus brushed past Sean and sat on the edge of his desk. "Remember the summer after Aimee was born? We were all at Aunt Priscilla's, and Clara caught Holly Jane Ferris kissing me. She said she knew all along I wouldn't have been faithful."

Sean sat next to him, shoulder to shoulder. The silence lingered so long, Zenus didn't think he would speak, but then Sean said, "Clara wouldn't have listened even if Holly Jane had admitted she was the instigator."

"Why do you presume the best of me?"

They looked at each other.

"Tell me I'm wrong," Sean said.

Zenus shook his head. He'd been too free with his kisses, but that was the most of it. Except for—"People considered me a rake. The ironic thing is Clara was my only one."

"Mine, too, which makes for a rather awkward conversation." He patted Zenus's back. "Clara was wrong, Coz. You have always been a loyal and faithful man, which is why I need you to marry Miss Oakes. Save me from her."

"I love Mary." Zenus stared absently at the floor he'd swept twice already today, after dusting, sharpening pencils, and scrubbing the coffee pot. To distract his mind from thinking about her, he cleaned. His office. His house. His canoes. Then when he was finished, he started the process over. His housekeeper had already warned him she would resign if she saw him washing dishes again. "I'm miserable without her."

"Then do something about it. Change." Sean opened the cabinet to his left. "I need coffee, and you moved the mugs."

Zenus released a slow breath. What was he to do about it? There was nothing to do about it. Earning a doctorate took, at minimum, three years. And with Mary limited to special lectures, it'd take her even longer. If he saw Mary again—more aptly, if he kissed her again—he would have to be made a saint to wait three (or even longer) years. He could not wait three years. He was not *that* patient of a man. Better to not see her at all. Made the whole resisting temptation easier.

Bless her, Jesus. Remind her today how much you love her.

Another cabinet door opened and closed. Then another. "Seriously," Sean groused, "this is what I deal with at my office. Things move. I'm not told. I don't mind change. Just let it make sense."

"I have the mill," Zenus reasoned, focusing on his woes, not Sean's. "Mary is working on her doctorate at Johns Hopkins. I won't ask her to give it up."

"Then you give up," Sean offered, suddenly next to Zenus. He held a floral teacup in front of Zenus's nose. "This is all I could find, and it has a chip in it. Why do you keep chipped dishes? Because you are loyal and clingy."

"I'm also adjustable." Zenus took the cup from Sean and dropped it in the trash can where it shattered. "See, I adjust. Mary isn't a chipped teacup. I can't let her go and shift my attentions to another woman. I am not fickle."

Sean gave him a confused look. "Who said you were fickle? I meant you give up *the mill*."

Zenus sent him a dry look. "It's my job."

"It's your *business*," Sean corrected. He fanned his arm across the room. "Don't make *this* your life. You have always had a talent for finding work. You don't have to sell the mill. Promote your foreman to manager; the man is sharp as a tack. Baltimore to Philadelphia is an hour's train ride. If you want to marry Miss Varrs, you will find a way to adjust your life."

Zenus hesitated.

Sean quirked a brow. "Or you can stay in your comfortable routine and be miserable. I'd prefer happiness to misery any day." He slapped the side of Zenus's arm. "Speaking of misery, there is always Miss Oakes. She's probably pretty when she smiles."

Zenus pushed off the desk and walked to the window, giving him a view of the mill floor, and the numerous women he employed. They regularly thanked him for their jobs. Not every mill owner took as much care of his employees. Baltimore was a growing city, only half the million populace of Philly. Had electric streetcars. Hadn't he read they'd put in a cable car system, too? He liked technology. He liked cities who welcomed it.

Move to Baltimore.

He had never moved in his life. He'd been born in the house he still lived in. He could change, though. Move. Go to Mary instead of asking her to come to him. Doing so had never crossed his mind before. It should have crossed his mind. Why hadn't it crossed his mind? Because—

He was, plain and simple, an idiot. A man. Someone who couldn't see beyond what he'd been taught as the correct gender roles. Truth was a wife didn't have to stay at home and manage a household while the husband worked. They could both have careers. He didn't mind not having children if she didn't want any. He was adjustable. And patient. And loyal. And fascinated with the sciencey things Mary shared.

He loved her. He wanted to spend the rest of his life with her.

The more he thought about the idea of moving to Baltimore, the more he liked it. The more he liked it, the more optimistic he felt. Of course, there were obstacles. Would Mary even accept his proposal? Would Aunt Priscilla support him? Eh, Arel. No sense worrying. No sense begrudging the obstacles.

This had potential. This could work.

"I love her more than the mill," he said, feeling the need to make himself clear.

"I was hoping you did." Sean looked at him with a roguish tilt to his head. "What are you going to do about it? Women like grand gestures of love. And flowers."

"I have no idea." Zenus tapped the window pane with his knuckle then looked to his cousin. "I'm leaving early Thursday morning with you and Aimee for Belle Haven. It's Christmas, and I need to make things right first with Aunt Priscilla."

Sean paused. Blinked. Grinned.

Until Zenus said, "And you are bringing Miss Oakes with us. If anyone can help you convince this Attila the Hun transcriptionist of yours to find another job, Priscilla Dane Osbourne can do it. She likes helping people."

Three snowy days later

Christmas in Belle Haven was like living in the North Pole with all the sights and sounds. And this year, the North Pole had come to Virginia. Everyone was delighted except Zenus. He'd like snow better if it wasn't so cold. And wet. While Sean and Miss Oakes helped Aimee roll snowmen, and Mrs. Binkley prepared the elaborate Christmas dinner, Zenus searched the house for his aunt. Now was a good time as any to talk.

"Aunt Priscilla?" he called out, as he climbed the stairs to the rarely used third floor.

"In here." Her voice came from the room in the middle of the hall, the one Uncle Harold's nurse and her daughter had lived in while caring for him during the last month of his life.

Zenus stopped at the opened door.

Aunt Priscilla stood at the end of the bed, holding a knitted shawl around the shoulders of her gray woolen dress, staring down at a quilt lying over the two-person bed. Sadness darkened her expression. "I've never shown this quilt to anyone."

"Would you rather I not come in?" he asked, not minding. It was warmer downstairs. And there was coffee and pie. And coffee.

She motioned him to join her. "I was thinking about giving it to Miss Oakes for Christmas," she said as he drew up next to her. "The poor dear is barely making ends meet. Of course, in the midst of poverty, one needs food, not a decorative quilt. She would take offense if I gave her money, but a quilt she could sell, don't you think? Oh, what am I thinking? She would never sell a gift. She is too gracious a lady, but I ought to give her something. Do you think she would like this?"

Zenus gave the quilt a cursory glance, then, looking to his aunt, he opened his mouth to say, "Of course," but paused instead. He turned back to the quilt. While he had only "assisted" her once in quilting, he'd learned a few things about quilts he had not forgotten over the years. (He'd been thirteen, and it was still the worst summer of his life.) Because of what he knew about quilts, he *knew* this one was a masterpiece.

It had to be her most glorious creation, comprised mostly of diamond-cut fabric and interspersed with random "set on" scenes of fruits, birds, the American flag, a house, and two hunters with their dog. Rural in design, in the right bottom corner was a white calico house, with blue calico shutters and indigo blue taffeta smoke coming in a stream out of a brown tweed chimney. Next to it, a silk, velvet, and wool garden with a rigid and jointless calico female standing in the middle. There was a brown and white dog seated next to her.

If it weren't elaborate and eye-catching enough, she'd edged the entire quilt with three-inch red fringe.

Zenus stared in awe. She could enter it in every county, state, and even the World's Fair, and taken the premium "hand-runnin'" each time year in, year out.

"You could win blue with this," he said. "It's . . . it's . . ." He literally couldn't find an adjective strong enough to describe it.

"I hate it," she said quietly.

Zenus looked at her. Looked. At. Her. "Why?"

She sighed.

Overwhelmed with need to touch it, Zenus ran his hand over the luxurious and soft diamonds of pieced white and ivory silks radiating out from the sun in the quilt's center. He then moved to the appliquéd fabric "painting" at the top. The horse and rider looked surprising like—

He frowned.

He walked back to the end of the bed to get a better look at the calico female beside the dog. How strange.

He moved again to the "painting" at the top. "I know you would have created the center sun and the green frame around it first, but the Frankenstein arrangement of diamonds and random-sized fabrics along the outer edge, and then these appliquéd scenes—" His gaze caught on a tree. "For heaven's sake, Aunt Priscilla, you have an entire embroidered sycamore right here," he said, pointing to it. "How did you create this in only eight months? Did you ever sleep?"

She gave him a blank look. "What are you talking about?"

"You didn't start this last May?"

"I began," she said slowly, and now looking at him oddly, "this quilt after your uncle's funeral."

Zenus's eyes widened. Over three years ago.

He ran a hand through his hair. "How could you have made a quilt of Mary when you didn't even know her yet?"

There it was, the odd look again on her face, as if he had lost his wits.

"What are you talking about?" she repeated. "These are the things Harold could sit at the window and see during the last five months of his life. I wanted to capture his memories."

He lifted up the edge to show her the horse and rider. "This is Mary."

Her eyes widened. "No, it's Alva Linwood."

"Alva Linwood never wears green. Look at the hair. It's brown. Alva Linwood's is blonde."

Without looking at the quilt, she stepped closer. She laid a hand over his heart. "You haven't let go, have you?"

Zenus swallowed, the quilt sliding out of his grip, yet the lump in his throat remained. He shook his head. "I love her. Every day it grows stronger. I can't sleep, eat, or breathe without thinking about her." And the kiss. He couldn't get it out of his mind. He cleared his throat. "I decided every time she comes to mind, I'd pray for her. She has to be the most prayed for woman in the world."

Aunt Priscilla lowered her hand, clearly disappointed in his response. "My dear boy, she has moved on."

"You don't know it for sure."

"You have to let her go."

"Why should I?"

She didn't answer.

Zenus fought to keep a hold on his temper. Yet he repeated, "Why should I?" with more heat in his tone than he would have liked.

She still didn't answer.

"Tell me," he spat. "Why should I? Don't hide behind your silence, Aunt Priscilla. If you are going to say something like this, you'd better well give me a reason."

Her eyes flashed with anger. "Because she can't have a career and a family. She has to choose, and God has gifted her with too great a scientific mind to be limited to cooking her husband's porridge. She is destined for great things. She can inspire so many other girls."

Zenus's voice grew quieter. "What you're saying is she's too good for me. *I* would limit her." He wasn't fit to be Mary's husband, any more than he had been fit to be Clara's.

"I love you," she said calmly. "I see now you are who you are, and you will always be." He knew she meant to be consoling. She came off as snippy.

Zenus swallowed and grit his teeth. "I'm a disappointment to you."

Aunt Priscilla opened her mouth, then, probably too stunned by his words, didn't speak.

She didn't have to. He could see the answer—and more—in her eyes. And then—he wasn't sure where it came from—his heart filled with understanding. With mercy. How could he not have seen her pain all these years?

He didn't because he had never looked, never even thought to look.

Zenus gripped the sides of her arms, kissed her forehead. "I am sorry," he said gently. "I'm so sorry I lived and your son died. If I had not demanded Harry switch seats with me, it would have been me not him. It should have been."

"Don't say that," she snapped, and then with a choked cry, she whispered, "Don't you ever say that to me again. God had his reasons." Whatever else she muttered, he did not hear.

Zenus wrapped her tight in his arms. He held her as she cried.

Finally, she released a ragged breath. "All these years I wanted you to go back to being the happy boy you were before the accident. Clara and Sean's elopement made you worse. When you aren't happy, I'm not happy."

He smiled even though she couldn't see him. "I am happy."

"Even without Mary?"

She had a point. He was miserable.

"I won't deny I'd be happier with her," he said, resting his chin atop her lavender-scented hair. "Do you want to know why you hate your quilt and I think it's a masterpiece?"

She drew back so she could see him. "Tell me."

"When I look at it, I see Mary, and my heart smiles." He stepped behind her and, with hands on her shawl-covered shoulders, turned her to face the quilt. "When you look at it, you see the last images Uncle Harold saw, and your heart grieves." He leaned down and kissed her cheek. "Give the quilt to Miss Oakes, so you can finally let go."

She looked over her shoulder at him. "You don't want it?"

Zenus grinned. "Why settle for the girl in the quilt when I can have the girl?"

"She may not want you."

"I'm willing to take the risk."

19

January 1892

Zenus did the logical thing a man does when he finds a girl he wants to marry. He surreptitiously studied her, followed her, and plotted and planned on how to make her his, all the while not saying a word. Because when he finally spoke to her again, the words would be perfect. And they would be, he knew with assurance, because he had plotted and planned, adjusted a few things, and planned more.

For four—*four*—weeks, he studied and followed, thereby proving he was a patient man.

Oh, to be fair, the first two weeks were more of him sitting in Gamble's Coffee House across the street from the Biological Laboratory than doing much of anything else, besides drinking coffee, eating steak and coddled eggs, and plotting the perfect marriage proposal. But, truly, he had nothing else to do. Mary spent the Christmas Recess at the Biological Laboratory with another female graduate candidate and one of their professors. (Male students and other professors came and went, too.) When she wasn't there, she was with Arel, who was on recess from classes at Mount Saint Agnes College.

By the second week, Zenus and Hastings Gamble of Gamble's Coffee House were on first-name basis and co-conspirators, having congratulated themselves on their successful camouflage and subterfuge skills for avoiding detection. While Gamble's welcomed all genders, races, and nationalities, never had a woman darkened the black-and-white marble floor.

Weeks three and four consisted of memorizing Mary's intersession schedule: lecture attendance, mealtimes, study hours, morning constitutionals, research assistantship, and friendly acquaintances. The latter wasn't on her schedule, per se. Details were the lifeblood of any study. And Zenus took his study seriously.

He'd even noticed how she paused each time at a certain house a quarter of the distance between the boardinghouse and campus. A two-story bricked Georgian. Elm in front. Up for lease. So when he spotted the longing glance on Mary's face, he had the answer on how he was to propose.

Zenus sent Hastings out on information retrieval.

On Monday evening, January 18, Mary and Arel attended a meeting in Levering Hall under the auspices of the Women's Christian Temperance Union in furtherance of a plan for organizing a system of Police Matrons for the city. Arel spoke vehemently in favor. Mary read a book. Or so Hastings reported. Information not at all helpful.

On Thursday evening, the pair attended the Charity Organization Society's meeting, also in Levering Hall. Arel spoke vehemently again. Mary read the same book. Or so Hastings thought. He hadn't been able to get close enough to check because "the vociferous blond owl" looked at him as if he hadn't bathed in a year (he had one this morning), demanded his name (which he gave because he had nothing to hide), and suggested he sit near the window. In the back. Again, information not helpful to Zenus.

On Friday afternoon, Mary left the Biological Lab at 4:58 and returned to the boardinghouse. She, likely, read more from her book (Zenus had spotted the title on the spine), while Arel stood outside Gamble's Coffee House handing out pamphlets on the evils of coffee. Hastings paid a Johns Hopkins undergraduate the exorbitant amount of five dollars to flirt with Arel until she left. Took thirty-eight minutes before she departed in a huff.

Impressed at his new friend's ingenuity, Zenus sat near the coffee house's hearth, ate dinner, and drank coffee and pondered why Mary was reading *Anna Karenina*.

The next morning, since the Biological Laboratory was closed and thus Mary would spend the day at the boardinghouse, Zenus bought a copy of *Anna Karenina*. He reread the opening as he sat in an electric streetcar to the corner of the street on which sat the two-story Georgian Mary had longingly admired. Book tucked under his arm, Zenus held the collar of his greatcoat up to his neck as he hurried down the snow-packed sidewalk to get out of the cold. After opening the front door, he examined his new property. A little painting needed here. New wallpaper there. Usable furniture for now.

Plan in mind, he left the book on the stairwell and securely locked the door.

He, however, did not walk from the house back to Gamble's Coffee House (took a hansom cab instead) even though it was only two blocks, because precipitation had begun to fall, and he had a strong aversion to the wet and coldness of snow.

But he was happy. Soon to be happier.

On Monday, January 25, Johns Hopkins spring classes would begin, including a new lecture series, initiating a whole new routine of Mary's for him to learn. More weeks to waste. Even though Arel would return Monday to Mount Saint Agnes College, Sunday—tomorrow—was the better Proposal Day.

So by midafternoon on Saturday, Zenus had examined the information he knew or had recently collected about Mary. He looked to Hastings Gamble, who he decided was of the highest moral character despite his Blackbeard resemblance, and, after one final swig of his coffee, said, "Application, my friend, is the next step in the scientific study."

Hastings leaned back in his leather chair near the coffee house's blazing hearth. He propped his boots up on the ottoman. "What about the bird?"

"I'm picking it up in an hour."

"No, the peevish one."

"Eh, Arel," Zenus muttered. "She is a problem."

"$1 + 1 = 2$ is a problem. That *thing* is a blight on mankind, emphasis man." Hastings grimaced. "Did you see this?" He jerked a sheet of yellow paper from the inside of his gray frock coat and slammed it down on the table between them, the silverware rattling, the only sound in the abnormally empty coffee house. On the pamphlet, in bold black ink were the words . . .

Coffee = Whiskey

Zenus gave him an apologetic look. "Arel Catherine Dewey can be zealous."

Hastings groaned. "She's driving away my customers." Then his eyes narrowed to slits. "Do I have to let her inside? Couldn't we just leave her out in the snow to freeze?"

"Murder is generally frowned upon in civilized societies."

Hastings slapped both armrests. "This calls for improvising."

Zenus looked to him, got a little nervous, and said, "It doesn't bode well for Arel."

"Are you concerned for her welfare?"

"Not so much." He paused for a moment then added, "But my soon-to-be fiancée will, so don't do anything to cause permanent injury or occasional nightmares."

With a "hmph," Hastings claimed their empty mugs and stood. "If we're going to do this, we need to get going. Tomorrow is the start of a new adventure for you."

As he walked to the kitchen, Zenus pulled out the jeweler's box containing the emerald ring he'd purchased for Mary. He had the ring, the girl, the perfect proposal planned. All he needed now was Arel not to ruin it all.

Someone was watching her.

Holding her breath, Mary peeked through the curtains in the Biological Lab's front parlor to the snow-covered and empty street outside. She'd felt the chill from feeling watched all throughout morning worship. Even during the walk from Lovely Lane Methodist Church to the laboratory building. Where was he? He had to be out there. She knew it. She could feel him. Even through the green wool of her dress. He was a hobgoblin lurking in the shadows, or at least what shadows there were under a gray afternoon sky.

She shivered and drew her hand back from the frosty glass.

"You look nervous," her lab partner Florence said from somewhere on the other side of the parlor.

"She thinks someone is following her," Arel clarified, "like Jack the Ripper."

Florence laughed. "In Baltimore? We have little crime for a city of almost half a million."

Arel snorted. "You need to leave the campus more often. All a person has to do is look around and see debauchery and decay. Taverns. Dispensaries. Whorehouses. Coffee shops."

"Arel," Mary warned yet kept her gaze on the street.

"What?" Arel said with what Mary knew was a shrug of her shoulders. "One of these days you're going to realize I'm right about the evils of coffee."

"I quite enjoy it myself." Florence sat on the settee next to Arel, or at least it sounded like it. Mary would have to turn around to be sure. "In fact, I recently read an article in *Hall's Journal of Health* saying the white of an egg followed up with a cup of strong coffee will nullify most poisons."

Arel, surprisingly, restrained herself.

A hansom cab with a white horse turned down the street.

Mary's pulse increased. She shouldn't be nervous. She had no reason to be fearful. Everyone she had met thus far at Hopkins had been welcoming. Never had she felt more at home than she had since moving to Baltimore. She missed Zenus, to be sure. During the Charity Organization Society's meeting Arel had dragged her to, she didn't get a single page read due to imagining what her life would be had she accepted Zenus's proposal. Pleasant. But not *more*. And she wanted more than the norm.

Christine Ladd-Franklin had proven a woman could have a fellowship at Hopkins even if her name wasn't listed in the University circular as an official student. Could hold her own academically against men and complete the requirements for a PhD. Could be a scientist, a wife, a mother. More than the norm was possible.

Maybe, in time, wanting it all with Zenus would abate, and she would be able to love again. With Prince Ercole proud and Mum accepting of her doctoral pursuit, she was free. Finally free. And blessed. And (mostly) happy.

She touched her chest. Oh, how her heart ached.

"I wish," she whispered, looking at the star-absent sky. She wished he had found a way to make a future together work. She wished . . .

Her breath fogged the glass.

The hansom pulled to the side, nearing the building. Nothing abnormal, but—

Mary shivered again. "I feel as if someone is breathing down my neck."

"It's because I am."

Mary flinched at the sound of Professor Martin's voice. She turned around and awkwardly smiled at her thesis advisor and champion on the faculty. Endowed with a joyous outlook on life, he had a simplicity and frankness reminding her of Zenus. She'd also been warned by Florence he held a sink-or-swim approach toward graduate students and a predilection toward alcohol, although she had never smelled it on him during lab experiments. Until now.

"My apologies," she murmured.

He patted the side of her arm, like an obliging older brother. "You look a wreck, Miss Varrs. You should call it a day."

"But—"

"Both Miss Bascom's and your lab work are flawless, once again." Those intelligent blue eyes of his fairly danced with excitement. "I am teaching Physiological Seminary, Tuesdays at 10, and Animal Physiology and Journal Club, Thursdays at 10 and 12. I have put you two on the class roll"—he looked apologetic—"but you must sit behind a screen, as to not disturb the men."

Mary said, "Perfectly acceptable," as Florence exclaimed, "Oh, thank you!"

Arel made a peeved sound. "I think the men should be the ones . . ."

Mary gave her a hard look.

" . . . who are honored women like Mary and Florence will graciously hide behind a veil—umm, sheet—to spare them temptation." Arel grinned then stood and shook Professor Martin's hand. "Arel, Arel Dewey. It's so good to see you again, sir."

He nodded politely. "You, too, Miss Dewey, and rest assured the veil will someday come down. Ladies, do take care traveling home." He looked to Mary and Florence. "The Naturalist Field Club meets at 2:00 on Saturdays. We are studying the fauna, flora, and geology of the neighborhood of Baltimore. You are both expected to attend."

As he left the parlor, a rat-a-tat-tat knocking sounded on the front door.

Mary jumped, startled.

Arel and Florence exchanged glances.

"I know. I should not be so nervous." Since she was closest to the door, Mary drew it open enough to see outside. A burst of cold air bit at her cheeks and nose. "Yes?"

A well-bundled driver handed her a letter. "Fare is paid. I'll be waiting in the cab." Without giving her time to respond, he hurried down the steps to his horse and buggy.

Mary absently closed the door, staring at the letter with one word neatly written on the envelope.

Mary

No postmark. She turned it over. No waxed seal either. Her heart tightened. Whether it was out of fear, nervousness, or hope, she did not know.

"Who's it from?" came from Florence.

"It does not say."

"Trash it," ordered Arel. "It looks suspicious."

It did, and yet . . .

With a slight tremble to her hands, Mary took care as she lifted the unsealed flap and withdrew the notecard. In the same neat handwriting—

Sciencey assistance needed.

Her breath caught. Zenus? Good gracious, he was here. Here. In Baltimore, and had been for weeks. He was the one following her, which made logical sense, which explained why she could feel a presence even when she couldn't see him. How many men had she seen and told herself she was only imagining they looked like him? But why would he come all the way to Baltimore to see her and not say anything? Then when he did finally "speak," it's by way of a letter. Now it made no logical sense. Unless—

He had a plan.

And her cheeks and nose suddenly didn't feel so cold.

A giggle burst in the center of her chest, working its way up to her throat, bringing a smile. She blurted, "I need to go," swirled around, and claimed her gray woolen cloak from where she had hung it earlier.

Arel grabbed her crimson one. "I'm going with you, and don't you try arguing with me."

<hr>

The hackney stopped at the quaint Georgian Mary thought would make a lovely home, even with a gray sky overhead. She climbed out of the cab. She looked to the driver and, being cautious, said, "Stay here until I give you word."

He nodded.

Mary cautiously stepped in the indented footprints in the snow, but Arel rushed past. She stopped at the door, swirled around, and, blocking the knocker, braced hands on the door frame. Each puff of breath a cloud. Arel Dewey, a human smokestack.

"This is dangerous," Arel warned.

Mary sighed. "Oh, Arel. I promise when the door opens, the man inside will be Zenus."

The door opened.

The black-bearded man standing there wasn't Zenus.

And yet Mary released the breath she didn't realize she was holding. Although she had never entered Gamble's Coffee House, she recognized the wintery-bundled owner, Hastings Gamble, for he, too, attended Lovely Lane Methodist Church and most special lectures open to the public. And she'd heard he completed all the requirements for a PhD, yet the university denied the degree. She never heard or asked why.

She waved at the hansom to leave.

In one quick swoop, Mr. Gamble placed his hands under Arel's arms, lifted her over the threshold, and all but dropped her inside. He blocked Arel from leaving. "Nice to finally meet you, Miss Varrs."

Mary stepped inside, and Mr. Gamble closed the door behind her. Electric lights were everywhere, but none were turned on. The parlor and the dining room each had a lit candle or two. A crackling fire in the hearth. On the staircase rested a leather copy of *Anna Karenina*.

"Here." Mr. Gamble handed her an envelope matching the earlier one.

Arel blurted, "Don't open it."

With a low growl, Mr. Gamble closed his hand around Arel's wrist, completely encircling it. He grumbled, "You're staying here."

"No," Arel seethed. "And you can't make me."

While Arel tried (unsuccessfully) to jerk free, Mary withdrew the notecard from the envelope. In the same neat handwriting—

Come to the kitchen.

For a moment, she could do nothing but stare at the words.

Then her heart began to race, beating erratically, stealing the breath from her lungs. Though eight months had passed, she was transported to Belle Haven. To Mrs. Osbourne's kitchen. To the moment they had kissed. Really kissed.

I will make this—us—work.

When he'd said the words, she'd believed him. But then he'd fled back to Philadelphia the next morning, she'd chosen not to hope they could still have a future. Hope wounded. Hope disappointed. But maybe not this time. Zenus was loyal and faithful and had some strange plan, she knew for certain. If he disappointed her, so be it. She smiled, and she could have schooled it if she had tried, but she didn't, because she chose to hope.

"Arel, stay here." Mary took a step, then eyed Mr. Gamble. He looked bored as Arel, who was two feet shorter and more than half his body weight, struggled to free herself.

"Do be kind to him," Mary said sweetly.

Arel froze. "But . . . he's the bully."

"Even more of a reason for you to be kind," Mary answered. Then she looked to Mr. Gamble. "It goes for you, too."

She then left them in the foyer and walked . . . skipped—oh good heavens, she could barely feel her feet as she hurried down the corridor she presumed led to the kitchen. She removed her gloves, her hands shaking too much to make fine work of it, yet she managed the job and lowered the hood off her head.

She stopped, closed her eyes, breathed deep to steady her nerves. To calm the giddiness bubbling inside, because she hoped and yearned and wished for a prince like she was a girl of eight instead of twenty-eight.

Mary gave the door a little tap before pushing it open. She stepped inside. Unlike the minimal candles in the front of the house, myriad ones covered the counters. Each candle sat atop a palm-sized, figure-eight-shaped sheet of paper. Boards hung from the ceiling like tree swings, each bore a flickering candle. Glowworms and fireflies.

Her eyes blurred.

She turned. She turned her gaze to the right, and she saw him.

Zenus stood, leaning back against the sink, his arms folded across the chest of his greatcoat.

Mary took a step toward him. Just one. She could run to him, but why ruin his plan, ruin his delight, because of her own eagerness?

There may have been a grunt and a howl from the parlor as the door eased closed behind her, but it didn't matter. Nothing else mattered except this moment. Except them.

He looked at her, and the space between them seemed to dissipate. She began to tingle. Float. It was awful.

It was wonderful.

It was also too much, so she said, "What is all this?" as she draped her gloves over the back of a chair, as she blinked away her tears.

"My flock."

"Your flock?"

He nodded.

"Of candles?"

He shrugged. "Winged beetles tend to hibernate in December."

"Yes, they do."

He withdrew a bird cage from in the sink and proudly said, "Here's my actual flock."

Mary smiled. "It's a pigeon."

He drew the cage up to his face and gave the bird a most peculiar look. "It's supposed to be a dove."

"Ornithologically speaking," Mary said, walking to him, "they are of the same bird clade, *Columbidae*. Dove tends to be used for smaller species and pigeon for larger ones."

"I love when you talk sciencey."

"Are you flirting with me?"

"Wooing, Miss Varrs, wooing." He gave her a mischievous—a simply rakish—look. "Is it working?"

She tilted her head and smiled. "Pigeons are social animals. It will need a mate."

"I think I can find one." Zenus placed the cage back in the sink. He took Mary's hands in his. "A year ago I told God I wanted to stop playing life safe. 'Grow your flocks' was his response. I thought he meant my business, so I took out a loan and bought new looms. I thought I was in God's will doing exactly what He wanted. Then a flood hit. Because of an act of God, I took a journey."

"To Belle Haven."

"To you."

He kissed her. It was sweet and gentle and tasted of mint, of hope fulfilled. And it was different than before because she was changed. He was changed. And the kiss changed. He pulled her roughly against him, or maybe she had. Good heavens, she had never wanted anything more than this moment. Him.

She drew back. "I love you," she said because she hadn't yet and the words needed to be released.

His fingers brushed along hers as he descended. Onto one knee. "You weren't what I wanted. God knew you were what I needed. I love you. Marry me. I've put a lease on this house because I want to court you, and I will wait as long as you need—"

"Yes."

"Yes?"

Mary laughed. "Yes, I will marry you and provide all the sci-encey help you need."

His breath sucked raggedly into him, and he stood. "How soon?" he said, and he didn't give her a chance to answer. "It doesn't matter. Because I am a patient man."

Mary entwined her fingers with his. She pulled Zenus to her and then to the table. "Sit, Mr. Dane, for we have a wedding to plan. I, for one, am not a patient woman."

⸺ ✺ ⸺

The Queen Anne chair across from him wobbled against the wooden floor.

Hastings Gamble stretched out on the sofa, crossing his propped up legs, getting comfortable. He wedged a pillow between his back and the armrest. No telling how long Zenus and Miss Varrs would be in the kitchen discussing wedding plans. He had a stack of wood by the fire. Might as well enjoy the afternoon with company and a good book.

He turned to the page in *Anna Karenina* and resumed reading. "Stephan Arkadyich's eyes glittered merrily, and he fell to thinking with a smile. 'Yes, it was nice, very nice.'"

The chair wobbled again.

He looked to where Miss Dewey sat, legs tied together, arms bound to the chair, handkerchief tied around her mouth. Not a drop of remorse could be found in her pretty brown eyes, but several strands of black hair—his hair—could be seen on the front of her red cloak. The spot on his chin where she yanked out a chuck of beard verily ached.

"Now where were we, Miss Dewey? Ah, with Prince Stephan thinking."

She glared at him, muttered incoherently though the handkerchief.

With a twist to the corner of his mouth, Hastings found where he had left off. "'There were many other excellent things there, but one can't say it in words, or even put it into waking thoughts . . .'"

Group Discussion Guide

1. Zenus believes he is doing God's will by taking out a loan to expand his business. Then the flood occurs. Have you been through a circumstance where God allowed a bad thing to happen that resulted in the growth of your personal character and faith? How can God be a loving God when He allows bad things to happen?

2. In chapter 3, Arel criticizes Zenus because, when he "speaks, people listen and follow and adore." Is this fair criticism or sour grapes? Can it be both? Why is it easier to see flaws in someone than in ourselves?

3. Mary needs Aunt Priscilla's aid in drawing her tomato illustrations. Why do you think Mary panics over asking for help?

4. Zenus believes "a man's appearance should not define him as a rogue. Nor should his past forever delineate him as one." What does he mean by that?

5. For Mary, college was a path to her chosen career. Considering she believes college will expand Arel's horizons and curb her self-absorption, why doesn't Mary push college on all of Arel's "sheep"?

6. Mary struggles with the multiple expectations of what a woman should be. Why are women so susceptible to others' version of "ideal"?

7. Zenus's routine bothers Aunt Priscilla, yet Mary doesn't mind it and even makes Zenus his oatmeal with precisely twelve raisins. Why was Aunt Priscilla so bothered? And was she right to constantly push her nephew to change? Have you ever felt it was your job to change someone?

8. As he sets out winning Mary back, Zenus follows his plan because when he speaks to Mary again, he wants it to be perfect. Mary, though, feels she's being stalked until she

discovers it's him. What is the difference between romantic doting and possessive obsession?

9. When Arel takes up the *coffee = whiskey* cause, she drives away Hastings Gamble's business. Have you ever been so zealous for a cause that you've hurt people? Is there any cause worth hurting people?

10. When Mary first views the Bride's Quilt, she sees it as "erroneous" and a "faux pas," yet by the end, the Frankenstein pattern becomes a "collage of beauty." Why does Mary's perception change?

11. Aunt Priscilla keeps a Crazy Quilt stowed away and won't show it to anyone because she hates it. When Zenus finally sees it, he knows it's "her most glorious creation." Why is Zenus's perception so different from Aunt Priscilla's?

Want to know more about author Gina Welborn?
Want to know about other great fiction
from Abingdon Press?

Please check out our website at
www.AbingdonFiction.com
to read interviews with your favorite authors,
find tips for starting a reading group, and
stay posted on what
new titles are on the horizon.

Be sure to visit Gina online!

http://www.ginawelborn.com/
https://www.facebook.com/ginamarie.welborn

We hope you enjoyed Gina Welborn's *Masterpiece Marriage*, and that you'll continue to read Abingdon's Quilts of Love series. Here's a sample of the next book in the series, Cathy Elliott's *A Stitch in Crime*.

—⚬⚬⚬—

1

Perhaps if she simply avoided eye contact.

Thea James turned her back on the partygoers, paying attention to the dessert buffet, instead. The Quilt-Without-Guilt Guild had surpassed their Christmas potluck standard. Among a bounty of petite cakes, cookies, puffs, and bars, Thea found her own offering, a plate of blueberry tartlets. They appeared untouched. Strange. She pulled them to the front of the culinary display.

"Thea! Why are you hiding out in the desserts when I need your help?" The familiar voice of fellow guild member, Heather Ann Brewster, hinted at desperation.

Turning with reluctance, Thea morphed into hospitality mode. "Blueberry tartlet?"

"What?" Heather Ann viewed the diminutive dessert, gave a small shudder, and then had the grace to look apologetic. "Ah . . . no, thanks. I haven't browsed the appetizers yet. Anyway, I can't think about food now. I'm too upset."

Thea shoved her reluctance aside. "What seems to be the problem, Heather Ann?" This time.

"You know the publicity banner we had made? The one advertising the quilt show next weekend? The one supposed to be hanging over the entrance to Old Town?"

"Supposed to be hanging over the entrance? I thought they put it up yesterday." Thea calculated the days left until the show opened.

Today was Sunday, and tonight's kickoff quilt show soirée started the festivities. The main event was scheduled for next Saturday. Folks needed to be aware of the date so they'd attend en masse.

"City utility workers were supposed to put it up. Oh, and it's beautiful, Thea. In bold letters it says, '1st Annual Blocks on the Walk Quilt Show, Pioneer Park' and the date."

"Good . . . very good. So why isn't it hanging up?"

"I had the letters made in red, too. Sort of reminds me of Janny Rice's redwork quilt, you know? Perhaps she'll place with hers. Beautiful embroidery." Heather Ann seemed lost in the vision, green eyes staring at nothing.

"Heather Ann. Focus, hon. You said there was a problem. As the quilt show chairperson, I want to help." Well, it was a lie. Helping was overrated. Thea wanted to eat some desserts. And she wasn't the chairperson. Another fib. Rather, the co-chair, along with Prudy Levasich.

Where was the elusive Prudy, anyway? Probably showing off her twin sister, Trudy, visiting from the East Coast. The co-chair's co-twin. If Prudy stuck around now and then, she could co-solve these problems with Thea.

"You have to do something! The Larkindale city planning commission won't let us put up the banner." The desperation returned to Heather Ann's tone, sending her voice to a higher key.

"Why not?"

"It's not up to code. They said the banner needs holes cut in it so the wind will flow through and not blow it down."

"Makes sense. Without the holes, it could act more like a sail," Thea said. "Can't you cut some?"

"I guess." Heather Ann looked uncomfortable. "But I don't know how big to make the holes. Or how many. The banner was expensive. I don't want to ruin it."

"Very responsible." Thea considered the options. "I have an idea. Call the Larkin Lake Resort. They're always putting banners up for some event. The Fly-Fishing Derby. And the Daisy Pedal Bike Race, right?"

"Oh, you're good." Heather Ann's expression turned eager, like a puppy about to score a treat.

"Whatever size they advise, be sure you use the white space and don't cut into those big red letters you chose. This way people will only see the letters and not notice the holes." Thea gave Heather Ann an encouraging pat on the shoulder. "Sound okay?"

"Sounds great. Thanks so much, Thea. I'm on it." Heather Ann dashed away, blonde ponytail bouncing, presumably to make the call.

Or grab a few appetizers.

Which seemed an even better idea to Thea.

"Well, aren't you just the little problem-solver here." Renée Fowler pushed up against Thea in jest, as she used to do when they were teens.

"Oh, stop." Thea grinned at her best friend since fifth grade, recently returned home from a long honeymoon tour of Europe.

She had missed Renée terribly. But something seemed off between them. Had the travels changed Renée? She certainly looked different. More elegant. Her brown hair, cut in Paris, was styled in a fashionable pixie cut. But weren't her large gray eyes filled with disapproval now? Or was the still single Thea a little jealous of her friend's marriage and new life?

Thea studied the crowd. "A wonderful turnout, don't you think? I've been watching for him, but have yet to see Dr. Cottle. Did he already check in?"

"How would I know, Thea?" Renée said. "I may own the Inn, but I don't keep up on what time every guest walks through the door."

Not a hint of a thank-you for recommending Renée and Howie's Heritage House Inn as lodging for their illustrious judge and guest speaker, Dr. Miles Cottle. Typical treatment from Renée since her return to Larkindale.

Thea waved to a friend of Gram's. "Everyone seems to be enjoying themselves. And no better place to do it than in Mary-Alice Wentworth's garden. Exquisite, isn't it?"

Glorious roses edged a pavestone patio, which surrounded a sparkling pond, highlighted by the spectacular fountain in the pond's center. Water poured endlessly from an urn held by a grace-ful, granite lady. The effect was more than tranquil. It was hypnotic. Tables with bistro chairs dotted the grounds, and this evening's attendees alternately chatted in groups or relaxed with a cool drink. A number of quilts were displayed near the walkway, staging a quilt show preview and adding a folksy feel. Her mother's string quartet played various classical selections with so much enthusiasm the occasional sour note went unnoticed.

Except maybe by Renée, who now winced as if she had stepped on a nail.

Oh-oh. Thea grabbed the dessert plate and shoved it at her friend. "How about a nice blueberry tartlet?"

"Tartlet?" Renée's distasteful look increased. "What's in the fill-ing? And look how thick the crust is, Thea. You must use very cold dough to make a flaky crust."

Crestfallen, Thea placed the plate back on the table. "Tasted good to me."

"They probably are good, for Larkindale. I do like the antique serving plate though," Renée said. "My tastes have refined so much from my exposure to other cultures. Like what I'm wearing, for instance." She smoothed out her simple black dress. "In Europe, everyone wears something elegant like this. Understated, you know? Your dress is much too frilly. Too yesterday."

"Oh." Thea's cheeks burned. Was it no longer okay to like yester-day's fashions best? Her vintage cocktail dress had been a steal from the family's antique store, James & Co. Antique Emporium. Certain the cut was flattering to her figure, Thea also thought the cobalt color and purple tulle overlay brought out the periwinkle blue in her eyes. Both Mum and Gram had agreed.

"But the puffy skirt is a great illusion. One's not sure if it's so full because of your curves or the dress's design." Renée put a hand on her hip and once-overed her friend. "I could never pull it off. It would just hang on my slender frame. But those strappy sandals are cute. A nice change from your clogs."

Thea was beginning to wonder why she was friends with Renée. And where was Dr. Cottle?

Thea studied the gathering again, but didn't see him. Their hostess, Mary-Alice, was also missing. Perhaps she was inside greeting him this minute.

Leaning toward Thea, Renée said, "Here comes your Cole Mason. So handsome. Did you see him chatting with Mayor Suzanne Stiles for more than a half hour? You better watch out, Miss Thea. Step it up or you'll remain Miss Thea for a long, long time."

"He's not my Cole Mason, and he can talk to whomever he likes!" Thea almost hissed at her friend as Cole approached them. His roving reporter role tonight was to cover the quilt show kickoff soirée for the *Larkindale Lamplight's* society pages. Surely he wouldn't report any petty problems from putting on the show. It could result in a definite damper on attendance at the official opening.

Moving past a sullen Renée and closer to Thea, Cole flashed his disarming dimples. Then appearing stunned, he stopped and said. "You look so . . . nice! Am I writing about the wrong subject for the *Lamplight*? How about a full-page spread of you in your dress?"

Renée rolled her eyes.

"No comment," Thea said, laughter in her voice. "What are you planning to cover?" Making her a feature story was not an option. He had to be kidding. Especially if she looked as chunky in her dress as Renée seemed to say. And the camera added what? Thea sucked in her stomach.

Cole's attention had diverted to the treat table. "What do you call this delicious-looking sweet?" He plunked a pink petit four on a faux-china plate. "I don't want to get the name wrong in my article."

Relieved, Thea named each dessert. Cole listed it in his notebook and took still shots with his smart-phone. Without embarrassment, he snuck a few more tempting treats.

"And this . . . ," she swept her hand in front of the tartlets with a flourish, ". . . is what I made. Blueberry tartlets. Care to sample one?"

So far, Renée stood silent. But apparently she'd reached her etiquette limit. "You don't want to eat those, Cole. They're made by our peanut-butter-and-pickle sandwich queen here. Need I say more?"

"In this case, I'll take two." Cole stacked the tarts on the last empty spot on his plate.

The tiny triumph tasted like sugar. But Thea wondered if Renée, with her newly acquired European sensibilities, was right.

"Perhaps I should have used raspberries instead of blueberries," Thea said. "Might have looked more appetizing."

"No. Then it would have looked like coddled blood," Renée responded.

Coddled blood? Coddle? Clotted? Thea shivered, remembering Dr. Cottle was still a no-show. What if something horrible had happened to him?

She surveyed the party once more. Mary-Alice's favorite nephew appeared to have captivated a small audience, his hands in motion, probably spouting his expertise on the family quilt, "Larkin's Treasure." The string quartet sawed with vigor. Thea spotted Prudy having a good old time talking away. Or was it Trudy? Thea's Aunt Elena, along with a few others, admired a magnificent Grandmother's Garden quilt displayed on the walkway.

But no Dr. Cottle.

Cole's voice cut through her concerns. "You know, these look so good, I think I'll take another one, in case we run out before I've had my fill." He balanced another tartlet atop the others and winked at Thea.

Renée blew out a sigh. "You are quite the risk-taker, Mr. Mason." She waved a dismissal and strolled toward the mayor, probably for a little update on her conversation with Cole.

This is it. It's all I can take. I'm leaving before one more person says boo to me.

Cole's hand briefly touched the middle of Thea's back, stopping her flight, his dark eyes inquisitive. "Are you quite sure she's your best friend?"

No. She wasn't sure anymore. But what could she say? Thea groped for a reason for her friend's bad behavior. In the search, she found an emptiness she couldn't name.

"Renée's . . . not been herself since she got back from Europe."

"A lingering case of jet lag. Could be the cause," Cole said.

Thea looked up, grateful for his kindness.

"So where's the famous Dr. Cottle?" Cole asked, changing the subject. "I've heard he can read the stitches on a fastball from the nosebleed section at Yankee Stadium."

"So they say. He's a major leaguer on quilts and quilting in our state," Thea said. "In fact, I should go see if there's been any word of him. Folks came tonight to hear his talk about the Wentworth legacy quilt."

"You go then. I'll pacify myself with a blueberry tartlet." Cole stuffed a whole one in his mouth and started chewing, pleasure written all over his face.

Did he like it or was he trying to cheer her up?

Maybe she didn't want to know.

Thea excused herself and strode purposefully toward the house. No eye contact. No eye contact. No eye contact. She managed to slip through the French doors, muting her mother's Mozart, and putting a wall between herself and the problems outside.

She closed her eyes. See no evil.

Beyond the glass door, a distant voice called out, "Has anyone seen Thea?"

She clicked the door closed.

Hear no evil.